A
Rip Roaring
Good Time

A Ripple Effect Cozy Mystery
Book One

Jeanne Glidewell

Cover and Book design by eBook Prep
www.ebookprep.com

March, 2015
ISBN: 978-1-61417-715-9

ePublishing Works!
www.epublishingworks.com

DEDICATION

This book is dedicated to my wonderful 152 Crew friends and neighbors, Janet Wright and Colleen Dudley, aspiring authors themselves, who help me by letting me bounce plots and titles off them. I appreciate that Janet and Colleen don't mind when I use some of their ideas in my stories. It was the two of them who convinced me, a former RV Park owner, to write a cozy series about RV enthusiasts, which I'm introducing with this first Ripple Effect mystery. I hope my Lexie Starr readers will enjoy this crossover novel, and my new cozy mystery series, as well.

ACKNOWLEDGEMENTS

I'd like to thank my editors, Judy Beatty, of Madison, Alabama, and Alice Duncan, of Roswell, New Mexico, who help keep me from appearing as if I flunked out of my English classes fourteen years in a row. I'd also like to thank Nina and Brian Paules, of eBook Prep, and ePublishing Works, for their expert advice, and professional eBook services. They are truly a pleasure, and a blessing, to work with.

CAST OF CHARACTERS

Rapella Ripple - As Rapella, a full-time RVer, who has an unlimited number of clichés in her repertoire, would say, "You're only as old as you feel". At sixty-eight, she's a real pistol, ready to be fired. She'll do whatever it takes to help her friend, Lexie Starr, out of a rough spot.

Clyde Ripple, a.k.a. Rip - Rapella's husband and the other half of the RVing couple. Having spent his entire career in law enforcement, he's a handy husband to have around when the you-know-what hits the fan.

Lexie Starr - She's been sticking her nose into murder cases for several years, tracking down suspects and killers. When she ends up on the wrong end of a murder investigation, her friends, the Ripples, arrive in their travel trailer (affectionately known as the "Chartreuse Caboose") to rescue her.

Stone Van Patten - Lexie's husband of just over a year. Together, he and Lexie own the Alexandria Inn, a bed and breakfast establishment in Rockdale, Missouri. His blood pressure has gone down significantly since Lexie gave up her part-time sleuthing habit.

Wendy Starr - Lexie Starr's thirty-year-old daughter who works in the county coroner's lab. She's the guest of honor at her surprise birthday party. But when the party plans go awry, she gets a bigger surprise than anyone could have anticipated.

Andy Van Patten - Stone's nephew, who moved to the Midwest after his uncle did, and fell in love with Wendy Starr. The rancher had planned to propose to her at the party, but a dead guest spoiled the special moment.

Mattie Hill - Wendy's best friend, who helps Lexie plan the surprise birthday party, is in charge of making out the guest list. Did she have an ulterior motive in wanting the despicable victim to attend?

Detective Wyatt Johnston - A Rockdale police officer, as well as a friend of the family. He's grown accustomed to pulling Lexie out of deep doo-doo. But this time, even *his* hands are tied.

Veronica Prescott - Daughter of the first murder victim to land the Alexandria Inn on the front page of the *Rockdale Gazette*. As Detective Johnston's girlfriend, she has to cook a lot of food, even though she consumes very little of it.

Trotter Hayes - A handsome piece of arm candy that left a sour taste in a lot of people's mouths. He finds out the hard way that his stepfather, Chief Smith, couldn't protect him from someone who thinks he's a pain in the neck.

Chief Leonard Smith - The victim's stepfather, who also happens to be the Rockdale Chief of Police. He's had run-ins with Lexie before and is determined to see her behind bars for the murder of his stepson. Does he truly think she's guilty, or is he just fed up with her meddling into his murder cases?

Joy White - The victim's date for the party. She's one of the "Three Musketeers", a tight knit trio of friends. Joy's an exercise instructor by day and something less reputable by night. Did she want to get back at the victim for forcing her to do something she'd later regret, in a tit-for-*tot* retaliation?

Alice Runcan - As homecoming queen in her senior year in high school, she was stood up at the dance by the victim. Humiliated by his deliberate insensitivity, she's long had an ax to grind with him. She doubles as the second of the Three Musketeers and the owner of a health-food restaurant, called Zen's Diner. Was Trotter's murder a case of *revenge is a dish best served cold*?

Rayleen Waters - This shrinking violet arrives at

the party with business-owner Falcon Jons, but years ago the third Musketeer had shown up with a deceitful Trotter Hayes at the homecoming dance, after he'd stood up Alice Runcan at the last minute. The musketeers gradually disbanded following Joy's unintentional backstabbing of her good friend. Vengeance comes in many forms. Was murder her payback of choice?

Falcon Jons - Owner of Midwest Aerospace, Inc. He's unimpressed when Rapella applies for a position at his firm. He takes Rayleen Waters to the birthday party, but is more interested in the victim's date, Joy White, whom he'd just broken up with when he learned she was cheating on him with the victim, Trotter Hayes. Did he find a clever way to eliminate the competition?

Georgia Piney - As the caterer, she delivered the food to the surprise birthday party. Could she have served up some sweet revenge for dessert?

Lori Piney - The caterer's daughter, who also had a motive to want to exact justice against the victim. But did she despise him enough to give him a taste of *her own medicine?*

CHAPTER 1

"We ain't getting any younger, you know. Aren't you about ready to hit the road?" I asked Clyde "Rip" Ripple, my husband of nearly fifty years.

"Don't get your bloomers in a bunch, my dear. All I need to do is get the jacks cranked up and the antenna cranked down, and we'll be ready to roll. We have plenty of time to get to the Alexandria Inn in time for the party."

"Well, get to cranking, buster. I'm anxious to get the Chartreuse Caboose on the road." I had nicknamed our RV this after we'd hand-painted it chartreuse one weekend in a fit of boredom. We'd highlighted it with a few scattered yellow sunflowers for a little added flare. If nothing else, it was easy to locate in a crowded campground.

We'd already eaten breakfast and, as usual, I heard a chorus of snap, crackle and pops before I'd even poured the milk on our cereal. It was just part of being a senior citizen, as was the prune juice we drank to wash down the whole-wheat toast that completed our morning meal. Bacon, eggs and pancakes loaded down with butter and maple syrup had gone by the wayside when our cholesterol levels achieved "walking time bomb" status. They were just a fantasy now, as were a lot of other things we'd always enjoyed in our younger days. Even our sex drives were more often in "park" than not. Still, for both being sixty-eight years old, we felt we had a lot more active lifestyle than most folks did at our age. We made sure there was never any room on our schedule for bingo and potluck dinners, staples of many senior citizens' social lives.

Rip and I, Rapella Ripple, are full-time RV enthusiasts, crisscrossing the country in our thirty-foot travel trailer. We both retired at sixty-two years old, the earliest we could and still draw our social security benefits. Rip spent his entire career in law enforcement, first as a beat cop, then as a detective, followed by seven years as the Chief of Police in our south Texas hometown of Rockport. He ended his career by serving ten years as the Sheriff of Aransas County.

I, on the other hand, have had a vast array of full- and part-time positions involving dozens of different occupations. It's not that I'm a high-maintenance, incompetent, or difficult employee; it's just that I bore easily. I've quickly tired of doing everything from pitching magazine subscriptions, where I made random phone calls and was rudely hung up on ninety-nine out of every hundred calls before I could even spit out a full sentence, to working as a clerk at a stained glass art gallery, where the "You break it, you buy it" policy applied more often to me than to the customers.

My favorite occupation was short-lived—a taste-testing job at a local ice cream factory, which I was forced to quit when I developed both lactose intolerance and a double chin. But lest you think I'm flaky or unreliable, of all of the many jobs I've had, I've only actually been fired once. And that was due to an unpleasant customer I was serving at a local restaurant. For some reason, she took it personally when I referred to her rowdy young son as an obnoxious spoiled brat who should be put in time-out until he graduated from college. Let's face it, some people are entirely too sensitive.

We found retirement to be less than it was cracked up to be after a full year of sitting on the couch staring at a TV, speaking to each other only briefly during commercials. Fortunately, we could watch the same shows every other month and not remember whether we'd seen them before. The most excitement we were apt to have in an entire week was visiting a nearby park to feed the seagulls, at least until one of us felt the need to go home and take a nap.

When it finally dawned on us that our rear ends were beginning to take root in the plaid fabric cushions of our couch, we decided enough was enough. After all, we were retired, not dead.

Within a month, we had sold our home, given

away most of our belongings, purchased a travel trailer, and hit the road. We made no plans, followed no schedule, just let each day take us wherever it might take us, which, on a number of occasions, was less than fifteen miles down the road.

Sometimes we moved daily from one RV Park to another, and from one state to another, when we got a wild hair up our rear-ends. At other times, we would rest a spell and recharge our batteries—and I mean *ours*, not that of our trailer, or the truck we used to tow it with—and we'd stay in one park for several months at a time.

We would often work as what is commonly referred to as "workampers", a name derived from a popular magazine that helped pair campgrounds with RVers willing to work there for various forms of compensation. We'd receive free site rent in exchange for helping in the RV Park office, cleaning shower houses, doing lawn work or whatever needed to be done. As you'll no doubt come to realize, "free" is my favorite word. Occasionally we're even paid a small chunk of change on top of free rent, which comes in handy with the outlandish price of gas these days.

But right now we actually had a schedule to keep. In the Cozy Camping RV Park in Cheyenne, Wyoming, just a couple of weeks prior, we'd met Lexie Starr, her husband, Stone Van Patten, and her daughter, Wendy. Lexie and Stone were celebrating their one-year anniversary during Cheyenne Frontier Days. When another camper was found murdered, Lexie and Wendy had become involved in the case, and I'd ended up involved as well, to the extent that we three gals nearly bit the big one in the process of discovering the identity of the killer. Two days after our new friends headed home to the Alexandria Inn, a bed and breakfast establishment they own in Rockdale, Missouri, I'd received a phone call from Lexie. That call resulted in Rip and me preparing to head east in order to attend a thirtieth surprise party for Wendy at their inn.

There was an RV repairman in Rockdale who worked at a station called Boney's Garage. We'd arranged to have him do some repairs on our trailer while we were there. Lexie had insisted we stay at the inn as their guests while our trailer was in the shop. Along with the word "free," I was also quite fond of its cousin, "guest." My favorite thing about being sixty-eight was the senior citizen discount that came with it.

Less than an hour later, we had Wyoming in our rearview mirror as we crossed over the Nebraska border. I had a feeling this trip would turn out to be one we wouldn't soon forget. Call it a premonition, or just a fit of fancy, but it was a feeling I couldn't shake. I was anxiously looking forward to finding out if there was anything to my anticipation, because boredom was nipping at our heels once again, and I was more than ready for a little excitement.

"According to this GPS thingy you bought yourself for our last anniversary, we are only a mile and a half from Rockdale. How can that be?" I asked Rip. I'd barely gotten my seat belt on, for goodness sakes.

"We pulled out of Cozy Camping forty-five seconds ago, dear. We're over six hundred miles from our destination. And, as you know, that's about twice what I like to drive in one day, so we'll pull over in a campground in Kearney tonight."

"Now it says we're only a mile from Rockdale," I insisted. As usual, I was pretty much just tuning out Rip's side of our conversation, as he nearly always did with me, too. "What kind of silly contraption is that thing, anyway?"

"Sweetheart, that isn't the distance to Rockdale. It's indicating that we're to stay on College Drive for a mile before taking the ramp on the right onto I-80 East."

"You couldn't have figured out yourself that we needed to go east on I-80 without that thing telling you? Ask me next time. I'd have been happy to inform you that if you went west on I-80 you'd end up in Utah, not Missouri. I could have saved you about a hundred bucks."

"Then we won't turn again until we reach Lincoln. We'll be in Nebraska all day," my husband explained patiently, as if I'd never spoken. As I suspected, not only had he tuned me out completely, he likely didn't have his hearing aids in either. For some reason, he found them unnecessary when there was no one around but me.

Rip often said it was fortunate that he had the

patience of a saint, and I had to admit he was probably right. But the GPS thingy still made no sense whatsoever to me. We'd been traveling around the country for six years. I couldn't recall driving around in circles, hopelessly lost, *before* Rip bought the GPS device. But I could remember a number of times *since* he's had it that the female voice has had him backtracking, making illegal U-turns and driving down dead-end streets while she'd been "recalculating" her butt off the entire time. Worst of all, she had him doing all this as he was driving to a location he'd driven straight to a hundred times before without her assistance. I didn't bring this up to Rip, however, knowing he wasn't paying a lick of attention to me anyway. Knowing him, he'd have only replied, "I thought maybe she knew a better way to get there."

"So why does your gadget say it's six-thirty? My watch reads ten o'clock."

"That's not the current time, dear. It's the E.T.A, estimated time of arrival, if we were to drive all the way to Rockdale, Missouri, tonight. I estimate we'll be arriving in Kearney around two-thirty, just in time for our three o'clock highball."

"Well, I'm all for that, but I think this GPS doo-dad was a waste of good money. It's too complicated, like that cell phone we've tried to use and can't even figure out how to call anyone on. Well, except for the time when you butt-dialed everyone on the contact list. It was the same day you accidentally placed a call to the Russian Prime Minister, Vladimir Putin."

"Yes, and if his secretary had put me through to him, I'd have had plenty to say to him. He needs a comeuppance, and I'm just the guy to give it to him."

"No doubt. Yesterday you talked to the fellow sacking our groceries for ten minutes about his haircut. By the time we got to the car, the ice cream was dripping out the little hole in the plastic bag. All I can say is, thank God Wal-Mart has such a liberal return policy on both Ben and Jerry's *and* cell phones."

"Sometimes I just like to be friendly. And I am not returning that phone, Rapella. We need to figure out how to use it. After all, we are two of the last remaining dinosaurs in existence who aren't totally tethered to their cell phones. Plus, it would be handy to be able to call and make reservations at RV parks from the road, you know. How many times have we driven miles out of our way to get to an RV Park with no vacancies? Cell phones are almost a must these days. And very handy in emergencies too, I'm sure."

"Fine. Whatever. It took you three months to figure out this silly GPS thing, so you'd best get started figuring out the cell phone right now if you want to learn how to use it while you're still on the right side of the grass."

Without replying, Rip put on the blinker as he gradually merged onto the I-80 exit ramp. He awkwardly extracted the cell phone from his front pants pocket and placed it in the center console. In the past, he'd nearly caused several pileups trying to get the ringing phone out of his jeans pocket while driving down the road. He'd drop it on the floorboard and weave from lane to lane trying to pick it back up. Then, instead of answering the phone, he'd nearly always hang up on the caller. It was like watching a toddler trying to operate the controls of a fighter jet; a lot of clueless button pushing with no idea what might happen as a result.

Even though I was basically talking to myself, I continued. "But I guess the GPS gadget was your anniversary gift, and if you like the over-priced toy, so be it. If you splurged this much for our forty-ninth, how much do you intend to blow on our upcoming golden anniversary?"

"Fiftieth anniversaries are rare these days, sweetheart. For that matter, marriages in general are rare these days. Stone and Lexie got me thinking about you and me taking a special vacation to celebrate the big occasion," Rip said. Funny how his hearing problem cleared up when the topic veered toward something he was interested in.

"But we're basically on vacation 24/7 now. We've been all over the country already. Where could we go that would be special? You know I don't trust airplanes as far as I can throw up in them. And I wouldn't feel safe on any foreign soil in this day and age. That old adage, there's no place like home, is especially true now. Because in so many other countries you'd have a target on your back and be lucky you weren't blown to smithereens when you stepped off the plane onto the tarmac. I don't understand why we all can't just get along. Live and let be, I've always said." I loved the open road, but the friendly skies were a whole different ball of wax.

"I agree wholeheartedly with you about traveling outside the good ol' USA right now, with turmoil and havoc taking place around the globe," Rip said. "But we can't let the threat of terrorism keep us from living our lives and doing the things we enjoy. If we do, the cowards win! For all we know, there could be a sleeper cell of extremists planning an attack right there in Rockdale, as we speak. But even so, the chances of being taken out by a terrorist are still relatively remote."

"You're absolutely right, Rip! I'm more apt to get killed in the H.E.B parking lot than I am by a suicide bomber. It's like negotiating your way through a mine field sometimes. I can't tell you how many times, while loading groceries in the truck, I've nearly been mowed down by stressed-out soccer moms chauffeuring a dozen kids around in their SUV's, fifteen-year old boys with brand new learner's permits, and even senile old ladies with glaucoma in one eye and macular degeneration in the other."

I might as well have been talking to the air conditioner vent for all the attention Rip was paying to me. He tended to have a one-track mind, so I listened as Rip continued expressing his plans for our anniversary trip.

"I was thinking about driving up to Alaska. We could take our time and enjoy all the sights along the way. We've never been there and I've heard the state is incredibly beautiful and full of fascinating things to see and do. I've always wanted to see the glaciers and perhaps spend a few days panning for gold."

"It does sound like a fun adventure. I'd like to see a dog sled team in action and go on a wildlife tour to see critters like moose, caribou, bears and bald eagles. But wouldn't a trip like that be expensive?" I asked.

"It wouldn't be cheap, by any means. It's a long trip up the Alaskan Highway, for sure. Almost fourteen-hundred miles, in fact. We'd pay a small fortune on gas and most likely have to replace a few tires on the journey, but we can afford it. A milestone anniversary like our fiftieth deserves an extra special celebration. You know, we only live once, and we can't take it with us. I've never seen a Brinks truck following a hearse, have you?"

"But I want to leave Regina cared for," I argued.

"Reggie's financially sound. She married a very industrious guy and they're making boatloads of cash. In fact, she's got more resources and investments than we do. There's no reason for us to sit on our money like old hens. Besides, what would you opt for instead? A new eggbeater? You've got to admit, my dear, a trip to Alaska would be far sight more exciting than that hard rubber spatula you bought yourself for our last anniversary."

We were well beyond buying each other presents. After he'd gifted me with a new weed-eater on Christmas years ago, and I'd given him a set of Corelle dishes that bounced when you dropped them, we decided we might as well start buying our own gifts. At least we'd be guaranteed to like the presents we exchanged.

"The handle broke on my old spatula and left me with only a metal one to use," I replied in my defense. "And you know metal is like kryptonite to a Teflon skillet. I sure don't want to be shelling out twenty bucks on a new skillet, too."

"Who do you think you're kidding, sweetheart? I was with you when you paid seventy-five cents for that skillet at a flea market. It didn't have much Teflon left on it then, and has even less now," Rip said with a chuckle. "I watched you break the handle off that crusty old spatula trying to scrape burnt cheese off the bottom of that crusty old skillet. I realize we aren't loaded, honey, but we can surely upgrade a notch or two above 'crusty' at this stage in our lives."

Rip was right, but as long as the skillet was still at least somewhat functional, I wasn't going to waste hard-earned money on a new one. He often accused me of being a tightwad, but I like to think of it as being financially responsible. My family was dirt poor when I was a child, and early on I knew I never wanted to go to bed hungry again, so I try not to throw money away unnecessarily.

As Rip set the cruise control at seventy on the pickup, I settled into my seat for the day's ride. I was looking forward to seeing Lexie, Stone, and Wendy again. The near-death experience the three of us had experienced had formed a strong bond between us, and attending Wendy's surprise thirtieth birthday party sounded really fun as well.

The rhythmic movement of our Chevy truck as we traveled down the interstate lulled me into a peaceful trance. I found myself daydreaming about what the next ten days would entail. I couldn't get past the feeling that an unexpected chain of events, such as a ripple effect, had been set into motion.

CHAPTER 2

"Are you ready to pull over and have a bite to eat?" Rip asked. He was rubbing his hip with his right hand as he drove with his left. "It's about Dolly's lunch time."

Our lives usually revolved around the four-times-per-day eating schedule of the chubby six-year-old grey and white tabby we traveled with. Being this cat's servants was pretty much a thankless job, but we adored her nonetheless. She always rode in the trailer when we were on the road. Otherwise, we'd be driven insane by Dolly's screeching and squalling as she plastered herself against the window trying to persuade people in passing vehicles to save her from such an injustice.

Although it's not recommended, I'd ridden in the trailer with her one time when I felt under the weather. For some odd reason, traveling in the trailer didn't affect her at all. She had curled up in the middle of the sofa and slept peacefully all day. I was convinced it was just a power play on Dolly's part; a reminder of who called the shots in our household.

"Yes, it's time for her majesty's twelve o'clock feeding," I said in response to Rip's remark. "You probably need to get up and move around a bit anyway. You can stretch your legs while I make us each a sandwich. We still have some leftover ham we need to use up before it turns green and fuzzy. As it is, it's taken on a slimy appearance and I've had to cut out a couple of areas that looked past their prime."

"Man, does that sound appetizing! My mouth's salivating just thinking about it. In the future, could you please refrain from describing the condition of my lunch quite so vividly? 'Leftover ham' is all I really needed to know," Rip said with a sigh. "Can we have a few chips with our sandwich, you know, just in case I can't choke down the decaying ham? Why didn't you pick up some fresh lunchmeat at the store yesterday?"

"Have you seen the price of meat these days? Ain't no sense wasting perfectly good ham when there are people going to bed hungry all over the world. It would be a crying shame to throw out edible food while other less fortunate people are starving."

"Okay! Okay! I give up. I'm not sure I'd call it 'perfectly good ham,' but I'm almost willing to go to bed hungry myself just so I wouldn't have to eat it." My husband could be quite frivolous with money when it came to groceries. I never understood his willingness to toss out food just because it was a few days past its expiration date. I've seen homeless folks digging through dumpsters who would be thrilled to happen upon the food he'd so casually thrown away.

"*We* are not homeless! If we get to the point we can't afford lunchmeat, I'll get a job sacking groceries," Rip would say when I brought this to his attention.

I admit I'm tight-fisted. Growing up, my family had been forced to scratch you-know-what with the chickens just to get by. Money was hard to come by, and my pappy couldn't keep a job to save his soul, and that's if mama could get him to look for one in the first place. It wasn't that he wasn't a hard worker, because he could work circles around men half his age. But if a hankering for something more enticing came along, such as an afternoon of fishing down on the creek bed, or perhaps a day spent bellied up to the bar in some dingy watering hole in town, my pappy would indulge himself and end up jobless more often than not.

When I married Clyde right out of high school, we were both just eighteen. I vowed to be responsible as possible with whatever money we were able to scrounge up. I never wanted to find myself down and out again, forced to live on handouts and the good will of others.

Like me, my dear momma loved my pappy unconditionally and never complained. She'd worked until her hands bled; doing anything she could to make money. She washed and mended other folks' clothes, cleaned out barns, and even stooped to begging on the street whenever we'd hit rock bottom, which was a frequent occurrence. Momma had done whatever it took to see that my siblings and I got an education. I was the youngest of five kids, and my mother passed away just after I got my high school diploma and my new husband all in the same week.

But even though I am financially conservative, I'm not cold-hearted or ungrateful. Since we had depended on the generosity of others to help us scrape by at times, I did my best to pay it forward. I donated money at least once a month to homeless shelters and food missions to help the needy scrape by, as we'd often needed help to do. We volunteered to work at the food missions frequently as well. However, helping the less fortunate was my only extravagance, if it could even be called that.

Traveling down the interstate a couple of hours later, Rip said, "Kearney is only about fifteen miles ahead. Do you want to pull over in a state park, or stay over in a discount store's parking lot to save a few bucks? I'd vote to splurge and stay in that nice Good Sam campground south of town along the Platte River."

"I think we can splurge for one night since we'll be spending the next week or so at Stone and Lexie's bed and breakfast," I replied. "Not to mention, we stashed away a nice wad of money helping the Harringtons out the last month and a half. If I remember right, this park on the river also has a nice pool. We could both use the exercise."

As "workampers", we'd made six hundred bucks, as well as getting a free RV site, at my cousin and her husband's Cozy Camping RV Park in Cheyenne, Wyoming. We'd kept the shower houses clean, and during the annual Frontier Days, we'd also bagged cubes from their ice machine and sold the bags of ice to campers. Cheyenne Frontier Days was the largest outdoor rodeo in the world, and the campground had been filled up to the gills with campers.

The annual rodeo was held in late July during the heat of the summer. Bags of ice sold faster than the Harringtons' machine could make it, and they often had to pay a local company to deliver extra ice just to keep up with the demand. As my cousin, Emily, told me, there were only two seasons in Wyoming - winter and July - and she wasn't exaggerating all that much. But summer to folks in Wyoming is subjective. In comparison, the hot and humid summers in south Texas would be akin to hell on earth.

As full-time RVers, when we weren't working for free rent at campgrounds, we often "dry-camped" to save money. Before leaving a park with full-hookups, we'd empty our grey-and-black-water tanks, and fill our fresh water tank. Along with our generator, we could camp without hookups for several days, which usually saved us at least a hundred bucks in campground fees.

We'd also utilize state and city parks, which were normally cheap, or even free, but where campers were often only allowed to stay a limited amount of time. Occasionally we spent the night in parking lots, where permitted, but it was always a special treat to stay in a fully-appointed RV Park.

We generally opted for Good Sam Parks where the campgrounds had to maintain high standards to maintain their Good Sam status. We carried one of their catalogs in our truck, which made finding a nice campground much easier. More importantly, we received a ten percent discount with our Good Sam card. We usually looked for campgrounds with swimming pools as well. We both enjoyed swimming for exercise, and with Rip's bad hip, swimming helped alleviate the pain of bone grinding against bone.

"By the way, Rip, when are you going to have that hip looked at? Are you planning to wait until you have to crawl to the bathroom just to take a leak?" I asked my reluctant partner. Like a lot of men, he avoided doctors like the plague. I'm sure he was afraid they'd find something dreadfully wrong with him that he didn't care to know about, or that, God forbid, required surgery or unpleasant treatment of any kind. "You know as well as I do that you need a hip replacement. It's not going to get any better on its own and eventually hip replacement is going to be inevitable anyway, you stubborn mule."

"Yeah, well, until it's absolutely necessary, I'm not going to allow anyone to cut on me like a butchered hog. In the meantime, I get along just fine with my trusty cane. So get off my case about seeing a doctor, sweetheart. In the meantime, help me watch for the right exit."

I knew he was changing the subject to avoid a good old-fashioned nagging episode by me. It's not like he hadn't heard my "your stupid stubbornness is going come back and bite you in the rear end" speech so many times before that he could probably recite it himself. So, instead of reiterating it, I responded to his request. "I thought that's why you bought that high-faluting GPS thingy? Ain't it supposed to tell you every move to make? Does it tell you when to pull over in a rest stop to pee, or do you have to figure that out all by yourself?"

Rip's selective hearing had been reactivated, so I just slipped on my bifocals that had been hanging from around my neck on an old shoestring I'd fashioned to hold them and began to read the road signs as they whizzed by. Within forty-five minutes, we were sitting in folding lawn chairs on the patio of our full-hookup RV site. Rip had leveled the trailer, attached the hoses and cords, and hooked up the cable TV, while I fixed us each our favorite drink. At the end of a long day on the road, we each always allowed ourselves a single highball, albeit the one allotted mixed drink was served in quart canning jars.

We didn't want to get staggering sloshed, but we did want enough alcohol to help us unwind and relax. My drink of choice was a tequila sunrise while Rip preferred a "Douchebag"—a cocktail containing four ounces of Crown Royal and such a tiny splash of Coke that a twenty-ounce bottle was a lifetime supply. In fact, I have a suspicion that the minute amount of Coke is added just so he can refer to the drink as a cocktail and not just four straight-up shots of pure whiskey. To test out my theory, I once served his Douchebag without the Coke and, sure enough, he hadn't even noticed it was missing.

It was warm and muggy in Nebraska that afternoon. It was the kind of heat and humidity that zapped your energy within minutes. Given the weather, my tequila sunrise was particularly refreshing. When I set the full jars of our iced cocktails on a small folding table we carried in the under-belly storage compartment, the sweat rolled off them like an NFL linebacker at training camp.

Fortunately, there was a nice breeze, a pleasant view of the Platte River, and much-needed shade under the awning on the door side of the Chartreuse Caboose. I had cranked out the full-length canvas awning after I'd removed the chairs from the same storage compartment beneath the trailer. This was a much more enjoyable atmosphere than one would find in an asphalted Wal-Mart parking lot.

We sipped on our drinks as we discussed our upcoming stay at our new friends' bed and breakfast. The Alexandria Inn was a massive renovated Victorian mansion from the turn of the 20th century according to Lexie. We talked about how nice it'd be to see the fascinating home and visit with our new friends.

After we'd exhausted that subject, Rip

explained the issues with the travel trailer he planned to have the local Rockdale mechanic take care of during our stay. His detailed explanation of each repair that needed to be done nearly caused me to nod off.

I finally distracted him enough to launch into a new, more intriguing subject. We discussed what Lexie had told us concerning the surprise birthday party she was hosting for her daughter.

"It sounds like it'll be a rip-roaring good time," my husband said.

"Yes, it does," I agreed. "I'm really looking forward to a little R&R while we're at the inn. It will be nice to kick back for a week or so and just hang around the inn like lazy slugs for a few days."

"Good luck with that," Rip said. "Since we came out of our self-induced hibernation, which most folks call retirement, I've never seen you manage to rest and relax for over about ten minutes in a row."

Little did I know, this would not be an issue. As things would turn out, there would be little time for kicking back, resting, and relaxing in the coming days. Being a lazy slug for a spell would turn out to have just been wishful thinking on my part.

CHAPTER 3

We pulled into Boney's Garage in Rockdale, Missouri, early the next afternoon. An older mechanic named Paul, who specialized in recreational vehicle repairs, was going to work on a long list of issues regarding leaks, squeaks, and reeks that had been accumulating over the last several months. The mechanic would work on the repairs while we spent the week at the Alexandria Inn. I'd been nagging Rip to work on the problems himself. Naturally, I would have liked to avoid the cost of a repairman, someone who, at seventy-five bucks an hour, had no incentive to hurry and get the job completed.

After a lengthy career as a member of law enforcement, Rip could bust them, cuff them, and stuff them like nobody's business. If you needed someone to scour your basement for potential serial killers after you'd heard a suspicious noise, or to talk a suicidal citizen at the bitter end of his rope down off the ledge of a tall building, Rip was the man for the job.

But ask him to get a toilet to flush properly, and he'll stare at it in a stupor as if viewing some unrecognizable object brought back to Earth from a mission on Mars. Watching this man stand hopelessly boggled in front of the ill-functioning commode with a can of WD-40 in one hand and a roll of duct tape in the other, one would never guess he'd utilized the object, and other ones just like it, many thousands of times in his sixty-eight years of life.

It was frustrating at times but I couldn't fault the guy for not being handy around the house. After all, for the majority of his life Rip's main focus had been to make it through each eight-hour shift without becoming a statistic while enforcing law and order within his jurisdiction. Somehow, he'd managed to get through all thirty-seven years on the force without sustaining a major injury, either accidental or intentional, in the line of duty. When he'd retired at sixty-two, he'd felt as if he was pushing his luck and the odds were against him.

Unlike my previous job at the ice cream factory, where all I took home with me was a tummy ache, a few extra pounds on my tall frame, and abundant chocolate stains on my blouse, his wasn't the kind of job you could leave at the office after you clocked out at the end of your shift. This was especially true after holding a tiny child in his arms as it succumbed from injuries sustained in a head-on collision caused by a drunk driver, or after having to kill a misguided teenager who'd pulled a handgun on him when Rip stumbled onto the young boy selling meth in an alley.

I was thankful my dear husband could put both of these heart-rending events, along with many other horrendous incidents he'd been involved in, behind him and enjoy his retirement away from all the stress and turmoil. Rip seldom watched the news on television after he retired. It wasn't because he didn't care what was going on in the world. He just didn't want to revisit old memories evoked from the overwhelming negativity of your average evening newscast.

I thought about these things as I watched Rip describing the eerie sound emitting from the air conditioner unit in our travel trailer, the eye-burning odor radiating from the refrigerator, and the water gushing from the pipes underneath the sink every time I washed the dishes.

From my line of view, as I leaned against a greasy concrete wall, Rip's balding head was barely visible over the hood of our pick-up truck as he conversed with the mechanic. At five-foot-seven, he was an inch shorter than I was but made up for his height deficiency with a doughnut-induced spare tire around his waist. Yes, it's true. Some cops really do rely on long johns and apple fritters for sustenance. My husband may have given up his job of maintaining the peace, but he'd yet to turn his back on a cream-filled doughnut.

I continued to watch as Paul, the older

mechanic, nodded his head frequently while Rip went into way too much detail about each issue. Paul's eyes eventually glazed over, as he'd no doubt tuned out the non-stop blabbering by Rip and started calculating in his head how much money he'd make at his hourly rate before my husband even finished working his way through the extensive list. I could see our bill growing with each faulty item Rip told the mechanic about.

"Hey, Chatty Cathy, over there," I finally shouted. "Could you kick it up a notch? He doesn't need to know every single item in our icebox. That stench smells more like burning rubber than that moldy chunk of head cheese I should have thrown out two weeks ago."

Without stopping to take a breath or even acknowledge I'd spoken, Rip launched into a long-winded story about the time he'd cut the cheese during a somber funeral service in Rockport. That anecdote cracked him up every time he told it. I still don't know how the man could turn on a dime mid-sentence.

Before my rising temper could begin to steam like the radiator the younger mechanic was working on in the other stall, I went outside and sat impatiently on a wrought-iron bench until Rip finally unhitched the trailer and motioned for me to get in the truck. He had already transferred Dolly to the truck, and she was carrying on as if a sewer rat had a hold of her tail.

Later, after a strenuous evening of sniffing and

checking out every square inch of the building, Dolly snarfed up her eight o'clock meal and was snoozing at the foot of our bed in one of the nicest suites in the inn. When guiding us to the suite, Lexie had assured us no one had died in it.

While Dolly was no doubt dreaming about her ten o'clock "go to bed" snack, Rip and I were relaxing on the back covered porch of the inn, enjoying some apple tarts and a couple of cups of stout coffee with our hosts, Lexie and Stone. We were discussing the events following the death of a snooty author at the campground in Cheyenne, Wyoming, a couple of weeks prior.

We'd recently picked up some tidbits of interesting news from my cousin, Emily, who owned the campground we'd all been staying in at the time of the murder. I had recognized Lexie's curious nature as being very much like my own, and I knew she'd want all the juicy details. As expected, she absorbed the information like a sponge.

The only good thing to arise from the tragedy was that we were becoming acquainted with our two new friends. After a few minutes, I noticed I was getting uncomfortably warm. I didn't want to complain to these nice folks, but I was sweating like a prizefighter and Rip was constantly wiping his brow with an old stained handkerchief he'd pulled out of his back pocket. Having gotten accustomed to the cooler, dryer climate of Cheyenne, it felt like it was a hundred and ten on that porch and as if I were trying to breathe through a soggy throw cushion. And drinking hot coffee hadn't helped the matter much.

When Lexie finally noticed a rapidly expanding wet splotch on the front of my shirt from perspiration trailing down between my breasts, she said, "Oh, heavens, you two must be sweltering. It took us a couple of days to re-acclimate to this muggy weather, and we were only in Cheyenne for a week."

"Yeah, this humidity is like a slap in the face after you've gotten used to not being able to work up a sweat if you tried. Right now I'm sweating like a call girl in church." I pulled my damp shirt away from my body and fanned it to emphasize my point. Lexie flashed me a warm smile while nodding her head in agreement.

"Let's retreat to the parlor inside. Stone usually keeps it like a meat locker in there." After she finished speaking, Lexie picked up the now empty coffee carafe and opened the French door that led into the kitchen.

With a couple of days on the road under our belt, Rip and I were both yawning and struggling to concentrate on the conversation. Rip spoke for both of us when he said, "We're kind of wiped out. If you two don't mind, I think we'd like to call it a day so we'll be fresh for the party tomorrow."

"You're right," Lexie replied. "We probably need to get a good night's rest too. We have a lot to get done tomorrow before all the guests begin to arrive at seven-thirty in the evening. Andy's going to tell Wendy he's taking her out to eat for her birthday and that I'd asked them to stop by here on their way to the restaurant to pick up a gift we'd gotten for her. When she opens the front door, the lights will flick on, everyone will shout 'surprise', and her thirtieth birthday party will commence. We'll be serving a catered dinner soon after they arrive, and there'll be plenty of refreshments on hand to satisfy everyone's appetites."

"I have underwear older than Wendy. In fact, I think I bought the pair I'm wearing right now during the Revolutionary War. And, according to Rapella, they've still got a few good years left in them. But, seriously, what a wonderful surprise to celebrate Wendy's milestone birthday," Rip said.

"Yes, and that's not even the biggest surprise awaiting her," Lexie responded with a sly smile and a twinkle in her eyes.

"Then what is?" Rip and I asked in unison.

"Once the party is in full swing Andy's going to hush the crowd to announce he wants to make a toast. Then he's going to get down on his knee in front of all their family and friends and ask her to marry him."

"Oh, what an exciting evening it's going to be!" I exclaimed. "As Rip said on the way here, it sounds like it's going to be a rip roaring good time. It'll be a night your daughter will never forget."

Little did I know at that moment my statement could not have been any more spot on.

CHAPTER 4

The coffee I'd ingested before hitting the sack had me tossing and turning all night. Wendy had warned me about Lexie's caffeine addiction. I realized then that if I drank a cup of her robust brew every time she offered me one, I'd down enough of the powerful stimulant to keep a small village awake for a week. I vowed to increase my water intake while I was at the Alexandria Inn instead of my coffee consumption.

Listening to Rip snoring contentedly as he relaxed in a deep sleep next to me made me want to kick him in the shin, or pull the pillow out from under his head. Misery loved company and I wanted that company to be as wide-awake as I was. I squashed my temptation and didn't disturb him, however. He had driven the entire way from Cheyenne while I worked on a wooden figurine I was carving into the shape of a goat. I had wanted to finish it in time to give it to Wendy as a birthday gift.

Wendy had showed me a photo of an ornery goat that lived on her boyfriend, Andy's, farm. She'd told me some humorous anecdotes about the temperamental critter she referred to as Precious. It had given me the idea to carve a replica of the animal to give her for her birthday instead of wasting money on something she already had or didn't want. As a young girl, I had learned to whittle and carve wood from my pappy, who could while away an entire afternoon turning a small log into a toothpick. It beat the hell out of working, he used to tell me.

With four older brothers, I leaned toward being a tomboy, so they'd let me go with them when they went to town to look for small jobs, or to talk strangers into giving them enough change to buy chewing tobacco. I tried some of the Beechnut they'd talked an old farmer out of one day. Not only did it taste like Wintergreen gum dipped in cow manure to me, it also had me puking my guts up for the rest of the day. After that, I didn't try quite as hard to be like one of the boys.

I was pappy's only daughter and he called me his little princess, even though instead of fancy dresses, I usually wore stained hand-me-down britches and tattered shirts my brothers had outgrown. But I stuck to pappy like a stamp and learned a lot of time-wasting skills from him.

Reminiscing about my childhood helped me to finally doze off around three and sleep fitfully until six. While I was clearing the cobwebs out of my mind, I decided I'd pull out something more appropriate to wear to the party that evening, but for now, I'd just slip on some old holey jeans and an aquamarine shirt with a sunflower on it. The jeans had come back into style. Even though the holes in my jeans were from wear and tear, I'd seen a pair just like them on a rack at Penney's for sixty-five bucks. The shirt, which I'd found at a garage sale for a quarter, had inspired me to paint our travel trailer in a similar design.

I think the old mechanic at Boney's garage had been impressed with our paint job too. I'd seen the younger fellow point at the trailer when we pulled into the station, and say something to him. Paul had responded with a huge smile and nodded in agreement. I knew when I'd talked Rip into painting it that it'd be a big hit. And to think, Rip had thought it would look ridiculous.

I reluctantly rolled out of bed to get ready for the day. Fifteen minutes later I had dressed, put my teeth back in after having let them soak in a glass jar on the bathroom counter all night, and pulled a comb through my naturally wavy salt and pepper hair. My hair looked just a touch saltier with each day that passed, and I'm not sure what it says about my character, but I really didn't give a rat's ass if it turned the color of a field mouse overnight—no pun intended.

I set Rip's hearing aids on the counter so he wouldn't forget to wear them while we were here. It wasn't a big deal whether or not he heard what I had to say, he'd told me, but he didn't want to miss out on the conversation with Stone and Lexie. *How rude*, I thought. I had half a notion to take the batteries out of his hearing aids and not tell him I'd done so.

Finished with my morning routine, I went down to the kitchen to have some coffee with Lexie. I needed to get rid of the fog enveloping my brain after such little sleep. As expected, she was sitting at the kitchen table with a cup in her hand.

Lexie looked a bit harried as she sorted through a conglomeration of lists and receipts on the table in front of her. She'd been muttering to herself when I'd entered the room.

"Good morning, sunshine," I greeted her. She was such a sweetheart, and the thought flitted through my mind that she looked young enough to be my daughter. But then I realized she could've been had I got knocked up at seventeen instead of eighteen. We hadn't seen our own daughter since we'd gone home to Texas for her fiftieth birthday in the late spring. But Regina had been so tied up in some real estate deals she was involved in, she'd hardly had time to visit with us. Reggie, as we've always called her, and her husband, Milo Moore, made a living "flipping houses" in town, whatever that means. Even though their livelihood sounded somewhat sketchy to me, they seemed to be doing well financially, so I kept my nose out of their business.

"Grab a cup of coffee, Rapella," Lexie suggested.

"Sure thing, but I'm limiting myself to two cups

a day while I'm here. I didn't sleep so good last night. If I tried to keep up with your caffeine consumption, I'd be buzzing around here like the queen bee hepped up on fermented nectar. But if you can handle a boatload of it, more power to you. Speaking of which, would you like a refill while I'm pouring mine?"

"Yes, please. I need another boost of energy to get all these details taken care of today."

"Can I help in any way?" I asked. "I have nothing else to do."

"Actually," she replied with a grin, "I was hoping you'd volunteer."

"What are all these lists you got here?" I asked as I pulled out a chair and sat down. "I hate to use a cliché, but you need to get all these ducks in a row."

Before Lexie could respond, a knock at the door startled both of us. After Lexie hollered for the visitor to come in, a young gal about Wendy's age walked in, and danged if she didn't have a fistful of lists in her hand too. *Probably a darned good thing I am here to help,* I thought. I said, "Good Lord! You gals must have ducks running amok all over the place!"

They both looked at me like I'd just spoken to them in Mandarin Chinese. Lexie introduced us, and the blonde young gal replied, "Nice to meet you Mrs. Ripple. I'm Wendy's best friend, and I'm helping her mom with the surprise party."

"It's a pleasure to meet you too, Mattie. Just call me Rapella, dear. Mrs. Ripple makes me sound old."

Lexie invited Mattie to sit down and asked, "Okay, dear, have you got a final count for me?"

Mattie nodded and replied, "As close as I'm apt to get, I think. I invited all of Wendy's friends who live in the area, of course. I knew the parlor here could handle a pretty big crowd. I factored in the people who definitely plan to come, the people who can't make it due to other obligations, and the people who will be here if at all possible. Then, assuming most guests will be bringing a spouse, boyfriend, or friend, along with them, I'm estimating between thirty-five and forty will be attending the party tonight."

"Okay. Thanks, honey!" Lexie said, looking at Mattie as she spoke. "That sounds perfect. I ordered enough cake to feed fifty and told the caterer to be prepared to feed dinner to that many as well. I also bought enough snacks, drinks, and refreshments to feed all of Rockdale. I knew the leftovers would not go to waste with the inn full of guests."

Lexie glanced at me with a smile and continued speaking to Mattie. "Every room in the inn is reserved for the weekend. Most of the guests are here to attend the party tonight. The Ripples will be visiting for a few days too. I'm sure the food will all get eaten one way or another."

"Cool," Mattie replied. "Did you think of anyone else I should invite that I overlooked?"

"No. I don't know whom all you invited, but I'm sure you know better than I who Wendy would want to come help her celebrate her thirtieth. I'm sure you covered all the bases. You did invite her boss, Nate, and her other co-workers at the county coroner's lab, didn't you?"

"Yes. Nate, his wife, and two other co-workers will be here for sure, and one plans to come if the seminar she's attending is over in time. Although it sounds grotesque to me, she was excited to go hear a renowned pathologist discuss new techniques in the art of dissecting cadavers."

"I'm glad Wendy had already heard that lecturer speak at an earlier event or we wouldn't have been able to pull her away from that seminar either. I don't know what these young people find so fascinating about carving a human body up like a Thanksgiving turkey to discover what caused their untimely demise. But I guess somebody has to do it."

"Better her than me, 'cause it grosses me out," Mattie said. She laughed and added—for my benefit, I was sure—"As a nurse in the neo-natal department at Wheatland Memorial Hospital in St. Joseph, our occupations are on opposite ends of the spectrum. I help them come into the world and Wendy tends to them after they depart. Sometimes I have to beg her not to go into detail about one of her latest cases. The one regarding the elderly woman who swallowed a cat food can lid was particularly gruesome."

"Yes, I remember her telling me about that one too," Lexie said with a dramatic shudder. "The old gal just lived a couple of blocks from here. No one knew she'd gotten to the point of having to eat cat food just to survive. They found her two Persians dead in the basement, one rotting and full of maggots, and the other one already reduced to a pile of bones."

"Egads! Those poor kitties didn't deserve to suffer such a terrible death. So what happened to the old broad after that?" I asked.

Mattie's head turned and she looked at me with an odd expression on her face, but I didn't have time to wonder why before Lexie answered my question. "The sharp-edged lid sliced Erma Digg's digestive tract up as if it were a razor blade, and she bled out on the way to the hospital. If we had only known Erma was in such dire straits, we'd have made sure she was taken care of and well fed."

Mattie nodded solemnly and said, "I'd have personally seen to it she had everything she needed to live comfortably no matter how much it cost."

Briefly, I wondered how a young nurse like Mattie could afford to be so generous. Then I shook my head and asked, "Didn't anybody think to check in on the old lady? Jeez Louise! Where I'm from, people watch out for their neighbors a little better than that, especially the ones up there in age. The whole town of Rockdale should be ashamed of themselves."

"I agree, Rapella. We all felt very bad afterward. I didn't know her well at all, but I should have popped in on her now and then anyway. I'd have kept her cupboards full had I taken the initiative to find out how she was faring. I guess hindsight's twenty/twenty, as they say. But back to the business at hand. I'll be inviting all the unrelated guests who'll be checking into the inn today to come to the party too, if they don't already have plans for the evening. I don't anticipate they'll all be joining us, but perhaps one or two might accept our invitation."

"What can I do to be of use to you ladies? Sitting here on my thumbs all day ain't gonna be much help to you." I was already tiring of just sitting around doing nothing. I needed something to do to keep busy. Rip was the same way, and bad hip and all, I could see him through the window limping around the perimeter of a large colorful garden in the center of the circular driveway. He was trimming the edge of the flowerbed with a weed-eater. I'd heard Stone tell Rip he could easily handle all the lawn work by himself, but my husband could be very persuasive—well, actually, he was just plain bull-headed at times.

I listened quietly as Lexie responded to my question. "I was hoping you could meet with the caterer this morning. Georgia Piney's not well educated, but she's really a sweet gal and a great cook. You'll like her."

"I'd be happy to meet with this Georgia."

"I need to pick up the sheet cake at Pete's Pantry. They made our wedding cake last year and it was delicious. I also need to swing by the bank to get some cash, and I have to grab a few items at the grocery store—fruit juice, chips, dip, and some other snacks. My best friend, Sheila Davidson, and her husband, Randy, are coming up from Fairway, Kansas. She's known Wendy since the day she was born, having been in the delivery room with us. Sheila makes a mean spiked punch that contains orange, pineapple, and mango juices, along with a hefty amount of grain alcohol. Her so called 'Citrus Surprise' packs a *punch* you will never see coming. Or at least not until you try to stand up and walk under your own power, that is."

"Thanks for the warning," I said. "I think Rip and I will stick to our tequila and Crown Royal, if you don't mind. Trust me, you don't want either one of us dancing on the table with a lampshade on our heads. Been there, done that, and believe me, it wasn't a pretty sight."

Rip had programmed the GPS in our truck to the address Lexie gave me, and the lady's voice took me to a small house on the other side of town. I only hoped I could figure out how to get back to the inn without having to mess with the over-priced electronic device. No telling where I'd end up if I tried to program the inn's address into it. A couple of wrong turns, and I'd be in Iowa before I knew it.

I wasn't totally convinced I'd pulled up to the right place when the gadget informed me I'd reached my destination. I'd expected to end up at some kind of business establishment with a "Catering" sign on the front door. Instead, the only sign on the front of this run-down place was a note on a piece of cardboard paper that read *"Bewear of Dog. No Solesiters - No*

Tresspassen," written sloppily with a green magic marker. I wasn't exactly a wordsmith, but it didn't take Noah Webster to recognize the fact that no word over three letters long was spelled correctly. I was sure now that I'd been directed to the wrong location even though Lexie had mentioned the caterer wasn't well educated.

I heard the low growl of what sounded like a very large canine as I stepped onto the porch. I was praying I wouldn't be mistaken for a *solesiter*. I was blessed, or possibly cursed, with a "no fear" personality, but there were always exceptions - such as being torn to shreds by large, fang-gnashing dogs that were protecting their territory and their owners. I was too hesitant to knock and had turned around to head back to the truck when I heard the door open behind me.

"Peanut, shut up!" The petite, dark-haired woman with a flawless olive complexion said as she stepped outside and shut the door behind her. "Are you Lexie's friend? She called to say you'd be stopping by."

"Um, yes, I'm Rapella Ripple. Lexie wanted me to discuss a couple of details about the food for the party tonight with you. She has written down a few items to cover on this list." I waved the list in her face as if I thought she doubted my reason for being there.

"Nice to meet you, Rapella. My name's Georgia Piney."

"Nice to meet you too, Georgia. Do you run your catering business out of your home? I wasn't sure I was at the right place."

"Yeah, this is my office for the time being," she said, as she spread her arms out to indicate the entire kitchen. "I can't afford to buy my own shop yet. Maybe some day, I hope. My schedule allows me to do occasional odd jobs during the day to help make ends meet. I take in ironing and do some tailoring work whenever possible. I'm putting a little money away every month, trying to build up a nest egg to put down on a little shop downtown one day."

"Good luck to you, dear. I love to see women with the ambition to be their own boss. I just met you but already I'd bet you'll succeed in accomplishing your dream."

"Thanks! Come on in and we'll talk in the kitchen. Don't pay no attention to Peanut. He's harmless other than possibly licking you to death."

Peanut might have been harmless, but he was huge and intimidating. Not to mention the fact I probably smelled like our cat, which I feared wouldn't bode well for me. I stepped inside tentatively as Peanut looked me over and licked his salivating chops, as if anticipating a tasty meal of fresh tabby-scented flesh. He had the height of a Great Dane and the girth of a Rottweiler. Judging by his unique characteristics, he could have a dozen other breeds in the mix too.

When Peanut leapt up to run his long slobbering tongue up my face he nearly knocked me over. His rope-like tail wagged back and forth like a whip, and I was sure I'd have bruises on my legs by the time I left Georgia's home. You know how one's skin gets thinner as they age. Occasionally, I could blow on Rip's arm and he'd be sporting a hematoma the next morning. As I was closing in on seventy in just a year and a half, my skin was thinning to the same degree as his. It seemed to me it now had the thickness of an onion-peel.

As we sat at the kitchen table discussing the items on Lexie's list, Georgia told me a little bit more about herself. She ran off and married a much older man when she was fifteen, dropping out of school to do so. She inferred that she'd never been much of a student to begin with. Since then, her husband had died of brain cancer, an adverse effect from years of exposure to toxic fumes in the factory where he was employed, and she told me she had only one living child.

Georgia Piney was a very sweet woman, as Lexie had indicated, and I enjoyed conversing with her. She explained how her husband's illness had left them with a lot of medical bills to pay. A lawsuit against the factory had been dismissed for having inconclusive evidence. Georgia told me that when Mr. Piney passed, she'd been forced to go to work, and she was still making payments to the Wheatland Memorial Hospital in St. Joseph, Missouri, for expenses incurred during his cancer treatment. With no high school diploma, it had been hard to find a job that paid much, so she'd taken up catering special jobs out of her house a couple of years ago.

I judged Georgia's age to be about the same as Lexie and my daughter, Regina—early fifties or thereabouts. Georgia told me she and Lexie both attended the Rockdale Baptist Church, and she had joined just a few months before the previous pastor had been murdered. I recalled Lexie telling me she'd been involved in the apprehension of the pastor's killer. After getting acquainted with each other at church events, Lexie had hired Georgia on a number of occasions to cater special events held at the Alexandria Inn.

It occurred to me then, knowing Lexie and her giving nature, the generous bed and breakfast owner had hired Georgia Piney as a way of helping her out financially. My cousin, Emily Harrington, who owned the campground in Cheyenne where Lexie and I had met, had told me what Lexie had done to help some underprivileged local families the previous holiday season. Hiring this kind-hearted and pretty, but financially-struggling, lady to cater her party would be exactly the kind of thing Lexie would do.

Georgia went over the list of items on the menu for the evening, including ham and turkey subs, potato salad, baked beans, deviled eggs, cole slaw, and a three-bean salad. She was also providing a decorated cake for the festivities and reminded me that Lexie was picking up an extra one from Pete's Pantry to assure there'd be enough cake for everyone. I could smell savory aromas wafting from the double oven as she spoke and saw large aluminum pans spread out across the kitchen counter.

There was a large metal pan with what appeared to be a warped bottom rocking back and forth on the stove. It was casting out drops of water that were sizzling as they landed on the hot burner. I assumed she was hard-boiling the eggs to be deviled later on. As if reading my mind, Georgia stood up and turned off the fire beneath the pan.

Sitting back down she noticed me studying the array of pots, pans, utensils, and other cooking paraphernalia scattered throughout the kitchen, including the stuff that covered half of the table where the two of us, and Peanut, were sitting. She smiled and said, "There's probably a lot more to catering a large party than you realize."

I shook my head and told her I'd tried the catering business myself when I was in my thirties. When the president of the local Rotary Club nearly choked to death on a small clip-on earring I'd lost in the chicken casserole, I'd decided to give it up before I got embroiled in a negligent homicide lawsuit.

"I was very happy to get the earring back after another Rotary member performed the Heimlich maneuver on the guy," I told Georgia. "The earring was one of my favorites. It was from the best pair of fake diamond earrings I owned. As you can imagine, I was upset while the president was choking, thinking I'd just thrown ten bucks down the toilet. And ten bucks was a lot of money back in those days. But thankfully, the earring came shooting out of the fellow like lava out of a volcano."

Georgia laughed at my remark as if she thought I was joking. Nearly losing one of my favorite earrings, from a ten dollar pair at that, was not something I'd josh about, I wanted to tell her. Oh, and I should probably add that nearly killing a feller really wasn't a joking matter either.

After we'd covered everything on the list, I patted Georgia's hand, told her it had been a pleasure to meet her, and that I'd see her later on in the evening at the surprise birthday party. I wiggled my way off the chair I was sitting on by tenderly removing Peanut's head and paws from where they were draped over my lap. He'd been perched there for half an hour while I'd stroked his head. It wasn't that I was an avid dog-lover. The independence and low maintenance of cats appealed more to Rip and me. It was just that Peanut seemed way too large for me to want to tick off by not letting him lay his head wherever he chose to lay it.

Earlier I'd foolishly waved off Rip's offer to show me how to program the GPS to lead me back to the inn once it had reached its original destination of the Piney residence. When I walked out the Piney's front door, I wasn't even sure which direction would return me to the Alexandria Inn. *I very well might end up in Iowa*, I thought to myself. I'd mindlessly followed the female voice's directions to get there instead of paying attention to the route she was taking me so I could retrace the steps without her guidance. The two-mile drive there had taken about five minutes. The drive back took considerably longer.

Unfortunately, my untrustworthy sense of direction was in full swing that morning. It took forty-eight minutes, three convenience-store stops for conflicting directions, seventeen wrong turns, one traffic warning for impeding traffic, two questionable U-turns, and *a partridge in a pear tree,* for me to get back to the inn. Oh, and did I mention the too-many-to-count rude hand gestures by other drivers?

Perhaps it was time to swallow my pride and have Rip sit me down and patiently explain how to work the damned silly gadget perched on the dashboard. It taunted me with its silence the entire trip back. It would have no doubt been snickering had it had the capability to do so.

"Lexie! Are you all right?" I asked frantically when I saw her face pale and her expression turn to one of horror. I had put my arm around her in case I needed to catch her if she fainted. "What's wrong?"

"Oh, no!"

"What? What's wrong, girl?" The guests were beginning to arrive and I'd have wondered if she'd just thought of something critical she'd forgotten to do in preparation for the party if not for the extreme panic on her face. Even a forgotten birthday cake wouldn't be that alarming.

"Look over there by the fireplace, Rapella."

"Okay," I scrutinized the young couple across

the parlor from where we stood. All I saw was a beautiful woman and an extremely handsome man. If not for the fact that I was married and four decades older than the dapper dude, I might have wanted a piece of him for myself. "What am I looking for? A testosterone overdose victim?"

Before Lexie could respond, Wendy's best friend, Mattie Hill, came up behind us and gasped, "Oh, my God! I can't believe he'd show up at this party."

"You surely didn't invite him, did you?" Lexie asked. I was still staring at the cause of their apparent concern, looking him up and down several times to try to determine what the two women were so up in arms about. Then I looked the fellow up and down a few more times just for the pure pleasure of it.

"Of course not!" Mattie said. "Apparently he came as a guest of Joy White's. I didn't even know Joy was dating that piece of—"

"Crap! What are we going to do?" Lexie asked, cutting Maggie off. "Wendy will be uncomfortable around him, as will I, but we can hardly ask him to leave, can we?"

"I don't know. Joy was one of our closest high school friends, and since he's her date, she'd have to leave the party too. And I know Wendy would want Joy to be present to see her get engaged and all. Maybe she won't be too uncomfortable with Andy here, because you know he'll be right next to her most of the evening. If Trotter says anything lewd, crude, or threatening to Wendy, Andy will lay him out like nobody's business."

I could tell Mattie was trying to convince herself as much as Lexie that whatever was upsetting them would turn out to be a non-issue. "I need to pull Joy aside tonight and warn her about that jerk before he does something similar to her. If she doesn't have something like pepper spray or a stun gun with her, it could get ugly. He's athletic and Joy is too, but she's kind of a girly girl, so to speak."

I couldn't stand it any longer. I had to know what was wrong with the hunk who was now leaning against the grand piano in a pose that could have graced the cover of GQ Magazine. I read old issues of that magazine every time I was in the waiting room at Rip's audiologist's office. The photos in that magazine were definitely candy for the eye, even to an old bird like me. I may be a senior citizen but I wasn't blind. Not yet at least.

"What in heaven's name are you two squawking about? Why wouldn't Wendy want that feller here?" I finally asked.

"Trotter Hayes is the stepson of our chief of police. Right before Andy moved back here from South Carolina, Trotter stopped in at the coroner's office to pick up an autopsy report for Chief Smith. If you hadn't noticed, he's not hard to look at." Lexie was almost whispering as she spoke to me.

"Trust me, I noticed."

"He asked Wendy if she'd go out to supper with him. She thought no harm could come of going out for a meal with an old schoolmate she'd known for years. She had her eye on Andy already, but they weren't officially a couple at the time. Andy still lived in South Carolina while Wendy had an apartment in St. Joseph. So Wendy agreed to the date. No strings attached, Trotter had told her."

"Aha! I'm guessing there was a 'string' he didn't tell her about," I said.

"Exactly!" Lexie replied with a nod. "When he took her home he tried to press himself on her to the point of ripping her brand new dress and yanking her undies half-way down her thighs. Trotter refused to take 'no' for an answer, saying he'd paid handsomely for her seafood supper, and that he was going to get what he had coming to him. Fortunately, she had always promised me she'd never leave home without a can of pepper spray in her purse. She was able to get to it and sprayed him squarely in the eyes. Then Wendy called 9-1-1 while he was pawing at his face."

"Good for her!" I said. "Sounds to me like he got what he had coming to him after all."

Then Mattie cut in with her opinion. "Well, it was a start, but not even close to what he deserved to get for such an assault. I think Wendy should have kneed him in the nuggets while he was rubbing his eyes. You know, just to make a point."

"I agree!" Lexie and I said in stereo. I glanced back at Trotter Hayes, who was staring at the piano lid as if admiring his own reflection in the luster of the shiny paint. He reached up and adjusted a small tuft of sun-streaked hair draped over his forehead so that it hung seductively over his left eye. I suddenly thought he was the ugliest creature I'd ever laid eyes on. Crazy how one's perspective could change so drastically in a matter of thirty seconds.

"So what happened next?" I asked. I'm ashamed to admit that when it came to juicy stories like this one, I wanted to hear all the gritty, gory, or even x-rated details.

"Our good friend, Detective Wyatt Johnston, recognized Wendy's address when the call came in, and he was the first to respond to it. The police department tossed Trotter in the tank for the night, and Stone took Wendy to the police department to file a complaint. Chief Leonard Smith and I have had disagreements in the past, so we decided it was best if I didn't join them. But as it were, it didn't matter anyway. The chief argued bitterly with the mayor, but the entire incident was ultimately swept under the rug and the jerk was released the next morning."

"Did Wendy tell Andy about the assault?" I wanted to know. I was thinking the party could turn out to be more memorable than we'd anticipated if she had shared the news with her protective boyfriend. If he were anything like my husband, he'd have a word of two to say to the rat, along with a promise to have his face rearranged if he ever touched his girlfriend again.

"I doubt she told Andy," Lexie said. "She felt humiliated and embarrassed about the whole thing and just wanted to put it behind her. But it might not stay behind her when she sees Trotter here tonight, I'm afraid. I can't promise I wouldn't do something totally horrid to Trotter myself, given half the chance."

As Lexie had been speaking, a young couple had walked up behind us. I was still staring at the man across the room, leaning on the piano as if he owned the place. I didn't even bother to turn around as the woman behind me spoke to Mattie.

"Hey, girl! Long time, no see. It's good to see you," the female said in greeting to her friend. She spoke with very little emotion, but politely.

"Hi, Alice. Glad you were able to make it after all," Mattie said in return. After the brief exchange, Alice turned to walk away, followed closely by her clearly annoyed partner. I turned to look at them as they strode toward a group of guests in the corner of the room and noticed that right behind them was another young couple, holding hands, and obviously smitten with each other.

"Oh, swell," Mattie said. Before either Lexie or I could ask her what she was referring to, Mattie nodded in the direction of the second couple who were now standing in the corner with the rest of the group. "As they say, the plot thickens. That's Falcon Jons, who I'd heard was Joy's ex-boyfriend. She must have broken up with him to date Trotter. I wouldn't want anything to do with Falcon, but he's a darned sight better choice than Trotter Hayes."

Lexie just shook her head. I could tell she was already regretting having planned this surprise party for her daughter. We both looked toward the corner of the room, beyond a large parquet floor that Lexie had told me was occasionally used as a dance floor. Falcon Jons was trying to find something in the back of his date's throat with his tongue. I wanted to tell them to get a room, even though all the suites in the inn were currently occupied.

"With the PDAs they're engaging in, I'd guess Falcon's trying to make Joy jealous. While he's kissing his date, he's watching his old girlfriend instead, apparently to see if Joy's witnessing him making out with a new girl, who incidentally used to be Joy's best friend. Jeez, you'd think they were high schoolers," Mattie remarked.

I had no idea what a PDA was but I assumed it had something to do with inappropriately making out in public. And I had to agree it appeared as if he was more interested in his old girlfriend than he was in his new one. He hadn't taken his eyes off his former flame, who to his obvious distress had yet to notice he was even in the same time zone as she was.

Lexie returned to the subject we'd been discussing before this Alice girl had interrupted us. "I don't want either of you to think poorly of me. I want to make it clear that I have forgiven Trotter Hayes because I feel it's the Christian thing to do. Nor do I want to go through life harboring hatred in my heart. But I'll never forget what he did to my daughter. When something or someone hurts my daughter, I hurt twice as badly."

"Hear, hear!" I said, lifting my water bottle in a mock toast.

"Same here," Mattie agreed as her wine glass tapped against my water bottle. "Wendy's like my other half, and when she's hurt I feel it just as deeply as she does." There was true sincerity in her remark. I knew it wasn't just rhetoric. I was happy when Mattie's mood lightened up drastically as she continued. "Well, I'm not being a very good hostess. I had better go greet the guests as they arrive."

Lexie replied with a nod, "Yes, we want them to feel welcome. And I better go in the kitchen and see if Georgia needs any help. She said her daughter, Lori, is bringing over a few loaves of fresh-out-of-the-oven sourdough bread for additional sandwiches, if needed. She went to school with Wendy and Mattie, but was four or five grades behind them. I've only met her twice before, and although she's rather somber, the young lady's as sweet as her mother."

"I'm looking forward to meeting her," I said sincerely.

"There's Lori now." Lexie nodded her head toward the buffet table where a pretty young lady was pouring juice into a large punch bowl. "Andy told me to look for he and Wendy to get here at about eight-thirty, since he'd made their dinner reservations for nine. We'll start the buffet line soon after they arrive and everyone's had a chance to wish my daughter a happy birthday."

"Sounds good. I love sourdough bread," I replied. I was starving and could hear my stomach growling, even over the clamor of the folks in the parlor. At that point I'd have welcomed a piece of moldy bread. A little scraping here and there and it'd be as good as new.

Eating supper at eight-thirty was unbelievable to me. Our supper was on the table at five o'clock, come hell or high water. If we went out for supper, we usually arrived at the restaurant by four-thirty to avoid the early crowd and the ill effects of going to bed with a full stomach.

We rarely ever ate anything after six in the evening in order to avoid the agony of a discontented esophagus as we tried to sleep. Acid reflux, like the thinning skin, arthritis, hardening of the arteries, hair and hearing loss, and many other equally enjoyable things, came as consolation prizes for getting older.

Heartburn later that evening was almost guaranteed for Rip and me. But I simply said, "Smells delicious. I'm looking forward to dinner. Why don't you let me check in on Georgia instead and see if she needs my help setting up the buffet table?"

"I'd rather you keep an eye out for Wendy and Andy's arrival while I assist Georgia. I'm concerned about her carrying those heavy containers of food by herself, and I need to cut the sheet cake. Georgia's a little wisp of a thing and I worry about her carrying such heavy loads."

"Get to it then, girl! You don't want her to get hurt and be unable to cater your next event," I said with a wink. "I'll watch out for the kids."

Lexie flashed me a sly smile. She realized then that her reason for hiring Georgia Piney was not lost on me. She thanked me and we split ways.

As I walked toward the window, I was thinking about what I'd like to say and do to Trotter Hayes for treating my girl, Wendy, the way he had. I figured it was probably best for everyone concerned if I avoided him. After a few tequila sunrises, I couldn't be trusted not to thump him on the head with Rip's cane if he got within ten feet of me.

CHAPTER 5

"*Surprise!*" A chorus of voices rang out seconds after the lights came back on. The flash of a few cameras filled the room, and nearly everyone else had their phone out in front of them, presumably to catch the look of astonishment on the guest of honor's face. But they'd have to have had a very fast shutter on their cameras, because that look of astonishment turned into one of complete shock in a split second. It was as if Wendy had seen the ghost of her late grandmother playing the piano across the room.

I have never before heard the word "surprise" go from one of jubilation to one of bone-chilling terror—all in two syllables. I saw everyone following Wendy's gaze toward that piano and I turned to glance that way also. I had to see what had caught everyone's attention.

I couldn't believe what I was seeing. It was the

body of Trotter Hayes, flat on the floor in a pool of blood. He was laid out right in front of the baby grand, with Lexie standing over him with a long serrated knife in her right hand. Next to the man's body was a broken goblet, one of the ones we'd put out next to Sheila Davidson's "Citrus Surprise" punch. Lexie had said her best friend's concoction packed a punch you wouldn't see coming, and I was thinking that the dead feller hadn't seen what hit him either.

As the entire crowd silently stared at the corpse with their mouths agape, Lexie's arms fell to her sides. Her face instantly drained of color and her hands relaxed. The knife she'd been holding clattered to the floor, making an eerie clinking sound as it broke the silence of the room. As everyone stood motionless, the tray Lexie had been carrying in her left hand fell to the floor beside the knife. It landed with a single thud. Suddenly Lexie's knees buckled and she fell to the floor like a house of cards collapsing.

As much as I hate to admit it, my first thought was "Hot Diggety Dog! Lexie did it!" Maybe she wasn't kidding when she said she'd be apt to do something completely horrid to her daughter's attacker if given half a chance. But I already knew Lexie Starr well enough to know that, although she might wish the guy great harm, she'd never resort to violence to carry out her desire. She'd slash her own wrists before she'd perpetrate such a vicious act against anyone, even that creep Trotter Hayes.

After several long moments of silence, the din

in the room rose to a deafening level all at once. Lexie's husband, Stone Van Patten, and Detective Johnston, who had been standing side-by-side about ten feet behind and fifteen feet to the right of Lexie and the victim, rushed to Lexie's side. As Stone assisted his wife, the detective removed his revolver from its holster. As he spoke into a hand-held radio he'd had clipped to his belt he briskly scanned the room for a hidden threat.

"Code Twenty. Repeat, Code Twenty. Ten-ninety-nine at the Alexandria Inn," I heard the detective say. I knew from being married to a career law enforcement officer that Wyatt was reporting a "Homicide" and an "Officer Needs Help" request to the dispatcher. He was also arming himself in case a psychotic mass murderer was on a killing spree in the Alexandria Inn. I couldn't say I blamed him.

Before the noise level could even drop a few decibels below that of a passing locomotive, a slew of first-responders swarmed into the room, asking everyone in the room to please calm down and refrain from disturbing anything even remotely associated with the victim. The party had come to an abrupt end. Alexandria Inn had just been upgraded from a party scene to a crime scene.

After Nate, the county coroner who was attending the party, ascertained the victim was truly deceased, the first order of business was to assess Joy White's condition, who had attended the party as the victim's date. She was sobbing and nearly hysterical when the EMTs responded to the scene only seconds behind three additional police officers.

The medics had her sit in a chair while one administered a shot, presumably a sedative to calm her down. It didn't appear to help one iota. The other EMT monitored Joy's vital signs. Five minutes later, Joy White was taken to a waiting ambulance on a stretcher, distraught and inconsolable. I'd later learn that the medics had feared her blood pressure was approaching a dangerous level. But by the time the ambulance arrived at Wheatland Memorial Hospital, Joy was calm and collected, and her blood pressure had returned to normal. She had been quickly treated and released.

To curtail nightmares as much as possible, two detectives curtained off the area around the body using two chairs and a tablecloth that Lexie had utilized to cover a small metal table. In doing so, they partially blocked the ghastly sight from the party guests. Trotter's face and bloody torso was no longer within our view, but his lower legs and bent left arm remained visible. That alone was enough to make the hairs on my arm stand straight up.

At that point, everyone in the inn was a potential suspect. Detective Johnston's investigative training took over as he directed the crowd to sit quietly on the floor and explained that we weren't allowed to leave the premises until told we could do so. He asked for silence and advised the partygoers to not discuss the tragic scene with anyone else in the room until after they'd been questioned and given a statement of what, if anything, they personally had witnessed.

We were asked to go over the tragic event in our minds and try to remember any sights, sounds, smells, or other sensations we'd experienced before, during, and after the fatal event. The detectives would ask us to relate those observations to them as we were called up one by one, out of earshot of the rest of the guests—standard protocol at a homicide scene, Wyatt assured everyone. The interviewing procedure would begin as soon as the scene was processed and the body was removed, he announced. When Detective Johnston finished speaking, the room began to buzz with the droning of numerous conversations erupting, from both the party guests and the investigating team. Wyatt blew his police whistle to quiet the crowd. The party was over before it had even had a chance to begin, but the Alexandria Inn was still a beehive of activity.

I doubt anyone saw much to report as the room had been quite dark when the murder was committed. Dusk was already turning into night and the only entrance into the parlor was through the dining room, where the lights had been turned off before the guests had even begun to arrive. Stone had hung blankets over the only two outside windows in the room to block out the light to guarantee total darkness when Wendy and Andy entered the parlor.

The lights in the parlor had been switched off

about fifteen minutes before the arrival of the guest of honor. Wyatt now requested that all of the lights be turned back on and the blankets removed from the windows to allow the crime scene investigators to better process the scene.

In my entire lifetime, I'd only personally witnessed detectives working one homicide case. That crime scene had involved the death of the self-absorbed author in Cheyenne, Wyoming, just three short weeks prior. I got the distinct impression that most of the detectives at this current crime scene had put Lexie at the top of their suspects list.

Rather than stand there like I was super-glued to the floor, I decided to join Georgia at the buffet table to help her clear off the food and serving paraphernalia. She was standing behind the table, appearing as dazed and confused as everyone else in the room. I watched Stone walk over to her woodenly. He handed her a check, which she reluctantly took. She glanced at the check and attempted to hand it back to him. Stone backed away, shaking his head fervently. Georgia eventually gave in, nodded her thanks, folded the check in half and stuffed it in her back pocket, then began putting the aluminum lids back on the serving containers.

When I approached her and asked if I could assist, she looked pale and unsteady. I pulled a chair up behind her and had her sit down until she regained her composure. She thanked me and mumbled that it didn't seem right to accept payment for a meal that was never going to be served. And now she had to decide what to do with all the food she'd brought.

Lexie was still in a state of shock, as was evident by the "deer in the headlights" expression on her face. At that point, she was in no condition to make any kind of decision regarding the food, and I didn't feel it was mine to make. I told Georgia to speak to Stone again about the issue when she got the opportunity, but in the meantime we might as well pack it all back up so it wouldn't go completely to waste. If it had been up to me, I'd have donated the food to the local mission that served meals to the homeless and underprivileged where it'd be very appreciated.

I helped Georgia load the trays of food into the rear of her van. She told me that Lori had forgotten the sourdough bread and had left to retrieve it just a minute or two after Wendy and Andy's arrival. For what purpose would the sourdough bread be needed at this point? I was wondering. Did Lori truly believe the party would go on as planned despite the bloody corpse on the dance floor?

When I re-entered the parlor from the kitchen, I came up behind the makeshift curtain blocking the guests' view of the body. I couldn't help but look at Trotter Hayes. His face was waxy-looking, almost translucent. He looked like a mannequin that had been knocked over at Macy's. When I saw the coroner nonchalantly stab a thermometer into the boy's abdomen, presumably his liver, I was glad I hadn't already eaten supper. I quickly retreated to a far corner of the room.

From there I watched Alice Runcan, the young lady who had spoken briefly to Mattie earlier, stand up and approach a tall, blond-haired detective. The officer appeared to be in charge of the investigating team as they carefully surveyed the scene and gathered evidence. The entire team wore latex gloves as they placed the items into clear plastic bags. Alice smiled in a very flirtatious manner as she showed the handsome detective something on the front of her cell phone. I don't know if it was her phone number, a photo of her flashing her breasts, or what. But judging by the provocative manner in which Alice was licking her lips and tossing her hair over her shoulder, not to mention the way the detective was practically drooling on her phone, I was guessing it was, at the very least, a photo of her winning a wet t-shirt contest.

The detective looked at the photo and began licking his lips as well. He took the phone out of the gal's hand to study it intently, smiling all the while. Yep! Definitely a booby shot of some type. If my instincts were correct, it was very inappropriate for the situation.

Then I looked across the room at the young man who had accompanied Alice Runcan to the party. I observed the stormy glare he was projecting across the room toward his date. Could the entire seductive scene have been played out by Alice to make her date jealous or to get under his skin for some reason? If so, her ploy was definitely working because her date looked absolutely livid.

To the man's chagrin, the detective appeared to be very captivated with Alice, and he spoke with her for a long time. As Alice spoke, he was writing occasional notes, or possibly just jotting down information on how to contact her later.

The remaining detectives began interviewing guests one-by-one, allowing them to leave the premises after they'd given a statement. As was the case with nearly everyone who was questioned, Alice Runcan did a lot of pointing toward the kitchen and then to the vicinity of where what's-his-name had been slain.

After being photographed from every perceivable angle, Trotter's worthless hide was carefully zipped into a body bag and carried out of the inn. The four burly men removed the body bag as if they were carrying easily disturbed and motion-sensitive explosive devices. I realized it was their way of showing respect for their boss's stepson. God help them if they were responsible for dropping the dude on his already brain-dead head. I'd have been more in favor of dragging his carcass across the floor like a bulky bag of potting soil, nudging it with my foot if it got hung up on the threshold of the front door. But then, I didn't have a job hanging in the balance like the detectives did.

Watching the victim being placed in the body bag had brought back memories of seeing nearly the same scene after the full-of-herself author had met her end in the RV Park. The two deaths in question certainly disproved the old adage that the "good die young". Both victims had had it coming, in my opinion. Karma could be a real bitch, if you know what I mean.

When Rip and I were questioned—individually, of course—there was very little we could attest to. I didn't think it was my place to inform the short, rotund detective questioning us what kind of deplorable person the stiff was before he met his maker. However, I'd have been happy to do so had the balding detective asked.

The portly detective frisked me and waved a high-intensity UV light around me like a TSA agent checking me for a weapon before I boarded an airplane. I was surprised he didn't insist on a cavity search or tell me to take off my shoes so he could scrutinize them for hidden weapons as well. The UV light he was using detected blood splatter, he explained, and was being utilized on every interviewee. Scanning the room full of stunned guests, every one of them looked potentially murderous to me.

Watching the same detective question Rip was like watching a man talking to himself in front of a mirror. Put Rip in his old policeman uniform, and I couldn't have told the two apart. I'm guessing the Rockdale detective favored doughnuts for sustenance as much as Rip did.

A few minutes later, I was standing in the front yard watching as numerous vehicles exited the parking area solemnly, like a funeral procession. I was soon joined by Wendy, Mattie Hill, and Sheila Davidson.

"How totally inconsiderate of that arrogant jerk to get himself killed and ruin the party. And here I was looking forward to sampling your 'citrus surprise' punch, Sheila," I said jokingly to lighten the mood a touch. There was a polite chuckle among the group, but the overall mood remained somber. We stood speechless for a spell before Wendy broke the silence by saying, "Well, speaking of 'surprise punch', if you all were aiming to surprise me on my birthday, you definitely succeeded."

I was saddened that Wendy's surprise party had gone by the wayside, thwarting Andy's plans to propose to her. I had hoped it would be a memorable occasion for her, one she'd remember fondly for the rest of her life. But what transpired was not at all what I'd had in mind. Wendy's surprise party was indeed memorable, but I doubted those memories would be remembered fondly.

I'm a little embarrassed to admit that I was not overly remorseful that Trotter Hayes had just looked karma in the face—and lost! No telling how many women, possibly even men, had a bone to pick with that loser. The very idea that such an ugly individual had been placed into such a beautiful body seemed unholy. But I realized God often worked in mysterious ways and that he probably viewed every living thing he created as beautiful, even perfect.

More than anything, I was upset that Lexie Starr had been taken to the police station for questioning. Even though the evidence all appeared to point her way, those of us who knew her personally knew there was more to this murder case than met the eye.

I was near tears when Wendy walked up to me and put her arm around my shoulder. She looked into my eyes and said, "Don't worry, Rapella. I'm sure that after Mom tells them exactly what happened from her perspective, she'll be released. I expect a call from her any minute, asking us to pick her up at the station."

"I know, honey. But I'm also sorry your party got spoiled the way it did."

"Stuff happens. It is what it is, I guess," Wendy responded. It was obvious that she wasn't overly gloomy about Trotter Hayes's untimely passing either.

Stone, Rip, Wendy, and I sat around the kitchen table. Detective Johnston had escorted Lexie to the police station, telling her it was only to make a statement about what she'd witnessed—a standard routine of the investigative process.

Stone looked as anxious as I felt. He said, "I've known Wyatt for long enough to judge his demeanor by his words, actions and expressions. He was a lot more concerned than he let on. In fact, he looked scared stiff—no pun intended."

"I hate to say this, Stone," Rip said. "I served as a police officer for thirty-seven years, including my last decade in law enforcement as the Aransas County Sheriff. I've worked very few cases of incredible violence such as this one, because fortunately, the crime rate in that county is relatively low. But I've seen detectives working many a crime scene and I got the distinct impression that all of the detectives, except Johnston, have put Lexie at the top of their suspects list."

"I got that impression too," Stone replied, nervously running his hand through his silver hair. His normally light blue eyes now looked almost battleship gray. A lone tear slipped out of his left eye and ran down his cheek, leaving a wet trail against his tanned face. Stone didn't wipe it off. It seemed as if he hadn't even realized the tear had escaped.

Rip, who often wasn't good at judging when to keep talking and when to shut up, adjusted his position in such a fashion that I knew his hip was bothering him. Then he said, "I saw Wyatt arguing with several of them before he put Lexie in his squad car. At one point, their voices were raised enough that I heard him say, 'You're crazy! I know her better than any of you do, and I can tell you she had nothing to do with killing the chief's boy.' Then he walked away from them, obviously teed off."

"Oh, good Lord!" Stone exclaimed. "I was so shocked that another guest was murdered in our inn, I completely forgot Trotter was Chief Smith's stepson. And that does not bode well for Lexie because she and the chief have been at odds on several occasions. Even when he awarded her a certificate of appreciation last year for playing a crucial part in getting a killer off the streets he hadn't appeared very appreciative to me. But perhaps it just seemed that way because he—"

"No, you read him right, Stone," Wendy said with a grimace, cutting Stone off. "I didn't tell Mom because I didn't want to take the wind out of her sails. But the chief fought long and hard with Mayor Bradley Dunn about presenting her with that award. I was actually surprised by the mayor's strong defense on Mom's behalf, as he's also had a run-in or two with her in the past. Dunn insisted that it was a well-deserved commendation. But Nate told me Chief Smith argued that he was tired of her intrusive meddling in police business and didn't want to encourage her to continue that ill-advised meddling. No disrespect toward Mom, but you've got to admit he had a point."

"Yes, unfortunately, he did. And apparently he lost the battle with Mayor Dunn."

"Yep! He nearly always does when pitted against Bradley. The mayor is not one to take 'no' for an answer," Wendy said. "However, this murder is extremely personal for Chief Smith. He's currently embroiled in a bitter divorce, but still, he just lost a stepson he loved as if Trotter were his own blood. I detested Trotter Hayes, but I can understand why the chief would be intent on getting the perpetrator behind bars as soon as possible. I would be too, if the victim were my child, even a seedy stepchild like in this case."

"Same here, Wendy. But I still think he should realize that someone of Lexie's character wasn't involved in the murder and let her go without further investigating of any motive she might have had to want Trotter dead," Stone said optimistically. "Smith can't possibly despise her to that degree."

"I'd agree with you, Stone," Wendy said ruefully. "But then we'd both be wrong. Don't think for a second he's forgotten the time we threatened to file a lawsuit against Trotter, because of—well, you know. And I imagine he's held that against Mom all along, too."

"Oh, good Lord," Stone repeated, dropping his head into his hands, which were resting on the kitchen table. "I'd forgotten about that incident too!"

We sat in the kitchen nursing our cups of coffee as one hour lead to the next. We could hear voices and even laughter as a number of detectives were reexamining the crime scene in the parlor. There didn't appear to be an overabundance of gravity amongst the investigating team. Of course, it stood to reason they might have very little use for the victim themselves, or possibly even for their boss, the victim's stepfather.

Three hours later, Detective Johnston finally called to inform Stone that Lexie was being held in custody while the investigation continued. Wyatt said he'd tried to get the detectives to let her go home if Lexie promised not to leave town, but his effort had failed. According to him, the other detectives thought it best to let the chief make that decision since the crime involved the death of his stepson, not theirs.

Chief Smith was not present at the police station because he obviously had other pressing matters. He was at the coroner's office, where Nate had taken his son's body. Wendy was also called to the coroner's lab to assist in the autopsy, which the police chief had demanded be performed immediately.

Even though he was no doubt grieving tremendously, he was apparently not going to let any grass grow under his feet in his eagerness to apprehend the person responsible for his loved one's murder. Unfortunately, according to Wendy, who had returned from the lab an hour after she left the inn, Chief Smith was convinced he already had the killer behind bars.

Wendy told us her boss, Nate, had sent her home from the coroner's lab soon after the procedure began. Nate told her Chief Smith had insisted she not be involved in the autopsy. He believed having her assist in the thorough postmortem examination while her mother was being held as the prime suspect was a conflict of interest, Wendy explained. "Apparently, the chief thinks I'd skew the autopsy report in Mom's favor to try to save her from the gas chamber. It's not that the chief wasn't correct that, at the very least, I would be tempted to intervene if it would help save my mother's hide. But regardless, to out and out suggest I'd so such a thing is preposterous. What a freaking a-hole!"

"The gas chamber?" Stone asked with a catch

in his voice.

"Just a figure of speech, Stone," his stepdaughter replied. "Actually, in Missouri, they'd give her the needle."

"The needle?" Stone gasped. And here I'd thought Rip didn't know when to zip it. I decided to steer the conversation away from the manner in which Lexie might be executed before Wendy dug an even deeper hole and pushed Stone headfirst into cardiac arrest.

"So why did they call you to come in if they didn't want you involved in the case?" I asked.

"It was merely out of necessity. When Nate made the initial thoracic-abdominal incision he noticed that the cadaver's blood and body tissue were bright red," Wendy said, as if we'd all automatically know what that implied.

Then the young dear turned morbid on us, detailing the standard autopsy procedure. After a few comments about opening the pericardial sac to determine blood type, removing and weighing organs before slicing them into sections and looking for petechiae, or tiny hemorrhages in the mucus membrane inside the eyeballs, I asked her to spare us the gruesome details and cut to the chase. I was getting ready to prepare sandwiches for everyone, and I didn't need visions of dissected eyeballs in my mind while I ate my lunch. I did change my mind about serving hard-boiled eggs with the sandwiches though.

"Oh, sorry," Wendy said apologetically. "Force of habit, I guess. I'm used to talking things like this over with my coworkers in the lab. Anyway, bright red blood and tissue in a cadaver indicates the presence of cyanide, but it has to be verified by smell. In the county coroner's lab there are Nate, the county coroner; a deputy coroner, Max, who's retiring at the end of the year; and a few assistants like me. In the entire department, I have by far the best sense of smell when it comes to detecting and identifying specific odors such as cyanide. Some people can't smell it at all, but I can easily pick up its scent if the poison is present."

"What does cyanide smell like?" Rip asked. He'd taken the words right out of my mouth and probably Stone's as well.

"It has a bitter almond scent to it. Kind of smells like Andy's dirty socks, actually," Wendy explained with a smile. "So anyway, they called me in to go 'under the hood' as we say. It's a process to trap the fumes in order to verify that cyanide was in Trotter's system. Then they told me I was not allowed to be involved any further in the autopsy, as I said before. I was extremely miffed at being barred from the case."

"I don't get it," Stone said, taking the words out of my mouth once again. "I thought his throat was sliced."

"It was. But only after he'd been weakened by cyanide poisoning, which was also detected in the liquid residue on shards of the broken goblet he'd been drinking from. My guess is that the perpetrator didn't want Hayes to bring attention to himself by thrashing on the floor while trying to get oxygen into his lungs. Also, and most likely, to prevent the risk of Trotter not consuming enough of the poison to kill him. That might allow for help to arrive quickly enough to save his life."

"Yeah, that wouldn't have been good," I remarked without thinking. The others looked at me for a few seconds before turning their attention back to Wendy.

"As soon as the victim fell to the ground, the killer had to have stepped behind Hayes and sliced through the carotid artery and jugular on the left side of his neck. The right side was unaffected, indicating the killer was most likely right-handed, as were all but four people on the premises at the time of the murder. Slicing his throat in this manner would not be an altogether easy task with someone of Trotter's muscular build, but it could be achievable, particularly if the perpetrator was in a rage and had adrenalin going for him. The old 'woman lifts car off baby' type of adrenalin."

Wendy told Stone that the chief knew Lexie had an ax to grind with his stepson. "And he believed that, due to Mom's impulsive nature, she could have easily acted out her desire for revenge in a fit of fury like I just mentioned." The news was not exactly what we all had hoped to hear.

Rip turned to Wendy and asked her if Missouri law allowed suspects to be held for forty-eight hours without officially charging them with a crime, and Wendy replied, "Missouri law only allows a twenty-hour hold time. But I'm sure that Chief Smith, being Chief Smith, will push the envelope as far as he possibly can. He'll likely pay no attention to that law whatsoever."

We were only marginally relieved to hear Wendy's response. I'd been silent during the conversation so far. I was brooding about how Rip and I might be able to help out with the situation. We were to be at the inn for at least a week while the mechanics at Boney's garage completed the repairs on our travel trailer. No sense sitting on our cans twiddling our thumbs during that time. And particularly not if we had a friend in need who could use our help.

At first I'd prayed the repairs would be taken care of as quickly as possible, given they were costing us seventy-five hard-earned bucks an hour. But now the penny-pinching trait in me had been swallowed up completely by the righteousness one. I didn't care how long the repairs took now that we had a more important issue to contend with while they were being completed. Neither Rip nor I had any intention of leaving town while Lexie was rotting away in jail.

Okay, I'll admit that perhaps "rotting away" was a little melodramatic, but I knew she wasn't a happy camper about being incarcerated, even if only temporarily. I could remember what my pappy always said after having spent time in jail for a public intoxication or disturbing the peace arrest, both of which occurred frequently.

Pappy would stuff a wad of Beechnut in his mouth, chew for a spell, spit on the ground—or on occasion his already grimy boots—and say,

"The big house is not a place you'll ever want to find yourself, Princess. Being locked up there is about as much fun as having a bear drop a load in your Easter basket."

I'd been too young to comprehend what he was saying. As a child it seemed to me that the "big house" would be preferable to the dilapidated, dirt-floored, three-room flea trap we lived in at the time. But if Pappy said otherwise, I figured it must be so.

CHAPTER 6

It was nearly midnight when Detective Johnston called to tell Stone that nothing further would happen until morning regarding the case, including a change in Lexie's imprisonment. He'd seen to it she'd had a comfortable cot and a decent meal since the catered supper had gone uneaten. I knew for a fact she'd skipped lunch as well, too busy to take the time to eat—as had I. He suggested we all get some sleep and that he'd call again in the morning after he'd heard the latest on the situation.

We agreed. We were all wrung out from being fraught with worry and shell-shocked by the vicious murder that had taken place in the parlor that evening. Stone had been especially concerned about his wife's welfare, naturally, but was also muttering about what affect yet another murder in the Alexandria Inn might have on their bed and breakfast business. I'd heard him remark to his stepdaughter, "Wendy, how many people do you think can get killed in the inn before customers are too scared to stay here? So far, the first two murders have not seemed to slow down the steady stream of guests, but eventually the word will get around that booking a room here is a bit like playing Russian roulette. We'll be deemed 'the house of horrors,' I'm afraid."

"Don't worry, Stone," she'd replied. "It'll all work out in the end. Mom, and the business, will come out just fine. Try to get some rest, as hard as that'll be for all of us, no doubt."

I'm pretty sure the only one who slept at all that night was Dolly. She'd had a very active day. The Alexandria Inn was a half-a-block long, and it had no doubt been a long, tedious task for her to get it all sniffed out. It was a vital part of the feline job description. And who could tell when the food fairy might leave an unanticipated cat treat in an obscure location? I'm sure this was Dolly's line of thinking since she appeared to believe she was always be on the brink of dying of starvation.

My mind was racing, preventing me from nodding off. At around three-thirty in the morning, Dolly had jumped off the bed to settle on a pile of clothes on the floor after being disturbed several times by my tossing and turning.

When I kick the bucket myself, Lord, please have mercy on my soul, I prayed. *Let me come back as a housecat.* How nice it'd be to only have to be concerned with a few things: a bowl full of

food, a comfortable place— up high preferably—
to nap, a clean litter box to poop in, and most
importantly, well-trained servants to wait on me
hand and paw. Even the mice could scurry all
over the house, unless of course, I had a
hankering to chase them down to wear off a
sudden burst of energy. *Ahh...what a nice life
that'd be*, I thought before finally drifting off into
a fitful slumber.

My sleep was rendered even more restless with
a dream about eyeballs being dug out of a corpse
with an ice-cream scoop, sliced in two with a
knife and placed on the top of a birthday cake
with a candle sticking out of each half.
"Surprise!" The unidentifiable people around me
shouted, as melted wax the color of fresh blood
began to run down the candles and onto the
whites of the eyeballs. Startled awake, I sat up in
bed feeling as if a ghost had walked over my
grave.

The situation had not righted itself as I'd hoped
by the time Rip and I joined Stone in the kitchen
for a cup of coffee early the following morning.
Our host looked dejected as he remarked, "It just
doesn't seem right to be sitting here in the
morning drinking coffee without Lexie."

"I'm sure it doesn't, my friend. We'll do our
best to get her back where she belongs as quickly
as possible. Any news yet?" Rip asked. I'd
noticed he had descended the staircase very
tenderly, rubbing his hip after each tentative step.
Maybe now I could convince the hard-headed

mule to make an appointment with an orthopedic surgeon. We were insurance poor, having paid premiums for health care we seldom needed for five decades. It was about time we recouped some of that investment.

"No, I haven't heard anything yet. Not a word," an impatient Stone answered Rip's question as he absentmindedly stirred his coffee nonstop for several minutes.

We sat quietly conversing about the situation for another half-hour. Just as I finished pouring all three of us a refill on our coffee, Detective Wyatt Johnston came through the door. He looked troubled. His uniform was mussed, the top buttons of his shirt fastened incorrectly, and his hair looked like he hadn't combed it in a week. He removed his hat before taking the fourth seat at the table.

"Bad news, I'm afraid," he began. "I heard Detective Russell tell my old partner, Clint Travis, that Lexie was expected to be formerly charged with first-degree murder later on this afternoon. Depending on several factors of course. The district prosecuting attorney will be reviewing the case beforehand to determine if charges are justified at this point."

"How can they charge Lexie with murder?" Stone asked. "Don't they have to have some kind of compelling evidence to present to the judge?"

"Yes, and therein lies the problem. A female party guest named Alice Runcan took several photos, utilizing her camera's flash while the lights were out and everyone was waiting in the pitch dark. And then several minutes later as the lights flashed on and we all yelled 'surprise,' she snapped one more. One of those first photos captured Lexie standing next to Trotter, handing him a goblet full of Crown and Coke. No one else was within ten feet of the two. In fact, Stone and I were the closest and we couldn't even make out Lexie bringing Trotter a drink."

"Oh, my," Stone said softly before Wyatt continued. "The last photo, taken a couple of minutes later, according to the date and time stamp, shows Trotter spread out on the floor with blood pooling around him. Lexie is still the only one near the victim, and she's holding the murder weapon in front of her with a joyful expression on her face."

"She'd been in good spirits all evening, prior to the murder, because she was excited about surprising her daughter on her birthday. What mother wouldn't have looked joyful at that moment?" I asked. "It's not like she was hosting a wake. It was a party, for goodness sakes!"

Wyatt nodded with a rueful smile and replied, "Try explaining that to the chief. In fact, I saw the photos myself, and I have to admit they're very damning. I was concerned from the beginning because we all saw Lexie standing there with the knife when the lights came on. And then, of course, she fainted, as I'm sure you all recall vividly. We all know Lexie would never commit murder, but after further investigation, the judge determined that Lexie was indeed the most likely suspect to have perpetrated the slaying of the chief's beloved stepson. She wasn't convinced murder charges were in order, but she agreed to give the detectives more time to investigate before Lexie could be released from jail."

"What are you saying, Wyatt?" Rip asked. "Was even more damning evidence found during this so-called 'further investigation'?"

"Unfortunately, yes. The drink Lexie handed to Trotter Hayes contained cyanide, and a large dose of it, at that. I'm sure Wendy related all that to you. But, also, two different sets of fingerprints were on the goblet, Lexie's and the victim's. The knife had a substantial amount of Hayes's blood on it, and also a trace of hers. The only fingerprints found on it matched the ones they took from Lexie yesterday when they booked her and the two Piney women, whose fingerprints on the knife were not unexpected, naturally, since they were catering the party."

"Oh, my," Stone said again, louder this time. "I don't understand, Wyatt. How could that happen? We both know Lexie didn't put that cyanide in Trotter's drink. I can't see any logical way she'd even have had access to the poison, much less have had the ill will to use it to kill the guy."

"Well, my friend, the Rockdale detectives, chief of police, judge, and district prosecuting attorney don't know that. To them the most obvious way Trotter was killed would be for Lexie to have obtained the cyanide some clever way, put a large dose of it in the Crown and Coke she prepared for him, gave it to him to drink, and then slashed her victim's throat in the event the poison didn't kill him. And/or be possibly treated at the hospital quickly enough to be saved so he could identify his would-be killer. Slicing his jugular vein would eliminate that possibility," Wyatt explained, echoing almost exactly what Wendy had told us earlier.

"The other possibility is that Lexie was framed, perhaps even unintentionally, by the real killer, and this is the angle I plan to base my investigative efforts on. The three of us in this room, along with Wendy and Andy, are probably the only ones involved in this situation who know without a doubt that Lexie is not a killer. But, as you can clearly see, the overwhelming evidence against her was more than enough to cause Judge Jueti to come to the decision she did."

"Did you say Judge Judy?" I asked Wyatt. *Judge Judy* was one of my favorite shows to watch in the afternoon when nothing else was on our schedule.

"No, Rapella," Wyatt answered with a little chuckle. "It sounds like Judy, but it's actually spelled J-U-E-T-I. Judge Jaqueline Jueti will be the presiding judge when and if this case goes to trial. It could be worse. Jueti is a fair judge and not easily persuaded by either the prosecution or the defense teams. She has no close personal ties to any of the local attorneys, which is often a contributing factor in a judge's decisions, I'm sure."

"So, what do we do now?" A weary Stone asked his friend with a touch of sadness in his voice.

"I don't know, Stone. I wish I could tell you everything is going to work out fine, but I can't promise you that. We'll just have to play it by ear. You can visit with Lexie at the detention center this afternoon. I should be the only employee in the station from one to one-thirty. You'll need to make it during that time frame so I can let you talk with her in private. Two other detectives on the investigating team report at one forty-five, and I don't want you there when they show up. So, to be safe, I'll have to get you all out of there in a half-hour—tops!"

"No problem, pal! I'd be happy just to get to see her and let her know we're going to do whatever we can to get her out of there," Stone said.

Wyatt nodded and replied, "Perhaps Lexie can give you a better idea of what really happened by explaining exactly what she did or didn't do, see, or hear. Naturally, she went over and over it with the detectives. But she was under a lot of stress at the time. Maybe talking with family and friends in a more relaxed environment will jog her memory. She might even suddenly recall something that is crucial in proving her innocence. And I'll keep you posted on what's going down as far as the investigating team and any potential charges being filed."

"Good grief," Stone replied. "After all my wife's been through looking into murder cases on her own, I never thought she'd wind up on the other side of a homicide investigation. And so soon after she assured me she was through putting her neck on the line to track down killers. I thought we were on Easy Street from here on out."

"Don't let this overly distress you, Stone. I know you have to battle high blood pressure as it is, and we don't need you stroking out on us right now." Wyatt patted his close friend on the back as he teased him. "Seriously, pal, try not to let this worry you too much. I'll do all I can to help get Lexie released and get the investigation headed down the right path, pursuing other potential, more probable, suspects."

"Thanks, buddy!" Stone replied as Wyatt exited the room. Rip and I looked at each other with matching expressions as Stone laid his head down on the table between his hands. In unspoken agreement, Rip and I decided to look into the circumstances surrounding this puzzling situation.

Wendy called from her and Andy's ranch near Atchison, Kansas. She told us she needed to feed the livestock and their dogs, but assured us she'd be at the inn in time to ride with us to visit Lexie while only Detective Johnston was on duty at the Rockdale Police Station.

Rip and Stone spent the time pacing nervously around the inn. To earn our keep, I cleaned all the rooms that had been occupied, scouring the tubs and toilets, putting fresh linens on the beds, replacing soiled towels with fresh ones, and straightening the suites for future guests. I'd heard Lexie remark that, as part of the vast amenities at the Alexandria Inn, they provided both breakfast and supper for their guests. It would be up to me to make certain the guests' expectations were met.

There had been eleven people at the dining room table for breakfast that morning, including Stone, Rip, and me. I'd chosen to prepare a simple meal of bacon, eggs, and pancakes, which seemed to satisfy everyone's appetite. I felt a sense of relief that they were all departing after breakfast. I'd also laid out a large package of frozen pork chops to fry for supper for Stone, Rip, and me. I was relatively certain Lexie would not be home to prepare supper herself, and fortunately, I had the leftover sandwiches from the party to serve for lunch before we headed to the police station.

Handling the kitchen chores was the least I could do to thank our hosts for their hospitality. I was happy to see that Georgia had thought to leave a beautiful cobalt blue platter stacked with individually wrapped turkey and ham sandwiches in the refrigerator, which would suffice for a mid-day meal before heading to the station to visit Lexie.

While I was frying bacon that morning, I'd noticed an open bottle of Crown Royal on the counter. I was surprised the detectives had not bagged and tagged it as potential evidentiary material, even though when the crime scene was being processed, the fact that poison had been used was still unknown. Thinking back, I recalled that the whiskey bottle had been obscured behind several large boxes of supplies brought in by the Pineys.

It occurred to me there was a chance, slim but not impossible, that the bottle could hold some form of evidence that might exonerate Lexie. Could one of the guests have poured the cyanide in it, unbeknownst to Lexie? This could have taken place earlier in the day, potentially even before the onset of the party. It appeared to be nearly full, as if only Trotter's drink had contained any of the bottle's contents.

A pair of latex gloves still lay on the counter, left behind by the caterers. They looked unused, so I put them on and placed the lid back on the bottle before placing it in a Ziploc bag. As the shape of the bottle was short and stout, it fit nicely in a gallon-sized bag. While we were at the police station, I'd give it to Wyatt to be scrutinized by the crime lab. Perhaps the actual killer's fingerprints had been left behind on the bottle. *Wouldn't that be a stroke of luck?* I thought. *And, a stroke of genius on my part, if I must say so myself.*

I'd find out soon enough it wasn't actually a stroke of luck after all. For one thing, the bottle of whiskey had been one of Rip's that he'd donated to the cause. More importantly, there was no presence of cyanide in its contents and the only sets of prints on the bottle were Rip's, Lexie's, and possibly those of the liquor store clerk who sold the bottle to my husband. The third set was smudged, most likely not recent, and didn't match anyone who'd attended the party.

I'm not retracting the "stroke of genius" part of my earlier statement, however. When I'd explained that I had found the latex gloves on the counter, the detectives confiscated them as evidence. They were unsure why none of the investigators had thought to do so at the time they were processing the scene. And to my credit, had the bottle contained fingerprints of any of the other party guests, and the detectives had also overlooked that bottle of whisky used to make the poisonous drink as potential evidence, then imagine how smart I would have looked in everyone's eyes. I'm sure they'd all have been just as impressed with my cleverness as I was.

CHAPTER 7

It was a couple of minutes after one in the afternoon when we all stepped into the Rockdale Police Station and were greeted by Detective Wyatt Johnston. He led us back to a locked holding tank, as Wyatt referred to it, where a forlorn-looking Lexie was sitting on a bench with her head in her hands. She looked up in surprise when she heard us enter the room.

She was alone in the cell, which might have been a fortuitous thing. No telling what kind of vermin might have been in the same enclosure with her. I shivered to think she could be placed in a position where she felt like she was in a cage with a lion that looked as if it were about to pounce. I'm pretty sure all five of us breathed a sigh of relief at the same moment when we'd discovered she was the lone inmate. *Inmate*? I thought. The next shiver I felt put the first one to shame.

The very thought of Lexie being left to her own devices against thieves, thugs, drug addicts, and other scum of the earth creatures, made my blood run cold. And the shiny, stainless steel commode in the corner of the room made me shake my head in horror. If I were sharing a cell with the kind of individuals I was visualizing, I'd refuse to use it even if it caused me to swell up like a water balloon until I finally burst and sprayed them all with urine like water spewing up from a slit in a garden hose. I was curious if there was a separate holding tank for each gender but didn't ask. We had more important things to cover in the half-hour we were allotted to chat with Lexie.

"Hello, baby," Stone said in greeting. "Are you doing okay?"

"Well, I guess I'm holding up as well as can be expected," she said somberly. Wyatt unlocked the cage and we all went in. The thought crossed my mind that it was as close as I ever wanted to get to being in jail. After I'd grown up, I understood exactly what my pappy had meant by not wanting to find myself in the "big house".

Lexie stood up and walked across the room slowly, as if she were stiff from whatever position she'd slept in the previous night. I wondered how she could have slept at all. She hugged her daughter and then fell into Stone's arms for a long and moving embrace. She finally backed away, and with tears welling up in her eyes, she said, "I didn't kill Trotter Hayes. I hope you all believe me. I might not have liked the fellow, but I would never take someone's life or even consider physically harming another human being."

We all replied with words of support, letting her know we'd never even contemplated the notion she might be guilty of murder. Lexie was the kind of person you didn't have to have been acquainted with for very long before you recognized the goodness in her heart and the purity of her soul. She and Stone were what Rip and I like to refer to as "good people".

"Have you heard anything about what's going on? Except for the few tidbits Wyatt's been able to pass on to me, I'm being kept entirely out of the loop. Surely the detectives are looking for the real killer, or killers, aren't they?"

"I don't think so, honey. I'm fairly sure they're convinced they've already apprehended the killer. And, in their eyes, that would be you, as you already know. Rip and Rapella have offered to do whatever they can to help us find out who the real perpetrator is, since the detectives are making no real effort to look for other suspects."

"Oh?" She said, glancing our way. She was probably wondering what two old geezers could possibly do to help her out of her precarious situation. One of us could barely move under his own power without a cane, and the other one, I must admit, was a little bit flustered by the entire incident. But I've always believed that if the will was there, the rest would fall into place in due time. And Rip and I definitely had the will to do whatever it took to identify the real killer.

Stone looked our way too, and I could tell by

his expression he was suddenly having second thoughts about letting us butt into the case. I was surprised when he turned toward Lexie and said, "You know I don't usually like to have you or anyone else who's not officially assigned to the case interfere with a murder investigation. But, since Rip was in law enforcement his entire career, I feel very comfortable with the Ripples nosing around and looking for clues that might lead to the apprehension of the actual killer of Trotter Hayes. Under the current circumstances, I feel like we have nothing to lose and everything to gain."

"Thanks for the vote of confidence, Stone," Rip said. "I do have a few tricks up my sleeve from the thirty-odd years of detective work and the boatload of criminal investigations I've been involved with. And then there's Rapella. How do I put this in a delicate and non-offensive way? Well, let's just say that Rapella is Rapella, and leave it at that."

Even though it seemed like a rather back-handed compliment, I beamed at my husband's words. I wasn't actually sure if I should be standing there with that stupid grin on my face, or walloping Rip on the head with my over-sized raggedy purse. The heavy thermos in my two-decade-old canvas bag would have definitely left a mark.

I was so rattled, I was lucky to remember my own name at the time, so I'd completely forgotten I'd brought the small thermos of stout coffee to give Lexie until I'd considered beaning Rip with it. A caffeine boost was something I knew Lexie would welcome and that she'd appreciate the gesture. I was correct. You'd have thought she'd just matched all the numbers in a lottery drawing when I handed it to her.

As Lexie sipped on the coffee, Stone and Rip asked her questions regarding what she could remember about the incident that had left the young, repugnant jerk dead on the parlor floor. I pulled out a small notebook, usually utilized for grocery and to-do lists, and wrote down a few important details as the rest of them discussed the crime. Ideas were forming in my mind as they conversed. A few of them even had merit.

"I had taken the sheet cake out to set on the buffet table, intending to cut the cake so it'd be ready to serve after Wendy blew out the candles on the regular birthday cake that Georgia had baked and decorated. Wasn't that a beautiful cake she made for you, Wendy? I loved the purple icing and the—"

"Don't lose focus, Mom. It was a terrific cake, but we need to get back to what you remember. Okay?" Wendy said. She was aware of how easily her mother could get distracted when she was nervous, I was sure, and didn't want her to take off on an unrelated tangent since our time with her was limited.

"Oh, sorry. So anyway, I then decided to wait on cutting the cake until the lights were back on because I didn't want to mess it all up or risk getting cut by the knife again."

"Again?" Rip asked. "What do you mean by

'again'?"

"Well, it was dark at the time, and as I was feeling around for the knife I'd seen Lori set next to the cake earlier in the evening, I sliced the tip of my index finger. I assume that's how my blood got on the knife that was used to kill Trotter." With tears in her eyes, Lexie held up the bandaged finger as if she were offering proof of her story.

"It's okay, honey," Stone said. "It wasn't your fault, and you had no way of knowing what was about to happen. You don't need to feel guilty about the young man's death. Go on with your story."

"So I decided to return to the kitchen to help Georgia and Lori Piney get everything moved to the buffet table, which was a challenging task in the dark. They were going back and forth to their cars to haul in boxes and trays. Trotter, who was standing by himself at that point, stopped me on my way to the kitchen. He asked me if I'd please bring him a drink, preferably whiskey," Lexie explained.

"And you told the scumbag you would?" I asked in a disgusted tone.

"Yes, I did, Rapella," she replied with a sigh. "I guess it's the ingrained 'polite and accommodating hostess' trait in me. We own a lodging facility, you know. And being over-the-top accommodating is what keeps customers coming back and recommending our B&B to others. In fact, we often—"

"Mom, please! Stick to the story about what

happened," Wendy insisted. "We haven't got all afternoon to talk with you."

"Oh, yeah. Sorry again! So, anyway, I continued on to the kitchen. Rip had brought me a bottle of Crown Royal earlier, and I opened it and made the drink for Trotter. I'll admit it actually flitted through my mind that if I'd had some kind of poison on hand at that moment, I'd have been tempted to add just a touch to his drink. You know, just enough to give him a severe enough bellyache he'd have to leave the premises before Wendy and Andy arrived. But, believe me, it was only fanciful thinking. I'd never actually do such an awful thing, even to a man like Trotter Hayes."

"We know you wouldn't, honey. Continue on," Rip replied.

"Okay. Just as I started to take the drink out to the parlor, Georgia walked in the back door with a large tray of pulled pork sandwiches. She asked me if I'd mind helping her carry in an even heavier tray of brisket. I told her I'd just made a drink for Trotter Hayes but I could spare a minute or two and would be more than happy to help. She flinched as if Trotter's name was familiar to her and that she wasn't a big fan of his either. It seemed clear that his reputation preceded him."

"Oh, trust me, Mom. It definitely did," Wendy replied. "Go on. What happened next?"

"After I went outside and assisted Georgia, we both returned to the kitchen. She exited the room to take some of the brisket sandwiches to the buffet table on a cobalt blue platter that reminded me of my antique bowl, an old family keepsake. Did you see that platter, Rapella? Remind me to show you the bowl I inherited from—"

"Really? Come on, Mom," Wendy said. "Stick to the story!"

"Did anything seem amiss when you came back in from outside with Georgia?" Rip asked Lexie as I continued to take notes.

"No, not that I recall," Lexie responded. "Although the spoon I'd stirred Trotter's drink with was lying directly on the counter instead of in the spoon rest where I'd left it. I only noticed it because it's kind of a pet peeve with me. It may sound trivial, but I don't like to have to continually wipe off the counters with disinfectant."

Then she shook her finger at my husband as if something had just occurred to her while she was reflecting back. "Wait a minute, Rip. I remember now that the pantry door was closed when we walked back inside with the tray of sandwiches. I'm almost positive it had been wide open with the motion sensor light on when I left the kitchen to help Georgia. So now that I think about it, it would only be illuminated if someone were moving around in there while I was preparing Trotter's drink."

"So, it's quite possible someone was in the pantry and heard you tell the caterer you'd just made a drink for Trotter and were heading outdoors for a short spell to help her carry in a tray of meat," Rip mused out loud. "That would have been the perfect opportunity for the drink to be spiked if the assailant was in the pantry when you made that statement. Where was Georgia's daughter at the time?"

"I had just seen Lori placing a stack of paper plates on the buffet table. She was arranging the plastic silverware, as well as the red Solo cups for the pop and beer. Stone and I always refer to those as Judge Ito cups because he always had one on the bench during the O.J. Simpson trial and —"

"Mom, please—"

"So, anyway, I assumed Lori was still putting things in order on the table in the parlor, such as the condiments, a few side dishes, and the glass goblets I'd purchased for Sheila's punch and the mixed drinks I'd expected to be serving. Georgia had provided deviled eggs, cole—"

"Had anyone else entered the kitchen earlier while you were mixing Trotter's drink?" Rip asked Lexie before Wendy could chastise her mother once again for getting sidetracked. The rest of us had been quietly taking in their Q and A exchange.

"I can't remember exactly, because I was running around like a greyhound on speed, but I do think a few of the party guests had wandered in and left shortly afterward. I was too busy to even turn around to acknowledge them, so I have no idea who they were. But I did at one point hear at least two females laughing at something they'd just been discussing."

"Did you recognize any of their voices?" Rip asked.

I could sense the thoughts racing through Lexie's mind as she tried to place their voices but couldn't. I don't think she'd ever met a lot of the guests so it stood to reason she wouldn't recognize many of their voices. Finally, she shook her head and said, "I did recognize one of the voices, but I can't recall now whose voice it was, not knowing at the time it could end up potentially being an important factor in a murder investigation."

"Of course, that's only natural," Rip added before motioning for her to keep reciting her story.

"Okay, so I took the drink out to the parlor and had to feel my way around to find Trotter in the near total darkness of the room. It was the sound of his obnoxious laughing that led me to him. After I handed him the drink, he thanked me."

"I'd think so," I interjected. "He should have been thanking you for not sending his sorry butt packing the minute he stepped on your property."

"Hush, Rapella! Go on with your story, Lexie," Rip remarked. The look he shot me spoke volumes. I knew the clock was ticking so I vowed I wouldn't interrupt with any more of my personal opinions, even though it'd be difficult to keep them to myself. I did, however, regret not whacking Rip on the head earlier when the thermos was still in my bag.

"After he thanked me, I basically just mumbled incoherently and returned to the kitchen for a short spell. I picked up a tray of small bowls containing pickles, olives, and butter mints. No, wait! I think it was a bowl of cashews, not olives. No, not cashews, it was roasted almonds, or maybe pistachios—"

"Oh, good God!" Wendy exclaimed in exasperation. "It doesn't matter if you brought out a bowl of cocoa puffs or crack pipes! Quit getting bogged down in insignificant details. Wyatt's going to run us out of here in less than fifteen minutes."

"Oh, okay. I'm sorry. I didn't realize I was on the clock. So I then went back out to the parlor and made my way over to the buffet table to set the bowls down. Afterward, I felt around in the dark until I located the knife lying next to the cake. I was going to take the knife into the kitchen to wash it off, realizing I may have left blood on its handle when I'd sliced my finger earlier."

We were all listening intently to her reciting the events that led up to the moment Trotter's dead body became the center of attention, leaving Lexie in a compromising position at the time the lights came back on in the parlor.

Lexie went on to describe those next few moments. "With the empty tray in one hand and the cake knife in the other, I was in the process of returning to the kitchen yet again. On the way, I nearly tripped over a large object on the floor which turned out to be Trotter's body. Just as I straightened up next to him, the lights came on unexpectedly and everyone shouted out to surprise Wendy. Then I remember seeing a number of flashes from cameras, including the one that captured me appearing to have just killed Trotter Hayes. If I had a 'joyful' expression on my face it was just because I was happy I hadn't done a face plant on the parlor floor when I stumbled over Trotter's body. And now I'm sitting in a jail cell trying to make sense of the entire sequence of events that led up to that moment."

My vow to keep my opinions to myself lasted less than two minutes. "You know, Lexie, if you hadn't agreed to wait on that big turd like he was royalty in the first place, you wouldn't be in this predicament now."

Lexie laughed and shook her head. "Oh, Rapella. Only you could come up with something like that! But thank you for making me laugh for the first time since before this whole crazy thing took place."

I hadn't meant to make her laugh, but I was happy to see a genuine smile on her face nonetheless. Glancing at Rip, I noticed there was no sign of a smile on his face. "Sweetheart," he said patiently. "What part of 'Wyatt's going to run us out of here in less than fifteen minutes' didn't you understand?"

"Hey, Lexie, honey," Stone spoke soothingly. "Wyatt told me it was a guest named Alice Runcan who showed Detective Russell a photo she'd taken on her cell phone. Do you know Alice by any chance?"

I interrupted again, despite my husband's scowling expression. "I remember watching that floozy practically seducing the detective on the other side of the parlor right after the cops arrived. She was rubbing her ample boobs all over that detective to get his attention, and her efforts were clearly successful. He was literally licking his lips while she was doing so. I'd gotten the impression she'd only used the excuse of showing him a photo on her phone in order to flirt with him."

Lexie nodded and asked, "But, instead, could she have been trying to frame me for a murder she'd committed? Maybe that's why she snapped the photo to begin with. She may have just seized that perfectly timed opportunity to point the finger in my direction, and away from her or anyone else in the crowd."

"I guess it's possible," I consented. "But I still think she was just trying to get in his britches."

"Lexie's point is something to consider," my husband said. He looked at me in disgust as he said to Lexie, "You never got the chance to answer Stone's question about whether or not you knew Alice Runcan before the party."

"Well, of course I'd heard a lot about her in numerous conversations with Wendy and Mattie over the years but I'd never met her in person before."

"She was a high-school classmate of ours," Wendy said. "Mattie and I buddied around with her on occasion but I never brought her home to introduce to Mom because we just weren't all that close."

"Our allotted time with you is about up but we'll discuss it more tonight when the kids all come over for dinner," I said.

"The kids are coming over for supper?" Lexie asked wistfully.

I should have thought before making that comment. We'd decided to invite them over so we could further discuss the murder and find out any new developments from Detective Johnston. Along with Wendy and Andy, Wyatt and his girlfriend, Veronica, were also joining us for a meal of pizza, bread sticks, and red wine. On the way to the police station, we'd decided to save the pork chops I'd thawed out and order our dinner from a local pizzeria instead. There was no time to waste on cooking meals when we could have the food delivered instead.

At the moment there were no guests at the inn. The two couples from out of town who'd been booked there for the night of the party had returned to their homes this morning, as had a few other guests who's stay over at the inn had only been coincidental. Before they departed, Lexie's best friend, Sheila Davidson, and her husband, Randy, had assured me they were just a phone call away if there was anything they could do to help out with the situation at hand. The Davidsons seemed like good people too.

I instantly felt bad about bringing up our plans for the evening while Lexie was locked in a God-awful cage. I could tell from her expression that she was upset about missing out on what would no doubt be a pleasant and interesting evening with the two young couples, all of whom Lexie adored as if they were her own children.

According to Lexie, Wyatt had been taking good care of her even though the chief had insisted she receive no special privileges. That made me feel a little better about her current situation. She told us Wyatt had brought her coffee at every opportunity, and even sneaked in some fast food for her just before we arrived so she didn't have to eat the customary lunch fare for inmates of the local jail. The previous evening, at the risk of losing his position on the Rockdale police force, he had even secured a warm blanket for her and laid a foam pad on her cot so she'd be as comfortable as he could possibly make her.

Thinking about Wyatt's kindness seemed to make him magically appear. He said, "Sorry folks! Gotta run you out of here before Travis and Russell report to work." As we proceeded to our vehicles in the parking lot, I thought about what had happened to throw the entire special event into such a chaotic conundrum.

As it stood, Andy had not been able to propose to Wendy. Obviously, he didn't want to ask her to marry him while her mother was in jail for murder. The very thought that those two youngsters' engagement was being forced into limbo until the real killer was apprehended and charged with murder saddened me. But it also strengthened my resolve to track down the killer soon so Lexie could be released and the kids could get properly engaged. I hoped to still be here when their engagement became official. In the meantime, Rip and I needed to break down any obstacle that blocked our path in hunting down Trotter Hayes's killer and bringing him, or her, to justice.

CHAPTER 8

Sitting around the large dining room table, which could easily seat another half dozen people, we talked about the case while we chewed on bland, nearly tasteless, thin and crispy sausage and pepperoni pizzas. They even looked like they'd been run over three or four times by a dump truck and then left on the pavement to cook in the sun for a week. They would have made better Frisbees than pizzas, but it didn't really matter. I didn't have to prepare them, and that's all I cared about. We all consumed our food mindlessly anyway, while we concentrated on our lively conversation.

Wyatt had no new information to pass on. He had a suspicion he was being intentionally kept in the dark about the case because of his relationship with Lexie and Stone. According to Lexie, the friendly detective stopped by the inn more mornings than not to drink two or three cups of coffee and eat as many pastries as she could come up with. She had told me he ate like a man who had just been rescued from a deserted island he'd been stranded on for weeks. Not just occasionally, but on a regular basis.

If the man was taking in as many calories as Lexie had indicated, he must have the metabolism of a hummingbird, which ate over twice its weight in nectar every day. Even having been told about the detective's appetite, I was still astounded when I saw him reach for his eighth slice of pizza. Now I realized why Stone had asked me to order so much pizza. At the time, I was assuming we'd have enough left over to eat for lunch the following day. Stone had also asked me to order two dozen cinnamon sticks, of which Wyatt had devoured seven already.

Wyatt was a big man, but seemed to be in incredibly good condition. He was tall, muscular, and very fit. The polar opposite of my husband, who was short, a tad doughy, and beginning to fall apart piece by piece, like a lot of folks our age tend to do. He wasn't terribly overweight, but his once firm muscles seemed to be atrophying from lack of use and leaning toward flabby now. Having to drag along a cane slowed him down, and the lack of exercise was starting to take a toll on Rip's waistline. I'd bought him three new leather belts in the last couple of years, one size bigger each time.

I had always made an effort to keep in shape. I swam whenever possible and tried to walk several miles every day. So far, it was keeping me in as good a condition as one could expect. I was determined to stay on Rip's case until I could convince him to see an orthopedic surgeon about his hip. It'd be advantageous for both of us if he were able to walk with me.

I came out of my reverie when I heard Rip ask Wendy how well she knew Alice Runcan. In response, Wendy wiggled her right hand in a so-so gesture, and said, "For the majority of the time, she hung out with Joy White and Rayleen Waters in high school. Mattie and I attended a lot of the same school functions they did. I haven't seen her in quite a while but knew her fairly well back then. Alice belongs to the same church that Mom and Georgia do, Rockdale Baptist. Mom told me that Alice keeps very busy with church functions. Mom said she seems to volunteer for every committee and helps out with almost every special event the church participates in."

"I'll bet she doesn't stay as busy with church stuff as she'd like to keep busy with Detective Russell," I remarked. There was something about the girl's flirtatious manner that had irked me. And now I was irked even more, with the notion she might have framed my friend heavy on my mind.

"Rapella!" Wendy gasped and then laughed at my comment and continued. "I can't believe you said that, but I really can't disagree. Mattie and I have always thought Alice Runcan was a little too brazen when it came to men. She's always been odd and unpredictable, but for someone so devoted to the church, she is surprisingly, um, what's the word—"

"Sluttish?" I asked.

"That will work," Wendy replied with a chuckle. "She's surprisingly 'sluttish' for such a devout Christian."

"That don't mean nothing though," I said. "I've known of several elders in our church back home who boozed it up all week long, cheating on their spouses frequently, and then acting like they're 'holier than thou' on Sunday. I hate to use a cliché, but as folks often say, 'you can't judge a book by its cover.'"

"That's for sure!" Wyatt's girlfriend, Veronica, said, speaking for the first time since we'd all sat down at the table. Veronica was very thin, almost skeletal, and I noticed she didn't even finish the one slice of pizza she'd put on her plate.

"Hey, girl," I said to the skinny young gal at the end of the table. "Eat up! There's still several pieces Wyatt hasn't snatched up yet. You could stand a little more meat on your bones."

Veronica flashed me a stilted, but friendly, smile. She didn't reach for one of the remaining slices, however. Wyatt looked at her, shrugged his shoulders, and took another slice out of the cardboard box for himself. *Oh well, not my problem*, I thought, and then rejoined the original conversation.

"Does Alice have a job that you know of?" I asked Wendy.

"Yes, she owns a restaurant called Zen's Diner. She just opened it up a few months ago. I've heard the business is struggling to stay alive, but I really don't know a lot about it. Zen's Diner is in a little town about twenty miles southwest of here called Ferry's Landing. It's on the Kansas side of the border."

"Sounds like it might be a gay colony," I replied.

"It's f-e-r-r-y, not f-a-i-r-y," Veronica said in response to my question that was actually meant for Wendy. She sounded disgusted when she continued. "It's a small town, for sure, but it's not a colony. And besides, it's not like gay folks need to be isolated on an island. They're not lepers, for God's sakes! They're folks like you and me who just happen to have a different sexual preference. Simple as that!"

An uncomfortable stillness fell over the room. Stone gave Veronica a questioning look as Rip did the same to me. Wendy and Andy wore matching stunned expressions, and Wyatt, who was impervious to the entire conversation, grabbed one final slice of pizza to place on his plate. For a few seconds I could hear my own heart beating.

Finally, I broke the silence. "I didn't mean anything derogatory by what I said, young lady. I had no intention of offending you, or gays, for that matter. I certainly have nothing against their kind. I've always felt that every person should choose their own path in life. In fact, Rip and I have several good friends who are gay and I love them all to pieces. To each his own, you know."

I felt like I was trying to dig myself out of a hole that I didn't even know how I'd fallen into.

For some reason, her tentative expression had changed to one of disgust the second I said I had nothing against their kind. I was aware I'd probably worded it all wrong. In this day and age, people sure seemed to worry a great deal more than they used to about saying anything that could in one way or another rub someone the wrong way. Lord knows, I hadn't meant to be insensitive or offensive.

As if sensing an argument beginning to brew, Wendy entered the exchange quickly by saying, "Ferry's Landing was named after just what it sounds like. The town was situated right where a free ferry crossed the Missouri River back in the 1800s. It was a large wooden ferry that actually transported carriages and stage coaches from one side of the river to the other. Naturally the ferry landing is long gone and there's a bridge there now. It's kind of an artsy-crafty community. Ferry's Landing was originally established by a group of artists and has attracted talented craftsmen of every imaginable medium ever since."

"Oh, so it's more like a Woodstock kind of place, with drugs, wild music, hippies, and all that kind of nonsense?" I asked.

"No, not really," Wendy replied, with a quick glance over to Veronica as if to judge her reaction to my comments. "Just a lot of talented people who like to display their work in the highly acclaimed art galleries for which Ferry's Landing is known."

"Well, they sound like hippies to me. You

know, the kind that smoke marijuana and eat Oreos while they haphazardly splatter paint across a canvas. Then, of course, they think everything they create while in a drug-induced stupor has some profound meaning. Most of what's called 'art' these days looks to me like crazy crap drawn by a drunken monkey that somebody handed a paintbrush to. A waste of perfectly good paint and paper as far as I'm concerned." From the glare Veronica graced me with, I knew immediately I'd stuck my foot in it again.

"Good Lord," Veronica muttered under her breath. But not so under her breath that I didn't make out what she'd said. With an exasperated-sounding sigh, she shook her head, very rudely I might add, and began to pick up empty plates to take into the kitchen. I had obviously offended the beanpole—again!

Whatever, I thought. I don't know why it's so, but I seem to have the knack for offending people who easily get their bloomers in a bunch. I guess I wouldn't make a very good politician. I don't think I could walk on eggshells all the time, afraid I might make some innocent remark that would somehow upset a large percentage of the population by not being "politically correct" enough. Becoming the focus of a "slip-of-the-tongue" scandal would just be a matter of time for me.

Suddenly, I wasn't sure I liked the anorexic-looking broad who had just exited the dining room. In fact, I hoped the next time Veronica opened her mouth it would be to put the last remaining calorie-loaded cinnamon stick into it.

"Coffee?" Wendy asked as I walked into the kitchen the following morning. She had stopped by on her way to work. It was just after six and she didn't have to report to the county coroner's lab until eight. She seemed frisky and full of energy.

"Yes, please," I said. Wendy removed another cup from the cabinet and filled it to the brim.

I sat down at the table and within seconds, Wendy sat down in the chair across from me. I had slept fitfully and felt a bit grumpy that early in the morning.

"Are you okay, Rapella?" Wendy asked. I guess she must have noticed the uncharacteristic scowl on my face that I'd been trying unsuccessfully to mask as a friendly smile.

"Yes, I'm fine. Just a little groggy from not sleeping well last night."

"Were you worried about upsetting Veronica?"

Wendy's question threw me for a loop. "No. Should I have been?"

"Well, well, no, no, not really," Wendy stammered. "I just thought the conversation between the two of you last night might have put you on edge. She can be a little sensitive, if you hadn't noticed. Veronica was a victim of a lot of bullying while growing up, primarily about her looks. She still hasn't been able to totally get past it."

"You're kidding me, right? A knock-out like

her got ridiculed for her looks? That's just crazy talk! She must have grown out of it 'cause ain't no one gonna tease her now about her looks, other than maybe her stick figure. I'll have to apologize to her for upsetting her, even though I'm not really sure what it is I said that put a burr under her saddle. I didn't realize she'd had a rough childhood. She seems very fragile to me, both physically and emotionally. By the way, when's the last time that woman ate a proper meal?"

Wendy chuckled, even though I'd been dead serious. She replied, "Veronica's not the type to carry a grudge, so I think I'd just leave it alone if I were you. And actually, she has put on a few pounds since we got home from Wyoming. She's really trying hard to get past her eating issues. I'll give her that. There was a time when she would have bypassed a slice of pizza altogether in lieu of a small, dressing-free salad."

"Yeah, I guess she does seem to have filled out a touch since I saw her there three weeks ago. Good for her, but she's got a ways to go to look healthy. Veronica's pretty as she is, but she'd be stunning if she could fill out a bit more and flesh out them sunken cheeks of hers."

"That's exactly what I told her. And also in her spare time, Veronica dabbles in abstract painting. She's attempted to get a few pieces of her work accepted in one of the most prestigious art galleries in Ferry's Landing and got a resounding, 'No thanks, lady, you best keep your day job,' in response every time. I'd have to agree with you, though. There seems to be no rhyme or reason to any of her paintings. I don't know about a drunken monkey, but I think both you and I could come up with something just as remarkable." With her last comment, she chuckled again, louder this time.

"So, back to Alice Runcan," I said. I had no time to waste talking about a young gal who had no insight into the murder of Trotter Hayes. I'm certain Veronica was at the surprise party, but I didn't recall seeing her there. Besides, I needed to dig some more information out of Wendy before she left for work. "What kind of restaurant is Zen's Diner?"

"I have no idea, but it sounds like a small town cafe to me. Why do you ask?"

"I was thinking that Rip and I might visit the diner for lunch today. You never know what you might find out if you ask the right people the right questions."

"Oh, dear. My mother's rubbing off on you, isn't she?" Wendy asked, while donning a mocking expression of horror. "I was afraid this was going to happen."

"Well, I have to say I do admire her spunk and dogged determination to get to the bottom of things when she's involved in a murder case like this one."

"Oh, dear," Wendy repeated dramatically. Then with a smile she added, "You can always Google Zen's Diner to find out more about the place."

"You want me to do what to what?" I asked. For a second I thought I might need to borrow

Rip's hearing aids since, after all, he hardly ever wore them himself.

When Wendy repeated herself, I shook my head and asked, "What are you talking about?"

"Um, you have a cell phone, don't you?"

"Rip does, but he knows little more than I do about how to use it."

"Okay. Well, in that case, I thought I heard you tell Stone you owned an iPad."

"I did," I replied. "But I didn't say I had a clue about what to do with it. I'm not sure I could even turn it on if I had to. My spend-thrifty daughter gave it to us last Christmas and told us we'd love it. So far, not so much! Can't figure out what we could possibly need it for to tell the truth. It's been taking up valuable space in our trailer since Reggie gave it to us."

"Go get the tablet, Rapella. I'll give you a quick lesson on the basics, like how to Google things so you'll be able to access information more readily—about any conceivable thing you could come up with."

That did sound like it'd be handy, especially in our current circumstances. However, the "tablet," as Wendy had called it, had never been charged and was still on the end table in the trailer. So she looked up the address on her "smart" phone for me. She then told me if I'd go and pick our iPad up from the trailer, she'd stop by on her way home from work and teach me a thing or two about how to utilize it. To date it had been doing nothing more than collecting dust.

A few hours later Rip and I were on our way to

Ferry's Landing. He had entered the address of the diner into his GPS and was following the step-by-step directions the lady's voice inside it was giving him. For once, I was glad I'd agreed to let my husband buy the gadget for his last birthday. Not that my approval to purchase it was necessary to begin with.

When we pulled up to the diner, it was nothing like I'd imagined. I expected to find your every day greasy spoon, the kind you find in every small town in the country. Small town diners are usually full of truckers and farmers in their overalls, eating biscuits and gravy and leaving greasy finger smudges all over their coffee cups. Also, there's usually old men who arrive there at the same time every morning and sit in the same seats. They lounge around there shooting the crap with other geezers for hours on end, paying a buck-fifty for a cup of coffee with eight free refills.

Turned out there wasn't one person in the cafe over forty when we walked into the diner. And if you'd have ordered biscuits and gravy, they'd have laughed and said something sarcastic like, "I'm guessing clogged arteries aren't a big concern of yours?"

At Zen's Diner there were beads hanging in the windows where curtains should have hung. There was the pungent smell of what had to be some type of incense burning. The acrid smoke hanging in the air caused my eyes to water and my stomach to roil. I was informed later by our waitress that the incense was lavender-scented to promote feelings of peace and tranquility. If that were the case, their attempt at aromatherapy, as the waitress called it, wasn't working, because I felt anything but tranquil.

Inside a see-through dome on the counter, where most restaurants would display slices of apple and coconut-cream pie, there were bowls of unrecognizable gooey gunk, including one that resembled porridge gone bad. I was particularly fascinated with a bowl of what reminded me of a Chia pet I once owned. *Why in the world would anyone actually want to eat any of the stuff featured under the clear plastic dome?* I wondered.

I'm not sure how the restaurant could be struggling financially, because we had to wait fifteen minutes to be seated. Granted, the seating space was limited, but still, fifteen minutes for lunch? That was ridiculous, as far as I was concerned. Under normal circumstances, we wouldn't have waited two minutes. There were other places to eat, after all. But today wasn't a normal circumstance.

I was convinced we stood out like ancient ruins in the long line of young people, who could only be described as "out there." And despite what Veronica or Wendy might think, they looked like hippies to me. I felt as if Rip and I had gotten trapped in a time machine that had transported us back to the sixties.

Once we were seated at a tall table, on chairs that practically gave me a nose bleed, I studied the menu and wondered if perhaps we should request one written in English. I didn't recognize one thing listed on their "lunch specials" page. The specialty of the day was the *Hummus Tofu Scramble*, which was described as a gluten-free, vegan, lactose and MSG-free casserole. Today's recipe included zucchini and those Chia-pet looking weeds they called bean sprouts. The photo of the dish looked like gobble-de-goop to me.

"This ain't no Cracker Barrel, is it?" I muttered under my breath. Rip shook his head as he studied the menu. Cracker Barrel was a favorite of many RVers. Not only was the food good, but the restaurants were also usually located close to the interstates and offered RV parking. It's a little difficult to run through a fast food drive-thru with a thirty-foot travel trailer hitched to your bumper.

Rip ordered a turkey bacon carb-free wrap and I ordered the specialty of the day. "I'll take the Hummus Tofu Scramble, please. Could you have the cook hold the hummus, tofu, and bean sprouts, and maybe double up on the zucchini?"

The waitress, who looked like she could be playing hooky from middle school, gave me a strange look and spent a great deal of time writing my order down on her small pad of paper. When I asked her if I could speak with the owner, she looked confused, as if she thought I intended to complain about the service we were receiving. She shook her head and replied, "She's not here right now. She's usually only here in the mornings during the breakfast rush. I'm sorry it took me so long to take your order but we are short-handed right now. Two of our servers just quit, and Alice hasn't been able to find new help."

A light-bulb flashed on in my head. I'd once worked at a cafe called Ken's Diner in my home town of Rockport. Zen's Diner, Ken's Diner— how much different could it be? I didn't recognize anything on their menu but I could fake it long enough to have a conversation with the owner, couldn't I? From her I'd get the answers I needed to assess any motives she might have had to kill Hayes, or alibis she might have to prove she didn't. Then I'd tell her I didn't think the job was right for me and quit just like the last two servers had.

I tapped Rip's shin with my foot and said to the prepubescent-looking waitress with hair dyed every color in the rainbow, "I'm actually looking for a job right now. I have a lot of experience as a waitress, and I think this job would be ideal for me. What do I need to do to apply?"

"Oh, gee. I don't know if you're exactly what Miss Runcan is looking for. I think she'd probably like to hire someone closer to my age."

"Unless I'm mistaken, employers can't legally discriminate against people due to their age. What did you say your name was, young lady?"

"Um, well, it's Chelsea, but I didn't mean anything like that. I'm sure sorry if I offended you."

"You did. But I'll get over it. Now, I'll ask again. What do I need to do to apply for the position?"

"When could you start?" Chelsea asked.

"Tomorrow morning."

"Let me call the owner. Hopefully I'll have an answer for you when I bring your meal. Okay?"

"That'd be perfect, honey. Thanks!"

By the time I'd finished my plate of gluten-free, vegan, lactose and MSG-free zucchini, which was surprisingly tasty, I was hired and due to start my new job as a server at Zen's Diner early the next morning. According to our psychedelic-haired waitress, Alice had been delighted to have me begin working as soon as possible. I had to wonder if Chelsea told her the applicant was older than dirt.

On the way back to the Alexandria Inn, Rip turned to me and asked, "Have you lost your ever-loving mind? You'll fit in working as a waitress in that restaurant like I'd fit in as a tap-dancing instructor. Not to mention we're due in Chicago by the 29th for the wedding."

"Don't worry, sweetheart. I don't plan to work there for very long."

CHAPTER 9

Not much had transpired in our absence regarding Lexie's imprisonment or progress in the murder investigation by the local detectives. The district prosecuting attorney had refused to allow any charges to be filed against Lexie until the investigators could bring him more corroborating evidence to consider. So far, he'd stated, all they were able to come up with was circumstantial evidence, nothing incriminating enough to warrant charging Lexie with homicide.

Stone was able to visit with his wife for a short spell in the evening. Rip and I stayed at the inn to lend our friends a hand with their bed and breakfast establishment. We worked together getting two adjoining rooms freshened up, which consisted of some last-minute dusting and tidying up, fresh linens, and placing a straw cornucopia-styled "horn-of-plenty" container, ready to be filled with fresh fruit, on the small antique table in each room. It was most certainly an all-inclusive lodging facility I'd come to learn.

I began preparing a simple supper for our two newly arriving guests; pot roast with potatoes and carrots, a Caesar salad, and freshly baked dinner rolls. I was liberally topping some bread pudding with rum sauce that I'd planned to serve for dessert while Rip handled the "checking-in" procedure for the two twenty-something-year-old sisters who were in town to attend a party celebrating their parent's silver wedding anniversary. The Spitz sisters were cheerful and bubbly, almost giddy, which made me feel like a cranky old curmudgeon in comparison.

Forty-nine-and-a-half years into my marriage to Rip, it often felt as if our wedding was just yesterday. However, on that particular evening, it seemed like lifetimes ago. I glanced in the mirror before I climbed into bed later that night and my normally clear eyes, the color of stonewashed Levi's, were now bloodshot and puffy. If I didn't know better, I'd think the reflection looking back at me was that of a recovering alcoholic who'd fallen off the wagon and been on a three-day bender. I was so tired and weary by bedtime that I slept like the proverbial log all night long.

After a nightmare-free night, I woke refreshed and recharged. The whites of my eyes were no longer red and the puffiness beneath had abated. I felt as if I were ready to conquer the world, beginning with a short stint as a waitress at a restaurant that served food more fit for rabbits than humans.

* * *

"You're asking me how the kelp and wakame omelet is here? Really?" I asked the young couple staring up at me as if I were actually in the habit of eating things that had no business being shoved into an omelet. "I really don't know, sweetheart. Personally, I wouldn't let any kind of seaweed pass through my lips if you paid me. I've made it to sixty-eight without giving up real food and I ain't gonna start eating this foo-foo stuff any time soon."

The young lady exchanged a look with her eating partner and said, "Sorry, ma'am, but we are very health-conscious and we're adamantly against the brutal slaughter of animals just to provide us with meat that's detrimental to our bodies anyway. We think it's very important to eat food with colors: green vegetables like broccoli and kale for the indoles and isothiocyanates that help prevent cancer, purple fruits and vegetables like plums and eggplant for the anthocyanins and proanthocyanins to keep your heart healthy and your brain functioning at optimal—"

I don't know who had pulled her chain, but I didn't have time to listen to a litany of fun food facts, so I cut her off. "Listen, sweetheart. I'd just as soon eat the geraniums in the planter by my kitchen window. They've got lots of colors; green foliage, red and orange blossoms, and even a few dark yellow leaves I ain't got around to picking off yet. Now I need to skedaddle and get your order turned in. Frankly, I don't know why anyone would want to ruin a perfectly good omelet by putting things like weeds out of the sea into it. Weeds that I think should stay in the sea where they belong. But, oh well, whatever floats your boat, I guess."

It was seven-thirty on a crisp Tuesday morning and I was already sick of waiting on people. Even the customers sounded like they were speaking in a foreign language. There wasn't a lot of coffee being served either, but I got a lot of requests for the drink of the day, a healthy alternative to coffee listed in the menu as "Slow-Steeped Diet Caffeine-free Herbal Pomegranate and Ginseng Green Tea with Honey and Stevia Leaf." *What the hell kind of drink is that?* I asked myself. Any kind of beverage that takes sixteen words to list on a menu is way too tooty-fruity for my taste.

Alice Runcan hadn't arrived yet, so I was pretty much obliged to wait on tables even though I didn't have a clue what the customers were ordering. The stuff on the plates I was delivering to tables reminded me of what my momma used to throw in the hog trough or the compost bin.

It was closing in on ten o'clock when I recognized the woman strolling into the diner wearing shorts that barely covered the cheeks of her behind and a tank top that her bouncing breasts were threatening to slip out of. Her skanky outfit left little to the imagination. Wendy had talked about Alice's devotion to her religion. I wondered if Ms. Runcan attended church bazaars in outfits similar to this one. I also wondered if she'd ever been tested for schizophrenia.

She marched right up to me and asked, "Are you the new hire?"

Duh...I thought, as I responded affirmatively.

"Well, then, welcome to Zen's Diner," Alice said. She looked me up and down before adding, "You're a little older than I expected, but I guess you'll have to do. I want to lay out the ground rules before you get too comfortable working here. For starters, if you are persistently late or snippy with customers you won't be around long enough to draw your first paycheck."

Jeez, what a bundle of fun she'd be to work for. Little did she know I wouldn't be around long enough to deliver a bowl of Quinoa steel-cut oatmeal to the scraggly-bearded dude in the corner booth, much less to draw my first paycheck.

I stood silently as Alice began to recite her list of rules. Before I was told I had to bow down and kiss her butt every time she walked into the diner, I said, "You sure look awfully familiar. Say, didn't I see you at Wendy Starr's birthday party the other night?"

"Well, yes, I su-su-su-pose you could have. I did attend the party. Tragic about what hap-hap-hap-happened that night, huh? So sad. I'm sorry I don't re-mem-re-memb...uh, recall seeing you there," she stuttered, suddenly appearing terribly nervous and on edge.

Of course she didn't. I'd had my back to her when she spoke to Mattie just after her arrival. Later, she was too focused on trying to "hook up," as they call it these days, with the handsome detective to take note of some ol' gal in the room that could be her grandmother.

"Did you know that poor feller, Mr. Hayes?" I asked innocently. "He certainly was a good looking thing, wasn't he?"

"Uh-huh. I've known Trotter for years, but who at the pa-pa-rty hadn't?"

"Well, me, for one. I heard he was quite the player. Just out of curiosity, did you ever go out with him?"

"Uh, yeah, for awhile I did. But he was supposed to be my date at Homecoming my senior year and the jerk-off backed out at the last minute, too late for me to find a replacement. As the homecoming queen that year, it was extremely embarrassing to show up at the dance without a date. He was a self-centered, overbearing blowhard if there ever was one."

Alice's whole demeanor had changed drastically. She morphed from a stern, unemotional taskmaster into a red-hot ball of fire with venom in her voice and hostility in her eyes. If she could spit out her vivid opinion of him without stumbling over it, her speech impediment was no longer an issue either.

"Oh, my," I said. I spoke dramatically just for effect. "Man, that'd make me furious! In fact, it'd make me want to get a little revenge. Knock that scuzzball down a notch or two. After all, you were no doubt the center of attention that night. I'd be humiliated to the bone to be stood up that way."

"Oh, but it gets even better."

"Do tell!"

"About halfway through the dance, Trotter strolled into the auditorium with one of my closest friends, Rayleen Waters, on his arm. He'd told her that he and I had split up even though he'd never told me that."

"Oh, my," I repeated. "In that case, I'd definitely want to open up a big ol' can of whoop-ass on that creep if I were you. And maybe an even larger can of it on your so-called friend, Rayleen Waters."

"Rayleen and I shrugged it off eventually and put it behind us. We blamed Trotter for lying to both of us and causing the rift between us to begin with. Joy White was a great friend of ours too. Joy was my very best friend, in fact. Rayleen, Joy, and I were called the Three Musketeers until we went our separate ways to attend different colleges, just a few months after that homecoming dance. I hadn't seen Joy in years, so I was naturally shocked to see her at the party with Trotter."

"Bad taste, huh?" I asked.

"No lie! She should have known better than to mess with him. Joy and I drifted apart after a while too, and hadn't seen each other in several years. But naturally she'd known all about the homecoming fiasco and also about Trotter's bad boy reputation. Then to top it off, Rayleen had attended the party with Falcon Jons. Another example of bad taste. I still can't believe she showed up with him of all people."

A bell went off in my head when I heard that unusual name. I recalled that he was the dude who was sucking on some girl's vocal cords, all the while staring at Trotter's date, Joy White. I now knew his date was a girl named Rayleen Waters, one of the "Three Musketeers" along with Joy and Alice. I had to tread slowly so as not to make Alice Runcan think I was anything but a nosy, gossip-craving senior citizen. "Oh, my goodness! So what's the deal with this Falcon Jons guy that came as Rayleen's date?"

"Let's just say he's got a screw loose. His elevator not only doesn't go to the top floor, it doesn't budge off the bottom one. Anyway, after what Trotter Hayes did to me on homecoming, I haven't given him the time of day. He was an inconsiderate, self-absorbed, narcissistic jackass if you ask me."

"Gosh, he sure sounds like one," I replied. "I'm guessing you're not too unhappy about his death then."

"Well, um, I can't hon-hon-estly say I was devasta-deva-um, you know, terribly upset about it, but that doesn't mean I'd want to see him da-da-dead or pers-personally ever consider mur-mur-mur-mur-mur —"

"Murdering him?" I finished her sentence for her because my patience was wearing thin. Her speech impediment had made a comeback. I was considering the fact her stuttering might be triggered by the telling of great big hairy lies.

"Yes."

"I see."

"Let's get to my list of ground rules again, Ms. Ripple," Alice said. "We need to get you back to work. We don't want to keep our customers waiting, now do we?"

In the blink of an eye, her personality returned to the one she was exhibiting when she first approached me. It was evident our discussion about the murder was over and I wasn't apt to get anything further out of this woman, whom I now considered a possible but unlikely suspect. She'd have to be insane to commit murder over such an insignificant event that happened over a decade ago.

"I'm sorry, Ms. Runcan, but I think I'm going to have to reconsider working as a server here. The arthritis in my spine is beginning to rear its ugly head, and the gout in my big toe seems to be flaring up all of a sudden as well. I'm afraid I'll need to look for employment in a position that requires less time on my feet. But I do appreciate the opportunity to find out if I could handle such a challenging occupation at this stage in my life."

I didn't even wait around long enough to hear her response. I threw the silly-looking apron I'd been given to wear down on the counter and walked out the front door. I felt as if I'd gained a lot of insight into what I considered a trifling motive to kill Trotter Hayes. But I had to admit it wasn't out of the realm of possibility for someone as emotional unstable as Alice Runcan appeared to be.

I got in the truck, glad my tedious morning as a

waitress was over. I quickly realized I had no clue how to get back to the inn. Once again, out of stupid pride, I had foolishly declined Rip's offer to show me how to program the return address into the GPS device. At the time he offered, I'd thought I'd be able to retrace my steps easily enough. Unfortunately, I discovered I'd overestimated my memory capacity by a great deal.

Sometimes I even worried I might be in the early stages of Alzheimer's Disease and there was no medical affliction I feared more. When you get to be my age, just forgetting where you left your glasses is cause for concern. More so when it happens six times a day and at least one of those times you find them propped up on the top of your head.

So I did what Rip had always done with electronic devices he didn't understand. I started randomly pushing buttons. I was about to give up on the GPS when the address of the Alexandria Inn popped up on the screen. I then pushed an option called "select as destination" and was delighted when the female voice told me to drive east for a mile and turn left on Weeping Willow Drive, which I remembered driving down earlier that morning.

I was following the directions being voiced by the GPS device on the way home when I decided to name the gadget Ms. Ratchet. Every time I made one small misstep, the bossy voice said, "recalculating," in what I considered to be a very snotty tone. She even forced me to make a U-turn in downtown Rockdale that I feared might get me thrown in the can alongside Lexie.

Back at the inn, I found the place eerily silent. The sisters were probably visiting their parents and a note written by Rip, lying on the kitchen table, read, "Stone and I are following a lead. Be back soon."

The note was encouraging. It made me hopeful they were on the right path to nailing the real perpetrator. I was anxious to find out what, if any, discoveries they'd made. I had a little insight of my own to relate but was convinced it was of little or no significance.

In the meantime, I wanted to sit a spell with my feet up and a drink in my hand. It'd been a long morning, and I'd been missing my afternoon cocktail. There was no tequila in the house so I grabbed a Miller Lite out of the fridge instead. I retreated to the screened-in back porch and stretched out on a chaise lounge. Dolly followed me outside and let out a series of pitiful squawks as soon as I'd gotten comfortable.

By the way she was flopping over like a fainting goat, I knew the chubby cat was trying to entice me into serving her two o'clock feeding an hour-and-a-half early. Now, I know what you're thinking. And I'll admit it's Rip's and my fault the cat is overweight. But you've never had to look into the adorable kitty's pleading eyes and deny the poor hungry thing some sustenance. It's damned near impossible to do. So, after I fetched Dolly a scoop of Science Diet Light, I stretched out on the chaise lounge again.

While I sipped on my beer and relaxed, I was
going back over my discussion with Alice
Runcan in my mind. I wished I'd thought to ask
her why the three close friends had not kept in
touch with each other in the years following high
school. I still talked on the phone with my best
school chum at least once a month. I could go
back to Zen's Diner for breakfast the following
day, but that might really raise a red flag with the
restaurant owner. She might even get the
impression I was stalking her. But, if nothing
else, maybe I could find out where Joy lived or
worked from Wendy and figure out some way to
get into a conversation with her.

I needed to try to think the way Lexie would if
our roles were reversed. It sounded to me as if
she had always been able to find clever, if
occasionally risky, ways to get the information
she wanted out of suspects. I went over the list of
possible suspects in my mind as my eyes got
more and more difficult to keep open. A short
time later her majesty's rhythmic purring next to
me lulled me to sleep.

Before I nodded off, I'd considered some of the
ramifications of the story Lexie had told us when
we'd visited her the previous afternoon. The fact
that Trotter's drink was spiked with cyanide
made it clear that whoever killed him had
planned the crime in advance. At the very least,
whoever killed him had attended the party
prepared to kill him if an opportunity to do so
without being caught presented itself. And to
their delight, no doubt, the opportunity had.

The killer could be any number of people. A guy like Trotter Hayes probably had a whole lot of enemies. The perpetrator might not have even been invited to the party, I realized. If they had knowledge of Trotter's plans to attend the event, they could have sneaked in the rear door, hidden in the pantry, spiked his drink, and left without ever being seen by anyone. But if that were the case, how could the killer know in advance Trotter would request a drink and Lexie would leave the drink unattended in the kitchen long enough for them to slip cyanide into his Crown and Coke? And, more importantly, who then slashed his throat? After more consideration, it seemed certain to me the killer *had* to have been at the party, instead of an intruder who slipped in, killed his victim, and slipped out, undetected by anyone else.

A coincidence of those proportions just didn't seem like a viable possibility to me. I decided we needed to concentrate on party guests who had previous issues with the victim. And it was beginning to seem like it could be a lengthy list. Unless something else popped up to indicate otherwise, looking into whatever motives the various guests might have had to kill Trotter Hayes is what appeared to me to be the best way to spend our time. The only way to discover motives a guest might have had was to talk to them, which might also result in finding out any possible motives other guests might have had. It was human nature for people to postulate and point fingers at others.

The next thing I knew I was being awakened by a tender kiss on my forehead. Startled, I pulled back abruptly and knocked my half-empty beer can off the wrought-iron table. Startled by the sudden noise, Dolly practically jumped out of her skin on the other side of me. She was trying to get traction to flee before she even hit the ground.

Rip laughed and took his handkerchief out of his back pocket to start swabbing up the spilt beer. I ran into the kitchen and came back with a dishtowel, knowing the handkerchief wouldn't be adequate to clean up the mess.

We worked together to sop up all the liquid. Fortunately, the floor was concrete and no permanent harm was done. Rip smiled at me as we finished and asked, "Drinking alone again, huh?"

I playfully punched him in the shoulder and asked him what they'd been up to all day. When Rip started to explain, I sat back down to listen to his remarks. The murder case was getting more intriguing every day.

"Stone and I drove over to the country coroner's office on the pretense of taking Wendy to lunch, which, by the way, we did. Guess what Wendy's favorite restaurant is," Rip quizzed me with a smile.

"Red Lobster?"

"No, it's a fast-food joint."

"Kentucky Fried Chicken?"

"No, it's a burger joint. Guess again."

"McDonalds?"

"No, it's a—"

"Oh, for God's sake, tell me!" I insisted, tiring of the guessing game.

"Duh—it's Wendy's! So anyway, while we were finishing our 'baconators,' Stone asked Wendy if she could somehow get us a copy of Trotter Hayes's autopsy report. We thought there was a remote possibility that something in the report might prove valuable in getting Lexie released from custody."

"Was there?" I asked impatiently. My husband had a bad habit of taking forever and a day to cut to the chase. Like Lexie, he tended to get mired down in the insignificant details. It was particularly annoying when I was waiting on pins and needles to find out something important.

"Don't know. We couldn't get a copy. As I expected, not even Trotter's father, Chief Leonard Smith, was permitted to receive a copy of the autopsy report in this homicide case. Wendy told us that, unfortunately, it was considered a conflict of interest for her to even view a copy. She hasn't been allowed in the lab since, out of necessity, Nate, the county coroner, called her in to assist by sniffing for the presence of cyanide. I'm sure you recall her telling us about her being the only one in the lab who could detect the telltale presence of a bitter almond scent."

"So you're telling me you accomplished absolutely nothing but boosting your cholesterol levels over burgers and fries?" I asked.

"Not exactly. Here's where it gets interesting,"

Rip replied. He was now resting in the chair beside me, sipping on a tumbler of Crown and ice and rubbing his bad hip as he talked. "While on the way back to the lab to drop Wendy off, she commented on the fact that Falcon Jons had been in earlier, also requesting a copy of the autopsy report. He said he was merely curious about his old classmate's death, but was denied a copy, too, of course. But Wendy said that Falcon had been at her birthday party, and Mattie had told her that Falcon was fixated on his ex-girlfriend, Joy White, who had come to the party with Trotter as her guest. Joy and Falcon had split up when he learned that she'd hooked up with Trotter."

"Hmm," I replied. "I recall Wendy also telling Lexie and me that Joy had just recently dumped him for Trotter and she wondered if Falcon wasn't trying to make Joy jealous by slobbering all over Rayleen Waters, his date for the evening."

"According to what Falcon told Wendy, he had planned to attend the birthday party alone. But then, Rayleen called him earlier that morning and practically begged him to let her attend the party with him. I'm not sure how happy she was about the overly zealous affection at the party that you told me you witnessed, because she'd never been particularly close to Falcon before that night, according to Wendy. Mattie had told Wendy she hadn't invited Rayleen to the party since they'd only hung out with her on occasion in high school and neither had seen her in years. Rayleen, Wendy explained, was kind of a loner who only interacted with a few select friends, primarily Alice Runcan and Joy White." As Rip talked, he kept referring to a yellow Wendy's napkin that he'd scribbled notes on.

"Joy told me this morning she hadn't seen Alice in years," I said. "And she didn't indicate having seen Rayleen recently either. Could the notion of reuniting with her high school buddies be why Rayleen was so determined to be at the party in the first place? Maybe she felt left out because she knew both Alice and Joy had been invited. I can understand why she'd want to be included."

Rip shrugged and said, "That's probably it, but if time allows, it might be worth looking in to." I nodded and wrote some notes in my own little notebook. I'd taken it out when Rip began outlining his day. I had remembered Lexie telling me in Cheyenne that she always utilized a notebook to keep track of all the details. At the time, I'd thought she was being too anal about her impromptu investigation. However, I was quickly learning the importance of keeping a meticulous record of every single issue and clue we unearthed in a quagmire like the one we were involved in. It helped to have all the intricate details in writing to refer back to should the need arise. Especially with so many young people involved in this convoluted web of friends and lovers.

While I scribbled down the particulars, Rip went inside to get me another beer, and I was guessing he would refill his half-finished drink too. When he returned I said, "Alice Runcan described Falcon as having a 'screw loose,' and Mattie had said he'd just recently been dumped by Joy White, who came to the party as Trotter's date. Joy was a reasonably close friend of Wendy's in high school, according to Mattie, who was the one who invited her to the party. But apparently Joy had no knowledge of the sexual assault Trotter had perpetrated against Wendy not long before Wendy began dating Andy."

"How have you come to that conclusion?" Rip asked.

"If Joy knew about the attempted rape incident and was close to Wendy, I can't believe she'd show up at her friend's surprise party with the man who'd assaulted her friend. If for no other reason, wouldn't she worry the same fate might befall her too?"

"Your reasoning makes perfect sense to me. Who'd have thought the little Mayberry RFD town of Rockdale, Missouri, could be such a cesspool of relationships gone bad?"

"Yeah, no kidding! It's more like Peyton Place than Mayberry. Still, I can't imagine any of their petty grievances escalating to the point they'd murder the feller. I'm wondering how Joy fits into this whole equation and what possible role, if any, she might have played in Trotter's death." I was thinking out loud as I was trying to fit the pieces together in my head.

"To me, Joy appeared genuinely grief-stricken about her boyfriend's death," Rip replied. "I don't know how she could have pretended to be that overcome with despair directly after the murder. She'd be a movie star if she were that convincing of an actress. They had to transport her to the hospital in an ambulance, if you remember."

"And because of that, she was the only person at the party who wasn't interviewed at the crime scene by the detectives. Could that have been her intention if she was somehow able to pull off such a remarkable acting performance?" I asked Rip. "Wendy's due here any minute. I need to find out more about all of the players in the picture from her. But first she's going to teach me how to use that silly iPad that Reggie gave us for Christmas."

"You mean that over-sized coaster you use to protect the end table from getting water marks?" Rip asked.

"Yes. At least it's been useful for something other than just taking up valuable space. Wendy assures me it will be very handy for researching all sorts of—"

"Before you know it, you'll wonder how you ever got along without it," I heard Wendy's voice from the doorway.

"Speak of the devil," I replied. "Are you ready to teach an old dog new tricks?"

"Good luck with that," Rip said to Wendy as he walked back into the house.

CHAPTER 10

As it turned out, one of those dreaded alpaca emergencies came up, preventing Wendy from being able to teach me about my iPad. She only had a few minutes to hang around the inn before she had to leave to meet Andy at a veterinarian's office. The animal clinic was in Atchison, Kansas, which was located near Andy's cattle ranch, where they lived. They had adopted two baby alpacas the previous fall and named them Mork and Mindy. Mindy had stopped eating and become very listless. The vet suspected gastric atony might be the cause, according to what Andy had told Wendy on the phone.

Wendy was scheduled to meet Andy at the vet's at five o'clock to find out what the prognosis was, and what, if any, treatment could be given. *If those two are going to be as hovering with their future babies as they are with their glorified llamas, they'll be helicopter parents for sure*, I thought with a chuckle.

As Wendy was telling me more about the alpaca's health woes, her best friend, Mattie Hill, walked in the back door and entered the kitchen. We exchanged greetings and Wendy said, "I asked Mattie to stop by to show you a few things about using your iPad. She's way more tech-savvy than I am anyway. She works with a computer daily, inputting data in the neo-natal department's computer files. Plus, she just lives a couple of blocks from here."

Before Wendy headed out, I was able to ask her a few questions. "How close are you to Joy White?"

"About the same as I am with Alice Runcan. Joy and I met in junior high. The two of us never hung out together much, but throughout our remaining school years, we ran in the same circles. Mattie has been my best bud since elementary school and Joy White was Alice Runcan's closest friend. But Mattie thought she should invite them both to the party since they still live in relatively nearby towns." Wendy and I glanced at Mattie, who nodded in agreement.

"How about Rayleen Waters?"

"Rayleen was sort of a loner and only hung out with Joy and Alice. Rarely ever did she have any interaction with Mattie and me, but we did have mutual friends, so we ran into her at school functions and parties fairly frequently."

Mattie, who'd been nodding the entire time Wendy was speaking, chipped in her two cents. "Rayleen always acted like a whipped puppy around us, as if she didn't feel she was as worthy as the rest of us. We all felt we needed to include her, if for no other reason than to boost her self-esteem and let her know we truly cared for her. I think her low self-esteem has something to do with what we heard Rayleen chose to do for a living. Don't you think so, Wendy?"

"Could be."

"Wendy is as close, or closer, than a sister to me," Mattie continued. "We were both only children. My mother died of complications during my birth, and with the umbilical cord wrapped around my neck, I almost did too. I don't know what I'd have done without Wendy to lean on all these years. I'm curious why you asked Wendy about Joy and Rayleen. Have you guys found out anything that might indicate one of them might have had a hand in Trotter's death...I hope?"

"No, not really," I replied. "I've just been trying to figure out how the personal dynamics of all the party guests fit into place. If there's any way possible, my husband and I'd like to help get Lexie out of jail and the real killer behind bars instead."

"I really do appreciate your help, Rapella. As does Stone," Wendy said. I wasn't sure if she was blowing smoke up my skirt or sincere about her gratitude. I could certainly understand if Lexie's daughter thought Rip and I were more of a nuisance than a help at this point in the game, but I smiled at her nonetheless.

"That's so sweet of you, Rapella. I wish you the best of luck," Mattie added. "Let me know if there's anything I can do to help. I practically lived with Wendy growing up, and Lexie was like a mother to me. I'd do anything for her. And when it comes to Joy and Rayleen, I agree wholeheartedly with Wendy's assessment of them."

"Wendy, was Joy someone you'd confide in if you had anything bothersome going on in your life that you felt you needed to talk to someone about?"

Wendy had a strange expression on her face when I asked her this question. It had been her mother who'd told me about Trotter's attempt to molest her, and I hadn't wanted to let on I knew about that traumatic experience. I could understand that it might not be something she wanted to share with folks like me whom she barely knew. But I got the impression she'd read between the lines when she replied that the only friend she'd ever felt comfortable enough with to confide in was Mattie. And, of course, she told me she shared everything with her mother as well.

I glanced over at Mattie who nodded her head again and added, "And I feel the exact same way. I've even confided in Lexie at times because she was the only mother figure I had growing up."

That cleared up my confusion about why Joy would come to her long-time friend's party with someone that friend had serious issues with. She probably knew nothing at all about Trotter's assault against Wendy. I didn't want to pick at that sore any longer and cause Wendy to close up and stop freely sharing information with me, so I switched my line of questioning to Falcon Jons and addressed both girls.

"Alice Runcan gave me the impression that this boy's bubble was not quite on the level. What are your impressions of him?"

Mattie expressed her opinion first. "The guy owns an aerospace engineering firm in St. Joseph, so he's not exactly the lowest rung on the ladder when it comes to brains. But, in the same vein, he seems to have made a lot of really questionable choices in his life."

"I agree," Wendy added. "He's a strange mixture of really smart and really stupid."

"I know the type," I replied. "I've known a few highly intelligent individuals who didn't have the common sense God gave a peanut when it came to their personal lives."

"That's Falcon in a nutshell," Wendy said.

"Pun intended!" The two young ladies spoke in unison.

"So, my dear, are you ready to show me my way around this iPod thing?" I asked Mattie after Wendy had departed.

"It's called an iPad, Rapella."

"Oh, yeah. Same thing though, ain't it?"

"No, an iPod is an entirely different device." She acted a little queerly, as if she'd just tackled an eight-hundred pound bear and wasn't sure what to do next with it. But her puzzled expression quickly morphed into a pleasant one. I could tell she was delighted to have such an eager student to instruct.

"Oh, yeah, well, *po-tay-toe, po-tot--toe.* I'm ready to learn about whatever it's called."

Mattie shook her head and launched into a long-winded explanation of how the device worked. I only caught about every tenth word, but I figured most of what she was explaining would never apply to me anyway. I really only wanted to know how to find information out there, in what I've heard referred to as 'cyberspace,' a place I wasn't at all familiar with. But I didn't want to be rude to the young gal, so I sat there with a dazed expression, no doubt, and nodded at what I hoped were appropriate intervals.

At first I really was trying to concentrate on what Mattie was explaining to me about my iPad, but words like hashtags, modems, USB ports, as well as swiping, flicking, tweeting and scrolling, were running around in my mind like a blind kitten looking for its mother's teat. She was explaining how I could bookmark my favorites, highlight, copy, and paste things to my clipboard, surf the web, put things in the cloud for safe storage, and, believe it or not, skype my daughter.

Do what to my daughter? I wanted to ask. The only reason I didn't is that I was afraid Mattie would give me a thirty-minute answer I wouldn't understand. Besides, I was sure Reggie wouldn't agree to having me "skype" her anyway. It had a painful ring to it.

I obviously knew what a cloud was, but I didn't have the foggiest notion how a person could put anything into one for safe storage. Even God couldn't put anything into a cloud that didn't eventually escape in the form of precipitation. Where is this cloud by the way? I wanted to know, but again was afraid of the long, detailed reply my question would evoke. I almost felt as if Mattie was so frustrated with me, she was trying to encourage me to give up the idea of learning new skills. *These computer nerds, like Mattie, are really into these things*, I thought. *I'll pretend I'm taking in all the confusing information she's putting out so I don't offend her. I've been offending too many people lately as it is.*

I spoke very little throughout the tutorial. I was too embarrassed to tell Mattie she was explaining all this technical mumbo-jumbo to someone who wasn't even entirely sure how to turn the complicated doohickey on.

"You know what?" Mattie asked excitedly. "You should get your own Facebook page! It would be a great way for you to keep in touch with your family and friends, and reconnect with people you haven't seen or even thought about for years. I can help you with it if you'd like me to."

"Well, I guess it would be nice to keep in closer contact with my daughter and my friends back home in Texas. Where do I buy one of those things? I noticed there was a bookstore in town. Can I pick one up there? Or perhaps at that office supply place on Main Street?"

"Um, no, Mrs. Ripple, you don't actually have to purchase a Facebook page. You just need to set one up. I'll show you how to do it. Then I can show you how to post photos and comments, how to 'like' other people's posts, how to share posts and tag people in your photos. I can even teach you how to block people from being able to access your posts."

"So you're saying I'm supposed to 'post' things on my Facebook page and then block folks from seeing them. What's the point?"

"Well, you wouldn't want to block all people, Ms. Ripple, just—"

"As I said before, I'd prefer you call me Rapella, dear. And this 'social media' stuff you've been talking about sounds like more than I want to tackle right now. So, let's just stick to showing me how I can use this thing to search for information. Wendy used the word 'Google,' I believe."

"Okay, but actually 'Google' is just one of the many search engines you can utilize. I prefer Bing, but there's also Blekko, Yahoo, DuckDuckGo—"

"Oh, swell." Suddenly I sensed a migraine coming on.

I was afraid it would require a lot more patience than Mattie Hill possessed, but she did manage to teach me how to type in anything I wanted to know more about and bring up multitudes of web pages containing information on the subject. I was sure the young lady had given up on me by that time because she flew through her demonstration as if the room was on fire and she needed to get out of it before the roof collapsed.

I focused as best I could and concentrated hard on the tasks she was explaining while demonstrating them step-by-step on the tablet. I felt a sense of pride and accomplishment when the tutoring session was over. It was exhilarating to know I now possessed a new weapon in my arsenal that might benefit me in my quest to exonerate my friend. And it was self-satisfying to discover I still had the ability to tackle challenging new skills and succeed in mastering them.

I also discovered how Mattie Hill could have afforded to take care of the old lady who swallowed the cat food lid. Mattie was not only financially sound, she was mind-numbingly rich. She wore a Cartier watch that featured a row of diamonds around the perimeter of its face and carried a Prada purse made out of ostrich hide, like some of the wealthiest movie stars I'd read about in those smut magazines at Wal-Mart. I'll have you know, I've never actually shelled out hard-earned money for one of those rags, but they helped pass the time while I waited in long lines in the checkout lanes. It's always amusing to learn who's cheating on who in Hollywood while they're married to another celebrity who's cheating on them at the same time.

When I walked Mattie out to her car to thank her and see her off, I wasn't surprised to see she drove a Bentley. Not being one to beat around the bush, I asked, "You win the lottery or something?"

Mattie laughed and replied, "No. It's even worse than that. I'm a trust-fund baby, as people like to call us."

"And that's a bad thing?" I asked, baffled by her glum demeanor.

"In some ways it is," Mattie answered my question as if ashamed of her lot in life. "My daddy's a very successful businessman. He owns a large manufacturing corporation based nearby in Mohawk, just east of here, but he travels extensively. He currently oversees seventeen factories across the globe, with an additional three in the works. I rarely ever get to see him, but I understand why he's too busy to come home very often. Personally, I think I'd rather have to work for a living, scrubbing toilets if it meant getting to spend more time with my father. You can't buy love or happiness, you know."

I never thought I'd feel sorry for someone who could buy anything she wanted without having to lift a finger to earn it. However, by the forlorn expression on this young lady's face, she wasn't kidding when she said she'd give it all up in a heartbeat in exchange for the kind of peace of mind only the love of a family can provide. Growing up, my family was often short of money, food, and other material items. But there was never any shortage of love, for which I've always been grateful. With the bountiful love my family shared, we'd always been able to overcome any obstacle that came our way.

I pulled Mattie toward me in a warm embrace. I could feel her pain. In many ways, I was much richer than she was and wished I could share it with her. Although it was none of my business, I said, "I hope I'm not overstepping my bounds, sweetheart, but I've got to ask you a question. Why do you work as a neo-natal nurse when you obviously don't need the money?"

"What else would I do to keep active? Besides, it's a passion more than a vocation for me, Rapella. I love working with babies. I not only get to care for them; on occasion I even get to help deliver them. It's like watching a miracle take place right before your eyes. I also see it as a way to honor my mother, whom I never had the chance to know."

"You poor child. I can't imagine losing my momma the way you did. I'm so sorry for your loss, sweetheart."

"Thank you," Mattie replied. "And also, when I first started my period years ago, I was diagnosed with severe endometriosis and had large cysts on both ovaries. I ended up having to have a total hysterectomy when I was seventeen. I'll never be able to give birth to babies myself, but I can still help bring them into the world in my own way. And I can always adopt, which I plan to do some day."

"Having a hysterectomy at that age had to be one of those many times you missed having your mother by your side to hold your hand and be there for you."

Mattie nodded. "Yes, having a different nanny every other month made it difficult to bond with any of them. I really had no maternal figure to turn to at times like that. Well, other than Lexie, that is. That's why I'm as determined as you to get to the truth behind this murder."

"We could certainly use your help whenever you can get free to join us. And I'm also proud of you for devoting yourself to premature and sick babies. You are a very special young lady, Mattie. Wendy is fortunate to have a friend like you."

"Thank you. I feel the same about her."

Mattie and I chatted a few more minutes about a few of the babies she'd treated who had, against all odds, miraculously survived and gone on to lead normal, happy childhoods.

Before she left, I remembered to inquire about something she'd said earlier regarding Rayleen Waters that had intrigued me. I learned that the young lady worked as an entertainer at a private club in the seedier section of town. Mattie reiterated her belief that Rayleen's choice of occupations might have been triggered by her lack of self-worth. Mattie didn't mention exactly what kind of entertaining the girl did but I had a sneaking suspicion.

Five minutes after Mattie pulled out of the driveway, I was on the iPad typing "Rockdale, Missouri, private clubs" and "St, Joseph, Missouri, aerospace firms". There were a number of private clubs in the area, but only one aerospace firm in St. Joseph. Thanks to Mattie, I soon found all the information I was looking for and I knew she would be proud of my accomplishment.

CHAPTER 11

I woke up the following morning full of piss and vinegar, as my pappy used to say. I was ready to hit the ground running, as he also used to say, but seldom did himself. The Spitz sisters were paid up for another night so I decided to serve biscuits and gravy and sausage patties for breakfast. Rip and I rarely had an excuse to eat as if our cholesterol levels weren't an issue. I think he was enjoying the abundant saturated fat and excessively sweet desserts even more than I was.

As I prepared the morning meal, I thought about the questions I wanted to ask Falcon Jons if I could somehow get an opportunity to speak with him.

On the Internet the previous evening, I'd learned there was an outfit in St. Joseph called Midwest Aerospace, Inc. and knew it had to be the one owned by Jons. After all, I hadn't expected there to be more than one in a

Midwestern town the size of St. Joseph, with an estimated population of just over seventy-six thousand.

I'm not a trivia fanatic but I'd enjoyed toying with the iPad more than I ever thought I would. And the more I messed with it, the more proficient I became at utilizing it. I found myself researching everything from the demographics of nearby towns to how many people could squeeze into a Volkswagen Beetle. Lexie drove a pale yellow VW Bug and it was very hard for me to believe the answer was twenty people, as stated in the Guinness Book of World Records.

When I'd realized I was getting sleepy and the topics I was googling had drifted far afield from what I'd actually set out to research, I'd plugged the iPad in to recharge and set the handy little critter on the nightstand. I quickly fell fast asleep.

After commenting at the breakfast table about the amazing number of people who had successfully crammed themselves into a VW Bug in Lexington, Kentucky, in 2010, it occurred to me that Lexie's car was sitting unused in the Alexandria Inn's six-car garage. I asked Stone if I could borrow it for the day and he replied, "Of course, Rapella. Rip and I each have a truck for transportation, and since Lexie's temporarily indisposed, her car's yours to use whenever you want it. Or, I should say, I hope she's only temporarily indisposed."

"Don't worry, Stone. We'll figure this all out soon. Paul, the mechanic at Boney's Garage, called this morning to let me know they were running behind and it'd be a day or two before they could even get started working on the repairs to our trailer. In the meantime, Rapella and I have chosen to spend our time helping get Lexie cleared. I promise we'll have her home before you know it," Rip assured his new friend. Then he shot me a look that indicated he had no idea how we were going to live up to the promise he'd just made.

Just then, the inn's phone rang and Stone took the call. He said, "Just a second, honey, and let me ask her. Hey, Rapella, did you happen to find Mattie's cell phone? She can't find it and thinks she may have left it here last night when she was tutoring you on the iPad. She's calling from the hospital."

"I haven't seen it. Tell her I'll look around and let her know if I find it. Get her work number for me, Stone."

After breakfast, I glanced around the desk where Mattie and I had sat the previous evening, but couldn't find a phone. While I called Mattie to tell her that it didn't seem to be here, Rip reluctantly entered Falcon's firm's address into the GPS in Lexie's car for me. His model was very similar to the one mounted on the dash of the yellow bug. After Rip had gone inside, I turned around in the driveway and headed north toward St. Joseph.

I had to laugh at the dried-up bouquet of purple loosestrife in the bud vase that Lexie had clipped to the air-conditioning vent on the passenger side.

I wondered if she knew the attractive blossoms were classified as a noxious weed. I'd later Google it and discover that in neighboring Kansas the invasive plant was not allowed to be transported into or within the state.

I followed Ms. Ratchet's directions to a T, and she led me right to the doorstep of the building I was looking for. On the front door was a sign that read "Now Hiring" and directed applicants to report to the office of Mr. Falcon Jons. Mr. Jons may have been young and a little "off," but he'd obviously done well for himself. The building was not especially large but it was very expensively decorated. The hanging pendant lights were encased in crystal glass cylinders, and as you walked into the entrance, you were looking across the room at a "crying wall" that consisted of re-circulated water running down a mosaic-tiled wall. Even the receptionist's desk was constructed of a brilliantly polished mahogany wood. At my request, the lady behind the immaculately organized desk pointed me in the right direction to the owner's office.

After a brief interval in a waiting room, I was told I could see Mr. Jons. When I walked into his office, Falcon placed the pornographic magazine he was sifting through into the top drawer of his desk and asked, "May I help you?"

"Yes, sir," I replied. "I wanted to speak with you about the job you are taking applications for to see if it's something I might be interested in."

"Seriously? I was kind of looking for someone younger. Like three or four decades younger, actually."

Ruffled by his comment, which was getting to be redundant by local employers, at least as far as I was concerned, I replied with a snide remark of my own. "Oh, so I take it that age discrimination lawsuits are not an issue for you?"

"Um, well, yes, I mean…"

"Go on."

"Please have a seat and we'll discuss the position I'm trying to fill. It's an entry-level position as a computer analyst in the Software Engineering Department."

"Perfect!" I replied. "I just learned all about that stuff last night!"

"Seriously?" He repeated. Falcon studied me for a few seconds and asked, "You sure look familiar to me. Where have I seen you before?"

"Oh, I get that all the time. I guess I just have one of those faces everyone thinks looks like someone they know." At Wendy's party he'd been so involved in playing tonsil hockey with Rayleen Waters, I was surprised he even recognized me.

"Hmm, I could swear I've seen you somewhere before."

"Well, it's possible. I did kind of think your name sounded familiar to me when I read it on the front door of the building." This was not the perfect opportunity to segue into a conversation about any motives he, or any other party guests, might have had to kill Trotter Hayes, but it was apt to be the best opportunity to come my way. So I asked, "Do you know Joy White, by any chance?"

Falcon's face flushed and his mouth dropped open. "Yes, yes, I do. We used to go together, as a matter of fact. How do you know Joy?"

I hadn't thought ahead enough to be able to spit out pre-fabricated details, so I said the first thing that came to mind. "I'm her godmother."

"Seriously? She never mentioned she even had a godmother. Are you a friend of the family?"

"Oh, yes. I've known her mother for years."

"How do you know Viola? Through the gun club?"

"The gun club?"

"Yeah. You know the one Joy's parents own in Atchison."

"Oh, yes, of course, the gun club," I replied nonchalantly, trying to wing it as best I could. "Yes, as a matter of fact that's exactly where I met Viola. I've been a member there for as far back as I can remember."

"They just opened the club last fall."

"Oh? Really? Just last fall, huh?" His comment flustered me, but I recovered quickly. "My memory is not what it used to be, son. Did I happen to mention I was very likely in the early stages of Alzheimer's? I can't recall if I've already told you that, or not."

"Uh, no, you hadn't. Even with your memory issues, you're actually here to apply for a job in the aerospace industry? Seriously?"

"Seriously" was obviously this dude's favorite word. "Well, yeah, I *seriously* am here to apply for the opening you've advertised! After all, I carry a notepad in my purse. I can always jot down any important details in the event I need to refer to them later. Now, as I was explaining about my involvement with my good friend, Viola's, gun club. I frequently compete in their, well, you know, those contests they have at gun clubs occasionally. The name of that competition slips my mind all of a sudden. It's that Alzheimer's thing, you know."

"Turkey shoots?" He volunteered.

"Yeah, that's it, Mr. Jons. Couldn't think of the name right offhand. I reckon I had a brain fart there for a moment. I'm quite good at shooting them turkeys, if I must say so myself. I've really got a dead eye for them little rascals, in fact. Are you aware that they're hard to kill if you don't shoot them directly in the head? They've got a brain the size of a pea, you know. And, more often than not, I nail them right between the eyeballs with my twelve-gauge." Even as I was blathering and lying through my false teeth, I knew I should have shut my mouth and given him as brief a reply as I could. I'm certain he already thought I was some century-old loony tune who couldn't recall what year it was.

Falcon stared at me for a few seconds and said, "I'm pretty sure they shoot clay pigeons, not actual turkeys in those competitions."

"Clay pigeons? Oh, yes, of course, clay pigeons. That's exactly what I said, isn't it, son?" *Why is the competition not called a pigeon shoot, then*? I wanted to ask the smart aleck. Of course that might be a dead giveaway that I'd never heard of a turkey shoot before, much less "frequently participated" in them. I had been correct, though, when I thought I might be pushing my luck by boasting about my shooting expertise, and running on and on about turkeys for goodness sakes! My only option now was to infer he hadn't heard me correctly. "You need to clean them ears out, boy. I'm guessing you could grow potatoes in them."

"Um, no, actually you said—"

"Well, never mind about what I said or how I know Joy." I was trying to divert the conversation back to what I'd gone there to discuss in the first place but Falcon wasn't making it easy for me.

"And, actually, a turkey's brain is the size of a walnut, not a pea," the know-it-all said.

"I was referring to a very large pea, young man. But enough of that! How do you know Joy? I kind of recall her telling me she quit seeing you so she could date some dude named Potter, Cotter, or something of that nature."

"His name was Trotter. Trotter Hayes. And she didn't dump me, I dumped her when I found out she was cheating on me with that rat. After we split up, she ended up getting pregnant by Trotter. I really cared for Joy and all, but I ain't raising some other chump's child, even if she did want me back."

"Which apparently she doesn't," I said somewhat sarcastically. "So, Joy had a baby with this guy? I can't believe she didn't call me to let me know of her good news. I am her godmother, after all. I'm also surprised Viola didn't tell me about her new grandchild."

"She hasn't had the baby yet. Joy only found out she was pregnant a few months ago. I'm guessing she's just going on four months now. Should start showing soon with what should have been my baby. That no-good bast—"

"Goodness gracious, son! You sound very, very angry with this Trotter fellow. You did say his name *was* Trotter, didn't you? What did you mean by *was*?"

"He's dead now."

"Oh, my! I hope you didn't have anything to do with his death! I'm not judging your character, mind you. But from what you just told me, I'd be tempted to whack him myself if I were you."

Falcon Jons thumped his fist against the top of his desk and took a couple of deep breaths before saying, "Let's get back to the business at hand. I don't have a lot of time to waste this morning. In fact, I have a meeting to attend in twenty minutes. So, Ms. Ripple, do you have a doctorate or, at least, a masters degree in aerospace engineering?"

"No, but I'm sure I could have gotten one of those degrees if I hadn't gotten knocked up at eighteen and had to get married right out of high school." Falcon Jons's expression suddenly resembled that of a man who'd just been told he had an incurable venereal disease. It took him several long seconds to come up with his next question.

"So, what experience *do* you have in this field?"

"None, really. But I've done about everything else, so I'm sure I could learn all I need to know about it very quickly. After all, I learned all about using an iPad in one short lesson."

"Good for you," Falcon replied. It appeared to me as if he was the one using sarcasm now. "Tell me what you know about cosmic astrophysics, microwave celestial bodies, and the electromagnetic spectrum."

He was obviously just messing with me now. We locked eyes for a few seconds, and then I asked, "Are you thinking the same thing I'm thinking, Mr. Jons?"

"Probably not."

"Well, I'm thinking this might not be the right job for me."

"No shit?" He replied. "This position sounded to me like the perfect fit for you."

Now I was certain he was being sarcastic with me. I didn't think Falcon Jons's condescending attitude was very professional for someone who was in the position of interviewing and hiring new employees to work at his firm.

"No, sorry. I'm afraid I'd bore very quickly working here. You know, in a position like this one in your Software Engineering Department that I'm so clearly over-qualified for. Good day, Mr. Jons. I'll see myself out." Falcon gave me the oddest look. It was as if the aerospace engineer was studying a new planet he'd never seen before.

Before he could respond, I stood up and walked out of his office. I could feel his eyes boring into my back as I walked down the hallway. I'm sure he was still racking his brain to come up with where he'd seen me before. Either that, or he regretted being so rude and disrespectful and causing a prime candidate for the job opening to walk right out the door.

I was pleased with myself for now knowing how to enter the inn's address in the GPS for the return trip, and was rather enjoying getting more and more proficient with the device. I was even getting used to Ms. Ratchet's bossy voice giving me turn-by-turn directions.

Rip was the only one at the inn when I walked through the back door into the kitchen. According to Rip, Stone had been allowed to visit Lexie at the police station again for a few minutes.

Meanwhile, Rip was sitting at the kitchen table scouring through some legal tomes he'd borrowed from an attorney friend of Stone's. He was searching for anything that might serve as a loophole in getting Lexie released from jail. So far, he told me, he hadn't had much luck. According to Rip, it seemed as though the majority of the loopholes only applied to the rich and the famous, many of whom seemed to be above the law and never had to worry about criminal charges sticking to them in the first place. As a career law enforcer, this was a particularly aggravating pet peeve of my husband's.

After Rip got through with his "justice is a joke" rant, he asked me how my morning had gone, and I explained to him what I'd learned about Joy White's pregnancy. I touched only briefly on how I'd applied and been interviewed for a job opening in the aerospace field, to which he'd replied, "Seriously?"

Rip's response hit a raw nerve. "How would you like that fourteen-hundred page, leather-bound law book shoved up—"

"Down, girl!" He smiled as he patted my head like I was an overly zealous Doberman Pinscher. "I was just teasing with you. Go on with your story about Joy."

"All right. As you know, she's the young gal who arrived at the party with the victim and was wearing a sad expression much of the time, even before her date got killed."

"I remember her. She was the hysterical young lady who got hauled out on a gurney."

"Yes, that's the one. Falcon Jons, who's Joy's former boyfriend, estimated that she should be about four months along in her pregnancy. I don't recall noticing if she was even beginning to show yet, but I didn't really pay much attention to her at all until she freaked out after Trotter was killed."

I didn't mention this to Rip, of course, but felt I might not have noticed if Joy was showing because, prior to learning what Trotter had done to Wendy, I was too busy checking out the chiseled facial features and tight buttocks on her date.

"I wonder if that pregnancy figures in to Trotter's death in any form or fashion?" Rip asked. "Also, the fact she was expecting might have been why the EMTs wanted to transport her to the hospital for further observation."

"I was wondering that too. I'm hoping to find out when I go to the YMCA this afternoon. I read online that Joy White is the instructor of an exercise program that just happens to take place this afternoon at two. I called the Y this morning and was surprised when they told me she had decided not to cancel the class, despite the vicious slaughter of her baby's father just a couple of days ago."

"That surprises me, too," said Rip. "I wouldn't think she'd be in any condition to go ahead with the lesson either, considering both her pregnancy and Trotter's death. What kind of exercise program is it? Aerobics? Spinning? Yoga, maybe?"

I wasn't sure what spinning was, but I was glad it wasn't that kind of class. I get dizzier than a loon just riding on any carnival ride that rotates in circles. I certainly didn't need any self-induced dizziness. So I replied to Rip's question, "No, thank goodness, it's just pole dancing. I reckon Joy will teach us how to dance with a pole. Kind of like dancing with an invisible partner, I guess."

After Rip had stopped laughing, I explained that the program was advertised with the catchy phrase, "Pole dancing is not just for strippers anymore."

After my husband stopped laughing again, even harder this time, I explained, "According to the program's description, pole dancing has become popular as a form of exercise that helps build muscle strength, endurance, flexibility, and self-confidence."

"That sounds wonderful, darling. Will you show me what you've learned from that program this evening, preferably right before we go to bed?" I knew Rip was teasing me, because he caressed my behind as he spoke. I promised him I'd give him a private demonstration of my new dance moves that evening at bedtime, because if nothing else, it'd be nice to shift our sex-drive gears out of *park* for the first time in a while.

At one time Rip and I had really enjoyed dancing. We'd even taken ballroom dancing classes when we were in our forties. With surprisingly good rhythm, Rip could really cut a rug before he became reliant on a cane. Now, without his "third leg," he couldn't walk from his chair to the refreshment table at the dance hall without groaning and moaning. I kept telling him I had no intention of spending the rest of my days pushing him around in a wheelchair because he was too bull-headed to see a physician about a hip replacement. So far, however, no amount of nagging had persuaded him to make an appointment with an orthopedic surgeon.

I had just enough time to grab a turkey sandwich and change into a sweatsuit I'd had for many years. The sweatshirt had a yellow and green Baylor University emblem, and running down the right leg of the sweatpants it read, "Go B ars." The "e" in bears had peeled off after about the hundredth washing of the tattered suit.

Grabbing the keys to Lexie's car off the table where I'd left them earlier, I told Rip I'd be back in a couple of hours. He wished me good luck and told me he'd give anything to be a fly on the wall at the pole-dancing program, just to watch me practice my new moves. I was flattered until he began to laugh again.

Shortly after I arrived at the gym, I watched as Joy entered the front of the building wearing dark leotards. The all-black outfit was certainly appropriate for the situation. Joy looked sad but she didn't appear to be in a state of shock, grief, or anxiousness. More importantly, her concave stomach showed no signs of what the celebrities in the gossip magazines were now calling a baby bump. Not that it was totally unheard of for an expectant mother to not show at all until her fifth month, or even later on rare occasions.

She must really need the income that teaching this program provides, I thought. Just to show up here to fulfill this obligation so soon after the death of her boyfriend seemed incredible to me. The very thought of having to raise their child alone had to be weighing heavy on her mind. I didn't know whether to admire her commitment or question the reasoning behind her apathetic behavior.

When I walked into the specified room at the YMCA a few minutes later, it was immediately evident that I was the only one attending the program who knew how to dress for a workout at the gym. Granted, I was the only senior citizen in the room, but you'd think these young ladies would have better sense than to wear such skimpy little outfits. They might as well have just shown up in their underwear, considering their attire left very little to the imagination anyway. I judged that there was enough spandex in the room to cover the gymnasium floor.

I had hoped to be able to speak privately with Joy White before the program began. If at all possible, I wanted to sneak out before the lesson commenced. I felt like the only adult in a room of toddlers, and I hated to show up all these youngsters who couldn't possibly have as much dancing experience as I'd had over the years. But it was not to be. When I approached her with the inquiry about speaking to her for a few minutes, she agreed to talk with me following the completion of the lesson she was planning to teach that afternoon. I really had no option but to participate in the ensuing program.

The next hour and fifteen minutes were grueling. I was sweating like a cold water pipe in the summer and grunting like a warthog as well. The younger women, clad in their cutesy little outfits, had shown nary a glisten of perspiration. Nor were they struggling to breathe like I was, gasping like a goldfish that had jumped out of an aquarium and was lying helpless on the floor.

I hadn't realized how out of shape I'd let myself get until after I'd finished a lengthy warm-up routine of push-ups, sit-ups, and squat thrusts. I'd gotten through the first two, but it was the squat thrusts that nearly did me in. I was ready to wave the white flag about the time Joy began demonstrating a few basic pole-dancing moves in the front of the class. She gyrated from one position to the next on a steel pole that stretched from the floor to the ceiling. Compared to the calisthenics I'd just struggled through, it looked vulgar, but relatively easy. About halfway through her routine, I wanted to tell her that she and the pole needed to get a room.

As I soon discovered, attempting a maneuver called the "caterpillar" was not as effortless as Joy made it look. Crawling up the pole upside down, using only your hands and knees to propel your body upward, while trying to keep from sliding down the pole into a undignified heap on the floor, was not the piece of cake I expected it to be.

When it was my turn to practice the assigned move on one of the four poles situated in opposite corners of the room, I approached one of them as several other participants walked up to the three remaining poles. For some reason, all eyes were on me, even those of the girls practicing the move on the other three poles. I was sure they were all thinking I was way out of my league. I hoped to prove to them otherwise. With unwarranted confidence, I grabbed hold of the pole with clammy hands, anxious to demonstrate to the younger gals how to flawlessly execute the move.

That confidence began to dissipate rapidly as I hung upside down in what I'm sure was a most comical version of the "caterpillar" position. At one point I'm pretty sure I saw my entire life flash before my eyes. Gravity had caused all the blood in my body to migrate south and pool in my head. I lost my grip just seconds before I'm sure I would have lost consciousness.

Lying in the aforementioned undignified heap at the base of the shiny pole, listening to the snickering of two dozen young floozies, convinced me to sit out the next few maneuvers and wait for the remainder of the program to run its course. It was a painful reminder that my body wasn't capable of doing all the things it could do when I was the age of the other ladies in the class.

Finally, Joy announced that the weekly program was over for the day and she looked forward to seeing us all next week, same time, same place. I hoped she wasn't really expecting to see me at one of her programs ever again in this lifetime. Throughout the lesson, she had continuously glanced over at me, presumably to verify I wasn't in desperate need of resuscitation—yet.

After the room cleared, Joy walked over and asked me what I wanted to talk with her about. I hadn't come up with a smooth way to launch into the topic of the recent death of her boyfriend and father of her baby. So I just dove right in, asking her, "Isn't all this strenuous exercising hazardous to your baby's health?"

Joy swallowed hard and asked, "My baby?" She was obviously taken aback by my question. "What are you talking about?"

I didn't have a game plan so I had to think fast on my feet. "I was at the gun club your parents opened last fall, practicing shooting clay pigeons, when I heard your mother, Viola, mention you were expecting a baby. So I was naturally surprised when I saw you were teaching this pole-dancing class."

Joy stared at me for an uncomfortably long period of time before responding. "Oh, goodness. I didn't even realize my parents knew I was pregnant. I lost the baby soon after I found out I was expecting a child, before I could even break the good news to them. After they took the baby, I decided telling my parents would serve no good purpose. I didn't want to upset my mom and dad by telling them I'd lost what would have been their first grandchild."

"I understand completely. I think I'd have done the exact same thing if I were in your shoes. And now that you've lost the baby's father also, and in such a violent way, you must be totally devastated. I truly am so sorry for both of your losses," I said to console her when she began to weep. I was relieved to find she wasn't as hard-hearted as I'd first thought she might be, and also that she didn't appear to recognize me from the night of the party.

"It recently occurred to me that you're the Joy White that Alice Runcan mentioned to me when my husband and I ate breakfast the other morning at Zen's Diner in Ferry's Landing," I said as casually as I could.

"Alice Runcan mentioned me?" She asked with obvious astonishment. "What did she say?"

"Oh, nothing too interesting. She just made the remark you were good friends. That's about it, if

I recall."

"How odd," Joy said. "She was actually my best friend throughout our school years, but I haven't seen her in a long time. She, Rayleen Waters, and I called ourselves the 'Three Musketeers' back then, but I haven't seen either one of them in years. As often happens after high school, we all kind of drifted apart and went our separate ways."

"Very common," I replied. "Same thing happened to me and some of my dearest friends. Of course, getting married right out of high school because I'd heard you couldn't get pregnant if you had sex standing up, might have had something to do with it. I was rather naïve back then, you see. But after giving birth, I had no time to do anything but care for our baby girl. Oh, dear Lord. I'm so sorry. What was I thinking? Here I am talking about caring for a baby with you having just lost one, and the baby's father as well. How thoughtless of me. Please forgive me, dear."

"That's okay. You know, I'm coming to terms with losing the baby, but it still hasn't completely hit me that Trotter is dead. I can't imagine who'd do such a thing to him. I know he wasn't perfect, but who among us is? It's still totally unfathomable to me," Joy said. She began to weep and tears ran down both cheeks. *Was her grieving an act?* I wondered. But just in case it wasn't, I didn't want to upset her any further. Anyhow, I had a gut feeling she had nothing to do with, and knew nothing about, who had perpetrated the death of Trotter Hayes. I didn't think there was anything to be gained by grilling her with more questions. Not to mention, I could hear a tube of Bengay calling my name.

Joy began to hiccup. She apologized for breaking down and asked me again what I'd originally wanted to speak to her about. I told her there was no need to apologize for grieving over the loss of a loved one. "Now is not the time to bother you with questions about advanced pole-dancing techniques, sweetheart. You need to concentrate on healing so you can get on with your life. My trivial concerns can wait."

Joy nodded and replied, "Yes, you're probably right. Maybe we can chat after next week's class instead."

"Yes, that sounds just fine, young lady," I replied. I put my right arm around her back and gave her shoulders a friendly squeeze.

She smiled through her tears and said, "I'm glad to see you enjoyed the class, Ms. Ripple. Are you seriously planning to come back for another lesson next week?"

"I'll be here with bells on," I said. Even though I gritted my teeth at her use of the word "seriously", I gave her a heartfelt, compassionate hug. *And maybe the week after that I'll star in "A Chorus Line on Broadway"*, I wanted to add. There wasn't enough Bengay at Walgreens for me to come back to this torture chamber again.

CHAPTER 12

An hour later, Rip found me lying on a chaise lounge on the back porch. I'd soaked in Epsom salts and then slathered myself with a topical pain relief cream. I'd found the old tube of Icy Hot in Lexie's medicine cabinet. It was called Icy Hot for a reason, I discovered. I greeted my husband when he stepped out onto the porch. I simply said, "Hey!" That one syllable used up all the energy I could muster.

"Hi, sweetheart," Rip said. "How was your morning?"

"Fine."

"Good. I was afraid it might be too strenuous for you," Rip said with insincere concern, I was certain. "But with all your previous dancing experience, and your innate ability to learn new skills, I knew you'd be a natural at pole-dancing. With your grace and flexibility, I can only imagine how delightful your—"

"Shut up, smartass!" I was in no mood to be teased about the exercise program I'd suffered through that morning. Instead of ridicule, I should be receiving praise for sacrificing my body for the cause. "And bring me an icepack. I think I pulled a groin muscle trying to put my left ankle around my neck in an ill-fated attempt to execute the 'hair chopper' maneuver."

"Oh, to have been a fly on the wall..."

Just before noon, the inn's landline phone rang. I'd been asked to answer any incoming phone calls in case it was a customer wanting to make a reservation. I picked up the portable phone I'd taken out on the back porch with me. I wasn't prepared to take down the customer's information, with the reservation book lying on the kitchen table while I was sprawled out on the lounge chair on the porch. I was glad it was Wendy instead.

"You busy at the moment?" She asked. I explained I'd been kicking back with my feet up but was available to do anything she might need me to do to help out.

"I'm meeting Mattie at the new Panera Bread on Main Street. Could you possibly join us for lunch? I have some new information I think you'd both be interested in."

"I'd be happy to. Stone and Rip are at the police station trying to get in to see Chief Smith. He's made it known he'd be in his office for a couple of hours this afternoon before going home to grieve privately and console his inconsolable wife. Stone told me that even though he knew it wasn't a good time to question Smith about Lexie's predicament, he wasn't sure when else he'd be able to get in to see him."

"Well, you have to admit that Chief Smith probably had a lot of details to take care of in his limited time," Wendy said. "It really wasn't the most opportune time to get in to chat with the man who'd just lost his son so violently."

"I understand why it might not be a good time for Chief Smith, but it's not his innocent wife who's locked up in that cage when she should be home where she belongs."

"I'll have to agree with you there, Rapella! It's not all about him like he seems to think it is. My poor mom is sitting in that holding tank and she doesn't deserve to be. Last night they put a raggedy young lady with no teeth and high on meth in the cell with her. She was released this morning, but I doubt Mom got a minute of sleep, even though Wyatt assured her he'd keep an eye out for her all night and wouldn't go home until her unkempt cellmate was out on bail. I'm sure the woman was probably harmless, but strung-out addicts can be unpredictable, you know."

"Oh, goodness, yes! Poor, sweet Lexie. My heart just goes out to her," I replied. "Is your news *good* news, I hope?"

"I don't know yet. Mom is at her preliminary hearing right now. I should know more by the time we meet for lunch."

"Let's keep our fingers crossed. And maybe our toes too. What time would you like me to meet you two?"

"One-thirty. This is Mattie's day off, and since she never found her iPhone, she decided to drive down to the Apple Store on the Plaza to buy a new iPhone 6. She said she should be back by one though. Got a pen handy so I can give you the address of the restaurant?"

"I don't want to hold you up while I drag my weary body to my purse to get a pen. I'm not operating on all cylinders right now."

"Why? What's wrong? Are you okay?" Unlike my husband, there was sincere concern in Wendy's voice.

"It was touch and go for a while, but I can almost see a light at the end of the tunnel now."

"Oh, my God! What happened?"

"I'm just pulling your leg, honey. I'm fine, just very sore. I'm sorry I scared you. I shouldn't mess with you like that, considering all the stress you're under. Anyway, I'll tell you about my morning in purgatory during lunch. In the meantime, I'll Google the restaurant's address."

"Wow, good job, Rapella! You sound like an old pro on that iPad now. I'm impressed how you took what Mattie taught you and ran with it. Good job, my friend!"

Wendy's flattering words were just the boost I needed to encourage me to drag my aching bones up the stairs. I had to change out of my faded and shabby, but incredibly comfortable, old duds, and get ready to meet the two young ladies for lunch. I was anxious to hear the news Wendy had to share, and also to tell Wendy and Mattie what I'd learned about Joy's miscarried baby.

From the second I disconnected the phone call with Wendy, I was praying for good news about the hearing. If Lexie were released, she'd be of invaluable help in our efforts to exonerate her. She had more incentive than anyone to leave no stone unturned in this quest for justice because, after all, she had the biggest dog in the fight.

God seldom lets me down, and he didn't in this instance either. My prayers had been answered. Lexie was being released from the Rockdale Police Station's holding tank at three o'clock. Wendy had just been notified by Detective Johnston that Judge Jueti had ruled in her favor and was appalled that the twenty-hour hold time law had been so blatantly disregarded. Lexie was not to leave town, pending further investigation, the judge had informed her. That certainly wouldn't be an issue because she had no reason to run. She hadn't done anything wrong.

According to the judge, Lexie was to be set free, at least until if and when more incriminating evidence was presented to her by the investigators. If that were to happen, she could then be formally charged with murder and transported to the county jail to await trial. Also, if that were to occur, Lexie would be at the mercy of a jury of her peers.

I had no idea how she'd fare being prosecuted for the murder of the police chief's stepson. The local citizens could hold the chief in high regard and want anyone who wronged him to be hung from the tallest tree or, instead, they could believe Leonard Smith was as big a scoundrel as his stepson. I just hoped Lexie would never be in the position to find out how the community felt about the victim's stepdad.

I really couldn't see that scenario happening. But Wendy told me that we couldn't be complacent about it. The chief was adamant that the detectives keep digging for evidence that would implicate Lexie in the murder. It sure seemed to me that he was dead-set on pinning the crime on my friend. *She must have really rubbed him the wrong way in the past,* I thought.

Mattie asked, "So apparently they don't think it's worth their while to investigate other potential suspects? I just don't get it!"

"It sure appears that way," Wendy replied. "I don't get it either, Mattie. We need to come up with something substantial enough that the detectives can't ignore and that will give them no other choice but to investigate other suspects. I hope you two are still willing to help out in whatever way you can."

"I'm all in," I assured her. "And I can vouch for Rip as well."

"Me too," Mattie added. "Whatever it takes!"

"Cool beans!" Wendy said with a sigh of relief. "I haven't got enough leave time to take off work so I'm going to have limited time to pitch in. They've barred me from having any involvement in Trotter's case. And yet they're piling my desk high with tedious paperwork to keep me busy and out of their hair."

"Yucko!" Mattie laughed. "I know how you feel about being a desk jockey, and I know you aren't too thrilled about being temporarily forced into that assignment."

Wendy shook her head and said, "You got that right! So, Rapella, tell me what went on this morning that wore you down to a nub."

I skimmed over the pole-dancing part of it and just mentioned I'd had to participate in a rigorous exercise session that Joy White was teaching. "It really was a taxing endeavor, and I'm afraid my age is beginning to show."

Wendy and Mattie gave each other a knowing look before busting out into uncontrollable laughter. The likelihood of the two knowing all about their friend's class hadn't occurred to me. Wendy finally caught her breath and said, "Tell me it isn't so. I read about that weekly program in the *Rockdale Gazette* a couple of weeks ago. You didn't seriously take Joy's weekly pole-dancing class at the Y, did you?"

Was "seriously" the word of the month? I wondered. It was rapidly becoming my least favorite word in the English language. Rarely was I at a loss for words, but I sat there in silence until Wendy repeated, "Well, did you?"

I'm certain my face turned the color of the tomatoes in my Greek salad. It was entirely too humiliating to go into detail, so I brushed it off with, "That's neither here nor there. I just woke up some seldom-used muscles that didn't even realize they were still alive."

"I can only imagine," Wendy replied.

"I'm sorry. But I really *can't* imagine it," Mattie teased.

When they stopped chuckling again, I told them what Joy had told me about losing her and Trotter's baby. I explained how between the loss of both Trotter and the baby, Joy was grieving and had become very emotional when I spoke with her.

Mattie's cheerful mood vanished in a heartbeat, like electricity being turned off at a breaker box. The stormy expression on her face when I turned toward her was startling. She was livid about something I'd said. Apparently, Wendy had noticed it too, and asked Mattie what was wrong.

"Joy may be upset about Trotter's death, but I doubt she's grieving the loss of their baby very much. As I mentioned before, Rapella, I work in the women's clinic at Wheatland Memorial. And I know for a fact Joy didn't miscarry their child. She had it aborted by some back-alley quack. Not surprisingly, she ended up in the hospital with complications from blood loss. Because the medical emergency was caused by an abortion, we heard about it in the clinic. The way I see it, if Joy's willing to kill her own baby, she should be willing to own up to it, too. I'm sure she's was fishing for sympathy when she told you she'd lost it. It's the poor baby whose life she took that I feel sorry for."

I could tell by Wendy's reaction she hadn't known about either the pregnancy or the ensuing abortion. "Hey! Why didn't you tell me about that, Mattie?"

"I'm sorry. I guess I thought I already had."

I suddenly thought back to something Joy had said that had stymied me. She'd made a remark about not telling her parents she was pregnant "after they took the baby" because it would serve no purpose. I was surprised I hadn't asked her about her inference then, but being bone-weary at the time was a viable excuse. I directed my next question to both ladies. "Do you know if Trotter knew about Joy's pregnancy?"

Wendy answered first. "I didn't know anything about it. I haven't seen Joy in ages, and I've refused to have anything to do with Trotter since—"

She stopped abruptly, as if not sure she wanted to address the attempted rape she'd experienced at the hands of the victim. As her best friend, I had no doubt Mattie was aware of the sexual assault, but Wendy probably didn't know whether or not I knew anything about the incident. I reached over and patted her hand. "Your mother told me about the assault, and I'm so very sorry you had to go through that ordeal. When your mother first noticed Trotter Hayes at the party she was instantly alarmed. If not for Joy, she'd have run him out on a rail, I'm sure. She didn't know how you and/or Andy would react to his presence."

"Andy didn't know anything about the assault either. Or at least not until after Trotter's death when I figured it'd come out anyway. I didn't want him to first learn about it from another source. And I'd have just ignored Trotter and stuck close to Andy. As it was, he was already dead when I walked in the door. I saw his body on the floor at the same time everyone else in the room did."

At that point, Mattie put her two cents in. Her voice was rising as she spoke. She was obviously emotionally affected by the aborted baby's fate. "I'd bet my Bentley that Joy told Trotter she was pregnant and he insisted she get rid of the baby. That sounds like his modus operandi when it comes to taking responsibility for any of his actions. Aborting her unborn child doesn't seem like something Joy would do unless she felt she had no other choice. I can't believe she'd go to that extreme to appease her boyfriend. Still, in the end, it was her decision to make and as far as I'm concerned, Joy chose the wrong option. I don't condone physical violence, mind you, but I can certainly understand why someone wanted Trotter Hayes dead."

"Yeah, I feel the same way," I said as Wendy nodded in agreement. Like Mattie, I'm completely against abortion too, but I didn't want to get her any more agitated than she already was. Other diners were already beginning to stare our way. I patted Mattie's shoulder and quickly changed the subject by asking Wendy if there was anything I could do to assist her. She asked me if I'd have time to run the glass platter back to Georgia Piney since I'd been there before and knew how to locate her house.

"She'd left those wrapped sandwiches in the fridge for us on the platter, you know, and I want to make sure she gets it back. I picked it up at the inn this morning and have it in my car. I was hoping you could take care of it after lunch since you're already halfway there." Wendy finished speaking just as Mattie's pager went off. She'd been called back to the hospital for an emergency in the neo-natal department. Another struggling baby needed a miracle-maker like Mattie to come to its rescue so he or she could live.

We parted ways after I collected the gorgeous blue glass platter from Wendy's back seat, and I headed toward the Pineys' home. Wendy had stopped by to program their address in the GPS before she walked to her own car in the parking lot. I'd told her I could do it myself now, but she must have had reservations about my competency with the newly mastered skill. Truthfully, I did too.

I'd been to the Pineys' home before, but wasn't altogether certain I'd remember the twists and turns I'd made to her house from the inn. And I was driving there from a different direction this time around. Ms. Ratchet told me where to go and guided me directly to the destination. *I might need to rethink the name I'd dubbed her,* I said to myself. *Maybe something like Angel would be more appropriate.*

But, if Angel ever insisted I make another risky U-turn in the middle of town, I can assure you it would have been me telling her where to go, not the other way around. I'd have directed her to a place angels dare not tread.

* * *

With Peanut raising a fuss behind her, Georgia greeted me at the door and invited me in. She wasn't surprised to see me, so I assumed Wendy had called her to let her know I was on the way over with her platter. Balancing the platter with my left hand, I'd massaged Peanut's head with my right. The petite little lady told me she'd just returned from her weekly therapy session. Naturally, Georgia's comment piqued my interest. However, my inner self, an inquisitive old hen, told my outer self, a respectful, non-interfering, youthful senior citizen, to not give in to the temptation to ask her what type of therapy she was undergoing. She didn't look the type to be struggling with any kind of addiction, but as I said before, one can never judge a book by its cover. And one *should* never judge a caterer by her appearance either. I hoped the nature of her therapy would come up in conversation without me having to pry into her personal life.

Georgia took the platter from my arms and politely thanked me for dropping it by. In return, I thanked her for being thoughtful enough to leave behind an ample supply of sandwiches for us when she ended up having to haul off all the uneaten food she'd so painstakingly prepared for the party.

Wendy had told me that when Georgia had declined to accept Stone's check for her services after the party was abruptly canceled following the tragedy, her stepfather had insisted the caterer take the check. He'd told her that she had held up her end of the bargain and was not responsible for what had occurred to end the party prematurely. When, as I'd suggested, Georgia had asked Stone about what to do with the unused food, he'd recommended that she donate it to the mission downtown that fed the homeless and consider it a donation toward the worthy cause on behalf of the Alexandria Inn.

That's exactly what had come to mind when Georgia had asked me that evening, and what I'd have told her to do if I had thought it was my call to make. Stone and Lexie were two of a kind when it came to being generous and caring.

I not only applauded Stone's decision to donate the food, I was also grateful Georgia had thought to leave a few of the sandwiches behind at the inn. They'd come in handy after Lexie had been "cuffed and stuffed," as Rip had always put it, and I'd had to step in and keep the masses fed. I suppose "masses" was an overly dramatic exaggeration but with more important things on my mind and to-do list, the responsibility had seemed overwhelming at times.

Unlike Lexie, I was only accustomed to having to keep two people fed. Make that two-and-a-half, if you count Dolly. Cats may be known for being finicky and independent, but all that flew out the window when Dolly experienced a hunger pang. Suddenly, instead of giving me the cold fur, I was her new best friend. It was a trait her majesty had inherited from Rip, her male servant. In Dolly's eyes, the emancipation of slaves was not something to be taken seriously.

When Peanut attempted to jump up into my

arms as if he were the size of a Chihuahua, my thoughts were instantly off my cat and on to the humongous dog that quickly had a paw on each one of my shoulders, licking my face from chin to widow's peak. I was grateful when Georgia dragged Peanut off me and put him in a large kennel to contain him.

Standing in Georgia's kitchen, I noticed that she had an almost full cup of coffee on the table and at least three cups' worth still in the Mr. Coffee carafe on the counter. I thought she might ask me if I'd like a cup, but I was wrong. It became apparent that Georgia, who had been practically a chatterbox the first time I'd met her, had no plans to prolong my stay by initiating a conversation or offering me a drink. I turned to leave, wondering why she'd invited me into the house in the first place. I reached for the doorknob just as Georgia's voice stopped me cold.

"Is Lexie Starr still in jail? Has she been charged with Trotter Hayes's murder?" She asked with a hint of hopeful anticipation in her voice. "I really hate that she got caught killing him. She's always been so good to me. But, the way I see it, if anyone deserved to have his throat slit, it was that guy."

"Excuse me?" I asked. I recalled Lexie's comment that Georgia had flinched at the mention of Trotter's name when she'd mentioned fixing him a drink. According to Lexie, it was as if she'd had issues with Trotter too. I understood the woman's earlier reluctance to speak now.

She'd probably been building up the nerve to ask me what was going on with Lexie. Out of pure curiosity? I wondered. I really couldn't tell, but my instincts told me she had a more personal interest in the case.

"I'm just wondering where the case stands at this point," Georgia said. Bingo! She'd wanted to find out if I knew any more about the case than she did, but she was nervous about asking me for some reason.

"I wasn't aware you knew the victim before his death."

Georgia grimaced and replied, "I really didn't know Trotter Hayes personally. I just knew *of* him from my daughters."

Her daughter, Lori, appeared to be in her mid-twenties, four or five years younger than Trotter, Wendy, and most of the other guests at the party, who all looked to be in the thirty- to thirty-five-year-old range. It stood to reason the majority of the party guests were classmates of Wendy and Mattie's. The two gals may not have even been acquainted with Lori if she'd been several classes behind them in school.

"Well, in the first place, Lexie is being released from jail as we speak. In the second place, she shouldn't have been there in the first place because there's absolutely no way my dear friend would have ever perpetrated such a vicious act. I'm sure you know her well enough to realize that yourself, Georgia. In the third and last place, I happen to agree wholeheartedly with your statement that Hayes had it coming. But that doesn't mean I condone someone killing the man in cold blood the way they did. That being said, the killer is still at large, and I can assure you it's not Lexie."

"I know Lexie's not guilty, Ms. Ripple. I didn't mean to insinuate that I thought she was. I merely misspoke. The detectives think she's guilty though. Don't they?" Georgia asked before answering her own question. "I saw Leonard Smith on TV just a couple of minutes ago. The chief was giving a statement on the courthouse steps. He certainly seemed confident they had his son's killer behind bars and was appalled the judge was forcing the police department to release her."

"Yeah, well, too bad for Chief Smith and his piece-of-work stepson!" I said, cutting Georgia off. But as if I hadn't even spoken, she continued.

"Chief Smith still believes her blood on the murder weapon proves she's the guilty party. However, Judge Jueti insisted Lexie's explanation of having sliced her finger while attempting to cut the cake, rather than cutting it as she was wielding the weapon against the chief's stepson, was credible enough to demand her release since there was nothing to prove otherwise. The chief also thought the photo that one lady took just as the lights flashed on should be enough to warrant her arrest. But the judge insisted it was purely circumstantial; possibly a case of the accused being in the wrong place at the wrong time." Georgia recited what she'd seen on TV very matter-of-factly, almost as if she'd taken notes and had been rehearsing her discussion with me.

"Judge Jueti is correct," I replied in Lexie's defense. I wasn't quite sure where Georgia Piney stood on the matter, but it appeared to me she was straddling the fence about Lexie's involvement in the murder. I had not yet heard about the press release, so I was happy that she was sharing the information with me. But I was also pondering about why she'd ask me what was going on with the case when she appeared to know more about it than I did. "Didn't the chief mention in his remarks that Lexie had been released from custody?"

"Um, yes." She answered simply. With that, she effectively ended the conversation by opening the door and telling me to have a nice day, and thanking me once again for returning the platter. She didn't seem to want to get into a debate about why she'd prompted the conversation by asking me what was going on with the case when clearly she already knew the answer.

As I stepped toward the door, a photo prominently displayed on the china hutch caught my attention. It was a photo of two pre-pubescent young girls in matching frilly pink and white costumes, grinning broadly as they showed off a number of colorfully decorated eggs in their woven Easter baskets. I was certain one of the girls was Lori, but I couldn't tell which one, because the other girl had to be Lori's identical twin.

Georgia visibly winced when she caught me

studying the photo. I thought back to when I'd come to her home to discuss the party menu. She'd told me she had only one *living* child when I asked her if she had children. The inference that she'd had at least one other child who was no longer alive had not really registered. At the time, I'd been making idle chatter to keep from letting our conversation slide into an uncomfortable silence as conversations often do when the two parties had only just met for the first time and have nothing in common to talk about.

In the discussion we'd just had, she'd mentioned having known of Trotter Hayes through her daughters, as in more than just Lori, the one I was familiar with. I had to assume Lori's twin had died and Georgia might not have wanted to converse with me about it. Due to the fact Lori's twin sister was obviously young at the time of her death, if the twin was truly dead, and not just "dead to Georgia", it was understandable that discussing the loss of her child might be too painful to bear. Identical twins share the exact same DNA, and the extremely close bond between most twins would have no doubt made her sister's death a devastating blow to Lori too.

If Lori's twin really was deceased, what had happened to her? I wondered.

I asked myself if questioning Georgia about the photo would seem too intrusive of me. Then I answered myself by thinking, *Of course it would, but when has that ever stopped me before?* I was a little too long in the tooth to change my nature now; to become all sensitive and non-interfering with other people's business when there was something important at stake.

"What adorable girls!" I said, pointing to the photo. "That's Lori, and what I'd have to assume is her twin sister, isn't it?"

Georgia nodded as her eyes misted over. I was mentally kicking myself in the rear end for not trying harder to restrain myself from asking her about the framed eight-by-ten print. I was standing there like a fool, trying to figure out what to do or say next, when Georgia surprised me by replying, "Yes. But Tori passed away about ten years ago."

As if reading my mind, before I could get the next question out of my mouth, she answered it by saying, "She took her own life."

"Oh, my! I'm so sorry, Georgia. I shouldn't have even asked about the photo. I was just curious, but I really shouldn't—"

"That's all right. You had no way of knowing."

I wanted to tell her I actually did have a way of knowing. Now that I could Google practically anything on the Internet, there was very little information I didn't have access to. It occurred to me then that maybe Georgia was unaware of this thing called the *World Wide Web,* as Mattie had called it. So, instead, I simply apologized once more and gave her a quick hug before walking out her front door.

CHAPTER 13

When I arrived at the inn, I found Lexie sitting in a wicker chair on the back porch, deep in thought, with a cup of coffee in her hand. She looked up when she heard me shut the door behind me.

"Oh, my goodness, it's so good to see you!" I said. "You are surely a sight for sore eyes, my dear."

Lexie stood up and folded her arms around me in a long and warm embrace. "It's great to be home and to be back in the company of those I hold dear. Not to mention, folks who don't reek of cigarettes, booze, vomit, and God knows what else. One of my cellmates had such a nasty stench it made me throw up in the shiny throne, with the stinkpot watching me all the while. Stone told me you and Rip have been busy trying to get to the bottom of this unbelievable ordeal. And Wendy mentioned you returned the Pineys' platter. I appreciate your help more than you know, Rapella."

"It was well worth the trip to the Pineys, I assure you!"

"Why? What happened?" I went on to tell her about my encounter with Georgia. She was even more surprised than I was, having never heard Georgia mention the fact she had a twin daughter who had died.

Lexie said, "And we chat after church every week. But I can see why it'd be a painful subject for her to discuss. Tori's death occurred well before I moved to Rockdale, so it stands to reason I wouldn't have read about it in the paper either."

"But wouldn't you reckon it was covered by the press at the time it occurred, especially when the suicide involved such a young person who left behind an identical twin?"

"Yes, it must have been big news at the time. Things like that don't happen regularly in a town this size. When it was announced the new Panera Bread you three gals had lunch at today was going to be located here, you'd have thought they were moving the White House to Main Street in downtown Rockdale. But that's a good thought, Rapella! It's something we need to look into for sure. Speaking of twins, are you sure you and I weren't twins who were separated at birth?"

I laughed at the ridiculousness of her remark and set my iPad down on the glass tabletop between us. "That's where this handy little critter comes in. Mattie gave me a lesson on its usefulness and I've been fiddling with it ever since. You won't believe what I discovered last night. I poked this doo-dad Mattie called an icon, and suddenly, out of nowhere, there were these images on the screen. Can you believe that I can actually play solitaire without even needing a deck of cards now? I guess Reggie put that game in this thing before she gave it to us last Christmas."

Lexie laughed. "Honey, with that iPad you have access to a zillion different games in what's called the 'app store'. See, it's this icon right here," she explained, pointing at the screen on the device.

I started to say that I knew what an icon was. Lexie had probably forgotten she was talking to someone who was well-versed in technical lingo now. To be polite, though, I merely nodded as she continued. "I could download a few games for you if you'd like. Or, better yet, show you how to do it yourself. Do you like Mahjong?"

"Love it! Used to play it at the senior citizen's center back home."

"Great! Then I'll download it to your tablet. How about Scrabble?"

"Oh, goodness, yes!" I loved beating the socks off Rip with words like qua and zoa. Most evenings Rip enjoyed TV shows where approximately two thousand rounds of ammunition are exchanged in shootouts between cops and criminals and, miraculously, not one character suffers a gunshot wound. He particularly enjoys scenes where healthy young thugs are run down by roly-poly police officers well past their prime. In real life, it'd be doubtful if they could run down a sloth.

Meanwhile, I'm scanning the dictionary for little-known words, seldom-used by mankind but having high-point-value letters, to use in scrabble competitions against my husband. I kind of enjoyed increasing my vocabulary at the same time.

"I'll add Scrabble then. How about a slots game or two?" Lexie asked.

"Nah, not wild about playing slots."

"Really? How come? I thought casinos were like magnets to people on social security."

"A lot of them perhaps. But not me. I suspect the games might be fixed."

"I can guarantee you, Rapella, all slots machines are fixed!"

"So why do people enjoy them so much?" I asked. "I've heard of people who lost every dime they had at casinos because they became addicted to gambling."

"People enjoy the excitement of possibly winning big jackpots," Lexie said.

"Big jackpots? Yeah, right," was my scuffing reply. "We were traveling through Mississippi a few years back and Rip thought it'd be fun to stop at a casino in Biloxi to splurge on their seafood buffet for supper. Afterward, just for kicks we decided to each put a ten dollar bill in one of their many slot machines."

"That sounds like it'd be fun," Lexie said.

"You'd think! But here's what actually happened. With my very first spin the machine made a bunch of dinging, bell-ringing sounds and lights were flashing like crazy. The screen up above read 'Winner.' For a couple of seconds I had visions of a brand new travel trailer in my mind. As much as I'd hate to get rid of the old Chartreuse Caboose, it *is* kind of like my husband, falling apart piece by piece."

"Your trailer's still quite eye-catching though." Lexie's response went without saying.

"So, anyway, there I was jumping up and down like an over-caffeinated lunatic who'd just won the Powerball lottery. People were staring at me like I was nuts, but I didn't care. After all, I was a 'winner' and going to be walking in tall cotton after the attendant had come over to the ringing, dinging, flashing machine and paid me off. Then Rip tugged on my shirt, and said, 'Bring it down a notch, darling. You only won fifteen cents.' Imagine that! I *won* fifteen cents after all the carrying-on that thieving machine went through. Winner, my well-padded behind! I didn't even get my entire twenty-five cent investment back. The screen should have read 'loser', or more appropriately, 'sucker'. Well, I cashed the rest of my money in and got the heck out of that rip-off joint! Rip foolishly played his ten dollars out and wasn't but about forty-five seconds behind me. You can bet we learned our lesson about slot machines that night."

For some reason, Lexie started laughing so hard she could barely breathe. I thought I might have to perform CPR on her at any minute. She finally caught her breath and said, "Oh, Rapella, you are such a delight to have around! You're absolutely one of a kind, sweetheart."

"Thank you." I wasn't sure what had tickled her funny bone and didn't know whether to be flattered or offended, so I changed the subject, "It sure is a blessing to have you out of that jail cell. I bet you're relieved to have that nightmare behind you."

Lexie's laughter turned into a somber sigh. "Yes, it's nice to be home. But I won't have this all behind me until the real killer is captured and brought to justice. In the meantime, the chief's going to be trying to conjure up anything he can to get Judge Jueti to change her mind about not arresting me."

"I don't see how they could dig up anything that would incriminate you in a murder you didn't commit. You are innocent, so how could they find anything that proves otherwise?" I asked.

"I think we'd all be surprised to know the truth about how many innocent prisoners are doing life behind bars for murders they had nothing to do with," Lexie said.

"I know you're right, but I still can't see what he could possibly come up with to make the judge think you're guilty."

"I don't know, but if there's a way, the chief will find it. Chief Smith and I have had not-so-pleasant dealings in the past. I've gotten under his craw several times, I'm afraid. The judge was almost swayed by a statement a witness made. Remember Alice Runcan, the gal who took the infamous photos? She was also the one who walked up behind us just as I remarked that I'd be tempted to do something totally horrid to Trotter given half the chance. Well, she was all too happy to pass that little juicy quote on to the investigating team too."

"But you were only joking!"

"Tell that to the judge, my friend," Lexie said, before shifting gears. "Let's just enjoy some much-deserved peace and quiet for a few minutes. I'll run and grab us each a refill."

"Sounds good to me." My vow to limit my caffeine intake while staying at the inn had fizzled out two days ago. I was now using it to keep my motor running so I wouldn't be tempted to lounge around on the porch and spend my time studying unusual words in the dictionary instead of thinking of ways to track down a killer.

When Lexie returned with fresh cups of coffee, her cell phone was ringing in her back pocket. After a short conversation with her daughter, she ended the call and told me what they'd been discussing.

"Wendy wants to come over here in about an hour to meet with the two of us. She plans to discuss with us what we know about our suspects so far, and what we should do to dig deeper. Mattie called to say she'd finish her stint at the hospital in just under an hour and asked to join us too in case she can help out in any form or fashion. I realize the three of you just met for lunch but I need to be brought up to date so I can be of some assistance too. After all, it's me who stands to gain or lose by any success we might achieve."

"Great idea! I was contemplating calling such a pow-wow myself," I replied. "Four minds are better than three any day."

As I sipped on my coffee, Lexie dozed in her chair, no doubt exhausted by the last few days of being locked up in a cage like a laboratory rat waiting for its execution. I went through the notes I'd scribbled in my notebook, hoping there was something there to spark an idea that would cast our net a little wider. A niggling thought in the back of my mind was becoming harder and harder to ignore.

That thought was that maybe the opposite was true. Maybe we needed to narrow our search instead of widening it. Couldn't there be someone right in front of our faces we were overlooking? Maybe some individual with the desire to see Trotter eliminated and the will and means to make it happen.

Our meeting began with Wendy relating everything she knew about the case and the investigation. There was little additional information we didn't already know about. She was clearly aggravated by the police chief and county coroner's joint decision to keep her as far removed from the investigation as possible, maintaining that her involvement in the case was an egregious conflict of interest. Her boss, Nate, tried to placate her by explaining the policy was in place to protect her as much as anything. She was fuming when she said, "Like hell that so-called policy's in place to protect me! Do they think I'm an idiot?"

"That's okay, honey," Lexie said, putting her arm around her daughter. "Maybe it's best you don't get in too deep under the circumstances. You are in line to potentially take the deputy coroner's place when he retires. I can't imagine anyone else being appointed to the position besides you."

"After this murder case involving my mother?" Wendy asked. "Are you nuts?"

Lexie's expression changed to one of despair. In an apologetic tone she said, "I'm so sorry, sweetheart. I didn't deliberately try to sabotage your chances on being promoted. If there's anything I can do to—"

"No, wait, Mom. I'm the one who needs to apologize. I know it's not your fault, and everyone else will know that too, as soon as the real killer is taken off the streets. And if I don't get the promotion, it's no big deal. Getting this infuriating monkey off your back is the only thing that matters right now." With her sincere apology, Wendy reached over and gave her mom a hug.

Afterward, Wendy continued, "As I think you all know, Stone and Rip tried to get in to see Chief Smith so they could discuss the situation with him. He told them he had no openings in his hectic schedule to see them at that time, which could be true given the circumstances, but could also just be an excuse to avoid a confrontation with the man he believes is married to his son's killer. The chief told them they'd have to make an appointment to see him sometime in the future, like two months in the future, according to Stone."

"Rip told me this morning they are trying to set up a meeting with the lead detective now, who is Detective Russell," I remarked.

"Good. I hope they have better luck with the detective than they did with Chief Smith," Lexie said. "Now let's see what Rapella has unearthed about potential suspects in the last few days."

Referring to my notebook, I said, "Okay, here's what I know so far about a few people I see as likely suspects. There's Joy White, who attended the party with the victim. She and Falcon Jons split ways when he caught her cheating on him with Trotter. She then learned she was pregnant with Trotter's child, which she had aborted almost immediately. Mattie believes she was pushed into agreeing to the abortion by Trotter."

"I'd bet my life on it," Mattie interjected.

"Me too," Wendy added.

"But when I conversed with her after the pole-dancing class, she seemed genuinely upset about Trotter's death," I said. "Although it appears she wasn't so upset she couldn't find it in herself to teach that class this morning. With occasional signs of glee, I might add. In fact, she laughed as loud as anyone when I attempted the 'hair chopper' maneuver."

All three of the other ladies began to snicker but reeled it back in quickly when they saw the annoyed expression on my face. In my own defense I said, "I only participated in the silly class for Lexie's benefit, you realize."

I could sense Lexie was trying to hold back a smile as she reached over and patted my hand and said, "I know you did, sweetie, and I appreciate what you had to go through for my benefit. Now let's get back to Joy White."

"Rapella said Joy seemed genuinely upset. But if she had anything to do with Trotter's death, I'd think she'd act as devastated as she possibly could," Mattie said. "I'm not sure Joy's scene-stealing act of grievance after his death at the party wasn't designed to make everyone view her as a victim. She'd want to come across as a victim, along with Trotter, instead of as a potential killer."

Wendy agreed and added, "And there's always the possibility we discussed before. She might have staged that dramatic scene to get off the premises before the police began taking statements."

"That's true," I said. "Joy managed to avoid the scrutiny the rest of the party guests were subjected to. Could that have been her ploy from the start? If so, she pulled the ruse off perfectly. Also, there could be a great deal of resentment on her part, especially if after the abortion took place, she was filled with remorse about killing her baby, which again Mattie doesn't think is something she'd do on her own without being coerced in to it," I said.

"Damn straight," Mattie said.

"Then we have Alice Runcan, who arrived with an unknown guest who appeared to me to be at odds with her at the party."

"Sammy Sparks." Wendy and Mattie spoke out in stereo.

"Who's that?" Lexie and I then asked at the exact same time. Great minds think alike, I've heard.

Wendy spoke first. "He's just a guy who recently moved to town. He owns the nightclub where Rayleen Waters is employed as an entertainer. But I really can't see any imaginable reason he'd have to kill Trotter Hayes, whom I doubt he was even acquainted with, unless Trotter frequented his club, which is quite possible. More likely, however, Sammy was just disgusted that his date was ignoring him."

I had to agree with Wendy's assessment. It would have irritated me too, had I been in Sammy Sparks's shoes. And there was the word "entertainer" used as Rayleen's job description again. "Entertainer" could mean a whole host of different things, I thought. So I asked, "Does she sing, dance, pull rabbits out of a top hat, or what?"

"She's a stripper!" Wendy answered. "Probably the last occupation any of us who knew her in high school could have ever imagined she'd be involved in."

"Rayleen was very shy and withdrawn back then," Mattie added. "But I guess people can change. And, by the way, I agree with Wendy's opinion about Sammy. He had no connection to the victim as far as I can tell."

"Okay. We'll mark him off our suspect list for now. Back to Rayleen Waters. Along with Rayleen, Alice and Joy were the other two gals in their Three Musketeers club, according to what Alice told me," I said.

"Yeah, that's what they called themselves back then," Wendy replied. "Mattie and I always thought their little club was kind of childish."

"I remember you two joking about their Three Musketeers club when you were in high school," Lexie said to the two friends. Then she turned to me and asked, "When did you speak to Alice Runcan?"

I didn't feel it necessary to go into the story about my short-lived employment at Alice's health-food diner, so I replied, "Long story. But during our conversation, Alice told me she was stood up at the last minute when she and Trotter were supposed to attend their high school homecoming dance together. As the queen of the dance that year, Alice was mortified. Even worse, her close friend, Rayleen Waters, showed up with Trotter later on in the evening. Even though it's been years since that snub, Alice still appeared to have a great deal of bitterness toward Trotter. Was it enough to kill him though? I don't know."

Wendy nodded and added, "Mattie and I remember that night vividly. Alice truly was devastated by the humiliation she experienced, and it was a bad deal all the way around."

"No doubt," I agreed. Then Wendy continued.

"As Stone and Rip probably informed you,

Falcon Jons told me Rayleen called and begged him to take her to the dance. Mattie hadn't invited her, which was fine with me since I hadn't spoken to her in years. Maybe Rayleen still harbored some animosity toward Trotter herself. Even though she and Alice eventually buried the hatchet, I doubt their friendship was ever as tight knit as it had been before what Alice had to think of as being stabbed in the back by Rayleen. It seems Trotter had lied to both girls, causing a serious rift between them for a while. It wasn't long after the homecoming fiasco that all three of the musketeers went their separate ways. That most likely left Rayleen with no close friends to hang out with, which she might have blamed Trotter for."

"Okay, that's something to keep in mind. I think we should check further into Rayleen's possible motive to kill Trotter." I consulted my list and added, "Then there's Falcon Jons, who owns the aerospace firm and is a bit 'off,' as you girls put it. He showed some serious hostility toward Trotter for stealing his girlfriend and getting her pregnant when I spoke to him. But Falcon was clearly not aware that Joy wasn't still pregnant at the party. He had estimated to me that she'd be four months along with what he claimed should have been his baby. He knew nothing about the abortion, I'm certain."

"When did you speak to Falcon Jons?" Lexie asked me, puzzlement etched across her face. "You've been a busy girl the last couple of days, haven't you? A woman after my own heart. Now

I'm more sure than ever we are twins who were separated at birth."

Wendy and Mattie chuckled and agreed Lexie and I were two of a kind.

"I hate to use a cliché, but we're what they call 'birds of a feather'. But how and when I spoke with Falcon is another long story that we don't have time for now. Let's just say, he didn't seem to think I was capable of handling a computer software engineering position he was interviewing applicants for."

"No shit?" Mattie asked with a great deal of sarcasm.

"That's exactly what Falcon said, Mattie, and I was not amused then either."

The smile on Mattie's face evaporated like morning dew on a hot summer day. She hung her head and said, "I'm sorry, Rapella. No offense intended. In fact, I'm very impressed and extremely proud of your new skill with the iPad. I must be a very talented tutor."

I could still sense a small degree of derision in her apology, but it was buried deep within a flattering compliment so I let it slide.

"Get back to Falcon Jons, Rapella," Lexie urged. I did as she requested.

"Falcon went to the party with Rayleen after she begged him to take her as his date. But I believe his sole purpose of agreeing with her request was to try to make his ex, Joy White, jealous. Why else was he making out so publicly with a gal he had no real interest in, all the while staring at his ex-girlfriend? Joy, of course, was there with Trotter, and that could have triggered a fit of uncontrollable rage in Falcon. After all, Joy had betrayed him by going out with Trotter behind his back. He could hold Trotter responsible for luring Joy away from him."

"Another possibility to keep in mind. But a crime of passion seems unlikely. Whoever killed him came to the party with the poison, ready to carry out the execution of a man they wanted retribution against. The throat-slitting was probably just an unplanned addition to insure Trotter's death," Lexie said. "I'm beginning to see a pattern here. It seems like nearly every young person at the party had some sort of issue with Trotter, and a possible motive to want him eliminated."

Wendy, Mattie, and I all nodded in agreement. And we all also agreed this fact would not make figuring out who the actual killer was any easier.

The niggling thought returned that we might be overlooking someone. Maybe a suspect who didn't appear to have a substantial enough motive to actually take another person's life. The motive could involve something really devious that none of us four were privy to.

At that point, we had very little idea of how Rayleen felt about Trotter, or about any deep resentment she might have had against her former homecoming date. Could Rayleen have held Trotter responsible for the gradual unraveling of the Three Musketeers' friendship? Neither Joy nor Alice had spoken with Rayleen in years, according to them. Could she even feel he had something to do with her resigning herself to becoming a stripper—perhaps due to a negative opinion of herself? Wendy and Mattie had mentioned that low self-esteem had always been an issue with Rayleen, and it wasn't likely to have improved much in the intervening years, particularly after her friendship with Joy and Alice had dissolved.

I thought Rayleen Waters deserved a little attention. Before the meeting broke up I asked, "Who feels like going out on the town tonight? Maybe we could even stop by Sammy Sparks's nightclub and grab a drink. I'm suddenly craving a tequila sunshine like you wouldn't believe. And I can't tell you ladies how long it's been since I've been entertained by a stripper."

CHAPTER 14

Rip, Stone, and Andy decided to join the four of us in going to the nightclub that evening. I'd like to think their decision was borne out of concern for our welfare, but I had a sneaking suspicion there was more to it than that. Now that he was retired from the police force, Rip couldn't possibly make up an excuse to visit a strip club that wouldn't land him in the doghouse for a month, and I'd imagine the same was true for Stone and Andy. The cheerful willingness of all three of the men to suffer through the evening as our escorts was a little disturbing.

When we arrived at the nightclub called Sparky's, we found a large table toward the back. It wouldn't have bothered me, but Wendy and Mattie weren't anxious to be recognized by their old classmate. They were reluctant to have Rayleen Waters spot the two of them sitting together in the crowd. The two girls were afraid she would think they were there to judge and ridicule her, and it could make her feel badly about herself. The two gals had no desire to hurt the stripper's feelings.

Fortunately, with the spotlights all aimed at the girls performing on stage, it was difficult to see your drink in front of you in the sheer darkness of the remainder of the room. How the barmaids found their way around without tripping and spilling the drinks all over the patrons was beyond me.

In retrospect, it might have been better had I not been able to find my drink in the darkness as often as I did. The "titty bar," as Rip had referred to it, served very strong, but tasty, tequila sunrises. They certainly weren't watering down their drinks or skimping on the alcohol. Before I knew it, I was beginning to feel a little woozy and must have been acting bizarrely because the other three ladies were eyeing me with concern on their faces. Rip was ignoring me but he had gotten accustomed to seeing me over-imbibe, as it had happened on a number of occasions. He was throwing back quite a few Crown and Cokes himself, I noticed.

The men took turns buying rounds as we sat through the first two performers' routines. The first one was an exotic dancer who made quite a production of removing her sequined and feathery outfit one article of clothing at a time. There was a long, drawn-out, agonizing amount of time in between each one. I could have washed, dried, and folded each item before she removed the next one. Each piece that hit the floor resulted in a rally cry from all the young men who were fixated on her performance. I was just glad when she picked up the pile of discarded clothing and left the stage.

The second performer was a striking, willowy black lady with huge boobs. I could recall as a child honeydew melons half their size taking home the grand prize at our local county fair. Since the woman's breasts were not even remotely in the same proportions with the rest of her body, I had to assume she'd purchased them out of a "Racks R Us" catalog. Her talent, if you could call it that, was giving lap dances to the salivating men on the front row. The men were shoving cash into her barely-there thong every time they got a chance.

Rayleen Waters was the next act to come out on the stage. As was with the first two acts, we sat through Rayleen's strip-tease routine without talking. It had been almost impossible to carry on a conversation in the lively crowd and ear-splitting volume of the band. We had eventually quit trying to communicate verbally.

I'm hardly a good judge of strip-tease performances, having never watched one in my entire life before that night. However, the thought crossed my mind that after a couple more rounds of drinks I could probably give a more spell-binding display of stripping than Rayleen. In my intoxicated state, I might have been tempted to get up on stage and give it a shot if not for the fact I was wearing a twenty-year old bra and a pair of undies in less than stellar condition. The elastic had torn away from the material in several spots and the once stark-white cotton now had a beige tinge to it from thousands of rotations in the washing machine. And the fact that I could practically tuck the waistline of my underpants into my brassiere was probably less than titillating too.

Soon after the thought of entertaining a room full of predominantly twenty- to thirty-year-old men by baring my sixty-eight-year-old body, and nearly as old underwear, had crossed my mind, I realized it was time to cut myself off. By now everyone at the table except Andy seemed to have a buzz on. Andy was our designated driver and drinking Sprite. He probably was praying that none of the other men in the crowd recognized him.

I staggered to the bathroom, joined by Lexie, who tripped over a swizzle stick on the way. Once there, we discussed the possibilities of finding a way to have a conversation with Rayleen. None of our ideas sounded plausible, and a few of them, fueled by too much alcohol, no doubt, were almost ludicrous. I didn't mention anything about my silly notion of going up on stage, because I knew Lexie would find that as amusing as she did the fact that I took a pole-dancing lesson earlier in the day.

Lexie was as blitzed as I was and she was laughing at nearly everything, including the fact that her stall had no toilet paper in it and she had to borrow some from me. I took solace in thinking the pole-dancing lesson that morning was probably what spurred the ridiculous idea of doing an onstage strip tease to begin with, along with too many tequila sunrises, of course.

As it turned out, we were able to discover an interesting detail without even speaking to Rayleen. As Lexie and I drunkenly zigzagged our way back toward the table, we both stopped in our tracks when we saw Joy White walk out on stage next to a stainless steel pole. The pole was mounted on a huge marble base that a couple of burly bouncers had just wheeled out on a dolly. We looked at each other in amazement and then scurried back to the bathroom as if we hadn't touched a drop of alcohol all day. We were anxious to discuss the ramifications of what we'd just witnessed. The noise level in the women's john was muffled enough that we could understand each other's words.

"I don't know why it never occurred to me that a single woman couldn't make a living off teaching a weekly pole-dancing class. To earn a reasonable income, she'd also need a more profitable job to make ends meet. What else would a pole-dance instructor do to earn a living other than perform as a pole-dancer?" I asked Lexie.

"True. And didn't you tell us earlier that Joy mentioned having not seen Rayleen or Alice in years?" She responded. "They're co-workers, for goodness sakes!"

"Alice Runcan, the third of the Three Musketeers, told me the same thing in almost the same exact words. It was as if both of their comments had been rehearsed," I said.

"But why would either of them lie to you about it? They could have no idea you're involved in investigating Trotter's death. In fact, I don't know how they could even know you and I were acquainted."

"No, me either. As far as Joy is aware, I only know her mother, Viola," I said.

"Why didn't you tell me you knew Joy's mother? How in the world do you know this Viola?" Lexie asked.

"I don't."

"Huh?"

"I only said I did after I'd told Falcon Jons I was her godmother and had known her mother for years. He mentioned that Viola was the mother's name, so I dropped her name when I spoke with Joy later. It was a tactic to segue into the discussion about her pregnancy. It's a long story and of no consequence now." As I explained this to Lexie, it was as if all of the alcohol I'd put away in the past two hours had been flushed out of my system when I'd used the toilet minutes earlier. I was stone cold sober and Lexie appeared to be as well.

The door opened then and Wendy and Mattie entered the small, but adequate, restroom. They were both excitedly talking at once, unaware we'd already seen Joy up on stage. It was their joint opinion that it was likely that neither Joy nor Rayleen made a habit of telling strangers what they did for a living. Mattie added a slightly offensive remark. "Telling an older woman your age, Rapella, that you worked in a strip club would be highly embarrassing to most young ladies. It'd be almost like telling your own grandmother."

"Taking into consideration that both girls, along with Alice Runcan, who also claimed to not have seen the other two girls in years, all seem to have an issue with Trotter, sure makes you stop to think," I said. "Could Alice have lied about not having any contact with her two old friends also?"

Mattie nodded and said, "From the close relationship they had for years, my guess would be she did lie about it. They live in the same county, after all! If nothing else, you'd think they'd occasionally run into each other at the mall, an area restaurant, or even while shopping for groceries at Pete's Pantry."

"My thoughts exactly," I said. "If all three ladies are lying, there's got to be a reason. Otherwise, what purpose would it serve? Could the Three Musketeers have banded together again to eliminate their common nemesis?"

"Are you suggesting the three of them killed Trotter together?" Mattie asked. "Like a tag team kind of slaying perhaps?"

"How could they have all done it together?" Wendy asked.

"Come on, my child," Lexie said to Wendy. She was following my line of reasoning easily. "Use your imagination. Joy White could have been responsible for getting Trotter to the party.

She was invited, not him. He only came as Joy's guest. Alice Runcan could have been hiding in the pantry and used the opportunity to add the cyanide to his drink while I was outside assisting the caterer with the sandwich tray. Then Alice could have scurried back to be in the ideal position to snap photos when the lights came on which could later serve as proof of her alibi. Meanwhile, Rayleen sliced Trotter's throat. You do recall how anxious Alice was to show the photos to Detective Russell, don't you?"

"And to rub her boobs all over him," I said. "Just as if it were a preview of coming attractions on Alice's part."

"I wouldn't put it past her," Wendy replied. "Alice has always been pretty promiscuous. So, where were Joy and Rayleen when the lights came on? Does anyone remember? In Alice's photo it was Mom standing next to him, not one of those two."

None of us had any recollection of Joy's or Rayleen's location when the lights came on and everyone had shouted to surprise Wendy. Nor did any of us know who might have noticed and could accurately place the two ladies at that critical moment so that we could question them.

I considered the fact everyone in the room was stunned at that point in time. All eyes were, no doubt, riveted to the spot where Trotter's dead body had lain bleeding on the parlor floor. I'd bet that Joy and Rayleen could have both shed all their clothes at that moment and not one person in the entire room would have even noticed.

"Could Alice, Joy, and/or Rayleen have been the voices you heard as you were preparing Trotter's drink?" I asked Lexie.

"It's possible. I'm sorry, but I was so busy at the time that I paid very little attention to whoever was in the kitchen with me."

We still weren't sure how to proceed with our impromptu investigation. We left the night club with more questions than answers. The six of us decided to sleep on it and meet the next morning for breakfast at the Alexandria Inn to come up with a game plan. There was a sick baby in the neo-natal ward at Wheatland Memorial that Mattie was emotionally invested in so she'd have to head to the hospital following the meeting. But Wendy told us she'd be calling in sick with a headache and upset stomach.

"With seven bloody Marys under my belt, I have a bad feeling I won't be lying about it either," she said with a groan.

CHAPTER 15

I woke up early the next morning and nobody else was stirring. The Spitz sisters left before daybreak, and there were no guests checking in for the next several days. Stone had told us the business was in its yearly back-to-school lull and wouldn't pick up again for a couple of weeks. I tiptoed into the kitchen and made a pot of Folgers in the Bunn coffee maker on the counter. After it had finished brewing, I took a cup out on the back porch.

Nursing a slight hangover, I went over the conversation we gals had engaged in while huddled in Sparky's restroom the night before. I was optimistically hopeful, but not at all confident, about the Three Musketeers theory I'd concocted. To pull off such an elaborate scheme would take precise timing, advance knowledge of who'd be where and when at nearly every moment, and a great deal of just plain dumb luck.

To plan an assault of this magnitude and have it come off without a hitch seemed too improbable to me. I still thought we should look into it, but not devote all our time and resources on a scenario so unlikely.

I had brought my iPad out on the porch with me and whiled away a good half hour playing Scrabble. I found it wasn't nearly as much fun when you were playing against a computer that could match you play by play. And unlike competing against Rip, I couldn't get away with making up words, complete with believable definitions, when I was in a tight spot.

Just as I was about to clinch a victory, my cyberspace competitor used the "O" in my word, "boat", to form the word, "QUIXOTIC", which to my dismay landed on a triple word score square. To totally rub my nose in it, the computer used all seven tiles for an additional fifty points. Even though I was now way behind my cyber competitor in scoring, I was happy to declare the game a tie when I heard voices in the dining room.

Lexie was pouring coffee and placing the cups at six places at one end of the massive table, which had a total of twelve matching chairs. The other four people were already seated. Wendy was enthusiastically chattering non-stop when I walked into the room.

"I was reading through the newspaper this morning and came across a blurb about a wedding tonight in the 'Daily Happenings' column. I couldn't believe it when I saw that Candy Kobialka was marrying Bobby Crushnut at the Rockdale Baptist Church at six o'clock this evening." Wendy must have thought no one would believe her remarkable find, because she laid the somehow newsworthy clipping down in the middle of the table.

"Why is that important?" I asked. "Was this soon-to-be Candy Crushnut at the birthday party?"

"Oh, my God! I hadn't put it together, but I hope for Candy's sake she keeps her maiden name. And, no, she wasn't at the party, but that's not important anyway," Wendy said.

If Wendy thought her news was not important, then why was she so passionate about it? Before I could ask, she answered my question.

"Candy Kobialka used to occasionally hang out with Alice, Joy, and Rayleen. Although the three girls seemed to think there was no room in their elite club for a fourth musketeer, they were close enough to Candy that I'm anticipating all three ladies will be at her wedding tonight. What do you think, Mattie?"

"I'd almost bet on it," her friend replied. "Or, at least Rayleen, who shared a locker with her our senior year."

"Exactly! That's what I figured when I saw the announcement this morning," Wendy exclaimed.

"How many bridal shops are there in Rockdale?" I asked. I knew where Wendy was heading with her news.

"Only one that I know of," Mattie replied.

"Why?"

"Give me a minute and I'll explain." I then Googled the shop and found a phone number for the store. Using the inn's landline phone, I called the number and asked the gal who answered the phone if they were handling the Crushnut wedding. When she confirmed that they were, I gave a thumb's up signal to the other five sitting at the table.

I spoke with the shop owner for a few minutes, telling her I was penning an article about the nuptials for the next day's issue of the *Rockdale Gazette*. I asked a few generic questions before asking for a list of names in the wedding party.

"Cool," I said after I'd hung up the phone. "It looks like Rayleen will indeed be attending the wedding. She's one of Candy's bridesmaids."

Rip shook his head in puzzlement and asked, "And how does all this benefit us in tracking down Hayes's killer?"

"I think it'd be interesting to see how the three girls interact if they all show up at the wedding, and chances are good that they will. They might huddle in a corner and discuss how well their murder scheme turned out, or blatantly ignore each other to prevent anyone from putting two-and-two together. If they just mingle socially like people who have nothing to hide, that will tell us a lot too. There's also the off chance of getting into a conversation with one, two, or all three of them." I explained my reasoning to everyone.

All five nodded and Lexie said, "I suppose it's worth a shot. If only two of us go, the rest of us could be exploring other avenues at the same time."

"Good idea," Wendy said. "Now obviously Mattie and I can't go since they all know us and will know we weren't invited to the wedding. And Mom and Stone would stand out like a sore thumb due to the hubbub around town regarding the murder. I guarantee Rockdale's ever-present grapevine is in full force right now."

"So," Wendy continued, looking directly at Rip and me. "Have you two ever crashed a wedding?"

I answered quickly, "No, but it's been on our bucket list forever!"

Rip turned to me and asked, "Won't it be obvious that we aren't even remotely acquainted with the couple getting hitched?"

"Not at all," I said. "Who in their right mind would attend the wedding of people they didn't know?"

"That's my point!"

"No, that's *my* point, Rip!"

"Huh?"

"Remember that old lady in the raggedy fur coat who attended our wedding and spent the entire reception at the refreshments table?"

"Yes, and I still think she hid the champagne bottle in her coat and made off with it before your pappy could make a toast to us." He turned to the other four at the table and explained, "We didn't have a pot to piss in or a window...well, you all know the saying. Rapella's pappy gave us the bubbly for our wedding present. It was the only highfaluting thing about our entire low budget, shotgun wedding. Neither Rapella nor I had any idea who the woman lurking around the refreshments was. I'm thinking now she was just some old down-on-her-luck lush who attended our wedding in order to high-tail it with the booze."

The other four at the table laughed, and then I said, "My point is that, throughout the wedding, even though there were only about thirty people in attendance, we both thought she was a relative of the other's. I'd heard you speak about your pa's estranged sister who he described as an eccentric old maid. The old lady in the molting mink jacket seemed to fit the bill, so I assumed it was her!"

"And I assumed she was *your* pappy's sister because she acted wacky just like him."

I smacked Rip on the side of the head with the back of my hand and continued. "We'll just act like we are long-lost relatives of either the Kobialkas or the Crushnuts, depending on who we might be talking to at the time, and try to avoid conversations with anyone who's not relevant to the murder case. Trust me, Rip, no one will even question our presence."

While we were attending the wedding, Wendy was going to try to contact a couple of her friends who were better acquainted with Falcon Jons, including one who worked as an engineer at Jons's aerospace firm. We weren't quite ready to quit sniffing up that alley yet. Mattie had to report to work in an hour and wouldn't get off until much later in the afternoon, so she'd be unable to help out that day.

Andy was hauling a dozen Herefords to the livestock auction that afternoon while Stone and Rip were going to try to find Detective Russell and have an in-depth conversation with him about the case. Stone, as the spouse of their only current suspect, and Rip, as a lifetime detective, hoped their combined credentials would earn them an audience with the lead investigator. Their attempt to get a foot in the door to see the detective the previous day had been unsuccessful.

Rip and I had limited space in the Chartreuse Caboose for clothing so our wardrobe selections were sparse. We had stopped by Boney's garage to pick up Rip's only suit, which worked equally well for both weddings and funerals. I chose to wear the dress I'd worn to the surprise party because my only other dress had gone out of style decades ago. I couldn't remember the exact year I'd bought it, but I'm pretty sure it was during the late sixties. As I recall, I'd purchased it from a thrift shop to wear to a protest against the Vietnam War.

We arrived at the Rockdale Baptist Church at straight-up noon, as the newspaper blurb had stated was the time the wedding was to commence. I told Rip we were at the church Lexie met Georgia in and both still attended services there, as did Alice Runcan.

As we stepped out of the truck, the Beach Boy's rendition of "The Little Old Lady from Pasadena" was playing on the oldies station, and I couldn't get the song out of my mind. I was humming that tune softly as we eased through the rear door of the sanctuary and took our seats in the back pew, just as the bride and groom were exchanging vows.

Rayleen Waters was standing with three other identically dressed gals to the right of the bride, as expected. I scanned the room quickly and saw Joy in a seat next to the aisle about seven rows back from the pulpit. *Fitting into this wedding party will be a breeze*, I thought. There were so many guests in attendance I was confident we'd be able to fly under the radar with no problem.

Even contact with Joy would not be a complicated matter. If I could convince her I knew her mother, I could surely convince her that Rip and I were long-lost cousins of the groom.

I continued to search the crowd for Alice Runcan but couldn't locate her. As the owner of Zen's Diner, I considered the fact she may not have been able to leave the busy restaurant during the lunch hour on a Saturday.

At the conclusion of the ceremony, the groom gave his new bride a brief, dispassionate peck on the lips. It was the kind of kiss he'd have been apt to bestow on his grandmother when he ran into her at his high school football game. I often gave Rip a more amorous kiss just for carrying the trash out for me. Clearly, an over-abundance of PDAs would not be an issue for this newly-married couple.

We melded into the throng of people exiting the sanctuary to gravitate down the staircase into the basement where the reception was to be held. While the invited guests mingled and greeted friends and relatives with hugs and handshakes, Rip and I meandered around the buffet line. It crossed my mind briefly that the newlyweds might be wondering about the old couple lingering around the food table. Like the elderly lady at our own wedding nearly a half-century ago, we probably appeared to be waiting for an opportunity to make off with the champagne bottles situated next to a number of crystal glass goblets. I knew Dom Perignon was not an inexpensive brand of the high-alcohol-content libation.

At one point, Joy White caught me staring at her when I'd spotted her across the room. Looking none the worse for wear from her several days of broken-hearted grieving, she nodded and I nodded back. Joy looked surprised to see me but made no effort to walk over and greet me. I hoped I'd get an opportunity to speak with her before the reception concluded.

Rip and I were standing together at the rear of the room when I felt a tap on my shoulder. I turned around and found myself staring right into the eyes of the recently declared Mrs. Candy Crushnut. She gave me a polite hug and said, "I wanted to thank you for coming to our wedding. It's such a pleasure to meet some of Bobby's relatives for the first time."

"And it's a real pleasure for us to meet his new beautiful bride as well. I'm Rapella and this is my husband, Clyde. Rip, as everyone calls him, is

Bobby's father's uncle's third cousin twice removed. Although we seldom see this side of his family, we were going to be in town anyway, so we decided to take the opportunity to attend your beautiful wedding." I spoke in a casual but friendly manner.

"Thank you. Where are you folks from?" Candy asked.

"Pasadena," I replied. There was no need to lie but it was the first place that came to mind, even before Rockport, Texas, our actual hometown.

"Cool," she replied. "I'm so glad you could make it, and I know Bobby will be delighted too."

The tone of her voice made it apparent she was getting ready to move on to greet other guests so I quickly changed the subject. "We were surprised to see Rayleen Waters here. Her late great-aunt and my mother have been friends forever. Coincidentally, we just saw Rayleen a few days ago at a surprise party for a mutual friend of ours. Tragically, one of the guests was killed before the party could even get started."

I glanced at Rip just long enough to see him roll his eyes. I was relieved when Candy took the bait and ran with it.

"Yes, it's been all over the news. That's just unbelievable, isn't it? At least they have the killer behind bars, I heard. But I've been so busy tying up loose ends for this wedding that I haven't had much time to pay attention to the news."

"I understand completely, sweetheart. Were you a close friend of Mr. Hayes?"

"No, not really, but I remember Rayleen went to homecoming with him our senior year. Caused a real dustup between her and Alice Runcan as I recall. But they got over it, and Rayleen had forgiven Trotter for causing the quarrel. In fact, she just told me recently that the two of them had discussed forming a committee to plan a fifteen-year class reunion to be held in a few years. She's been real torn up about his death the last several days."

As Candy was speaking, a petite, dark-haired woman, about twenty feet from us, caught my eye. As the woman turned slightly to her right, I recognized her as the caterer. I almost cut Candy off when I asked her, "Oh, do you know Georgia Piney?"

"Not too well, personally, but she's friends with my parents. Georgia and her husband were clients of my father, who's a partner in the Hocraffer, Zumbrunn, Kobialka and Wright law firm. He represented them when they sued Trotter Hayes and his family after their daughter, Tori, committed suicide, and then again in their lawsuit against the fertilizer plant after Mr. Piney was diagnosed with brain cancer. Well, I need to make the rounds and welcome all the guests, but it was nice meeting you both."

Before Candy could turn around, her new husband came up behind her and put his arms around his bride's waist from behind. She reached back with her right hand and patted his cheek, and said, "I've got to go talk to some other guests, Bobby, but you'll want to visit with your relatives from California."

"I'm sorry," he replied, looking at Rip and me as if trying to place us. "I didn't even know I had relatives in California."

"Oh, yes. Rip is your uncle's third—"

"Which uncle?" Bobby asked.

Oops! I didn't see that one coming. I knew he'd recognize all of his uncle's names, and with a zillion and four names to choose from I was fairly certain of guessing the wrong one. I considering trying "Bob" because a large majority of Americans have an Uncle Bob in their family and there was a decent chance that Bobby was his namesake. But if Bobby turned out to be in the minority and said he only had two uncles named Theodore and Winston, how would I respond?

So instead of replying, I did the only other thing that came to mind. I grabbed my chest and leaned over, groaning dramatically, with a couple of sudden lists to the side for effect. Fortunately, Rip knew me well enough to realize what I was doing and didn't pull the phone out of his suit pocket to dial 9-1-1. Bobby looked alarmed though, and probably wasn't keen on having some little old lady from Pasadena keeling over dead at his and Candy's wedding reception. He reached out to grab hold of my arm to help me regain my balance. Panicking, he asked, "Are you okay? Should I call for an ambulance?"

"No, I'll be okay in a minute," I gasped between groans. "I have these sudden chest pain episodes quite often. But my husband will help me out to the truck to get my nitroglycerine spray and I'll be fine."

"Yes, that's right, dear. We need to scurry on out there before the pains intensify as they're prone to do," Rip said. He put his arm around me as if I couldn't stand without assistance. He then turned to Bobby and said, "Congratulations on your marriage, son. I need to get my wife off her feet right away, but it was nice to meet you, and we appreciate you inviting us to share your big day."

Bobby looked bewildered, but he shook Rip's hand and told me he hoped I felt better soon.

Rip's bad hip made his limping even more pronounced as he practically drug me to the door. Actually, he needed my assistance to walk, not the other way around. Bobby Crushnut watched our departure with great apprehension until the door closed behind us, no doubt relieved to be seeing the last of his oddball relatives from Pasadena. As soon as we exited the building, Rip looked at me and asked, "Really? You couldn't have just faked a senior moment and forgot the uncle's name?"

I ignored his jab, mainly because I was upset with myself for not thinking of Rip's suggestion. If I had, we'd still be in there, possibly chatting with Joy or Rayleen.

Rip went on to say, "If nothing else, I think we can now pursue other possible theories instead of your one with the Three Musketeers banding together to kill Trotter. It sounds to me like Rayleen had no burning desire to kill Trotter Hayes if they were communicating about a class reunion down the road. As far as not admitting they've seen each other recently, I'm sure Joy and Rayleen don't spread it around to strangers that they work together in a strip club. And most likely neither one of them has run into Alice lately. But Candy did mention a lawsuit between Trotter and the Piney family."

"Candy also mentioned one between the Pineys and the fertilizer factory Mr. Piney worked for. I do recall Georgia telling me that they felt toxic fumes at the factory attributed to her husband's brain cancer. It very likely has no bearing on this murder case, but we're fixing to find out!"

"I was afraid of that," Rip said with a sigh. "What are you planning to do now? Or do I even want to know?"

"I'm giving it some thought. I'm sure either Lexie or I will come up with something."

"No doubt."

"There's a connection there somewhere to Trotter's death. I'm just sure of it. My Three Musketeer theory was just a hunch, but I'm wondering if we might not have Georgia Piney dead to rights with this latest discovery."

"I hope you're right this time but I have my doubts," Rip replied with another sigh. "Get in the truck now, darling. I need to get you home before those chest pains escalate and you have a massive coronary on me."

CHAPTER 16

No one was home when we returned to the inn. Rip's bad hip was throbbing from being on his feet for so long at the reception and then having to drag his incapacitated spouse across the room. He went up to our suite for a nap. I unplugged my iPad from its charger and took it out on the back porch with a Miller Lite to quench my thirst.

I Googled every applicable word combination I could think of and was only able to come up with one short newspaper article about the lawsuit between the Pineys and Trotter's family. Although it didn't say so exactly, and few details were given, it gave me the impression that the Pineys held Trotter Hayes responsible for their daughter's suicide. Trotter's mother was mentioned but not Chief Smith. Since Trotter was the chief's stepson, I reasoned the incident may have occurred before the chief married his mom.

It also stood to reason the young girl would

have had an autopsy performed on her body following the suicide. To verify my assumption, I called Wendy. She was at a male friend's house discussing his opinion of Falcon Jons. According to Wendy, the guy agreed that Falcon was more unpredictable than most. But Wendy's friend didn't think Falcon would viciously murder a person no matter how upset he was with him. It was just not in Falcon's DNA to be cruel, he had said.

I told Wendy what we'd learned at the wedding reception and asked her about the policies regarding autopsies and suicide victims. "Yes, we're required to perform an autopsy on anyone who takes their own life. Primarily the practice is done for insurance purposes, but on rare occasions the autopsy results conclude that the death was not self-inflicted as previously declared."

"Could that have happened in the Tori Piney case?" I asked.

"It's possible, but highly unlikely. I think I'll return to the coroner's lab for the last few hours of the workday with the excuse I don't want to fall too far behind with the paperwork stacking up on my desk. I'll tell Nate that my headache went away and my nausea cleared up soon after. And then, since no one pays any attention to what I'm doing on the computer anyway, I'll do some searching. With any luck at all I'll be able to bring up the autopsy report on Tori. You never know, something interesting might come of it."

"Couldn't you look up Trotter's autopsy report

the same way?" I asked.

"No, not yet anyway. The findings haven't been officially recorded yet."

Wendy promised to call if she had any luck locating the report. While I waited impatiently to hear back from her, I fiddled with the iPad. I Googled "brain cancer" just for the heck of it and read through possible causes for it. Then I Googled the name Tori Piney and found a 2005 article about the lawsuit regarding Tori's suicide, and a few old articles dating back to 2003 and 2004 that listed honor roll students alphabetically. Both she and her twin sister had made the grade, I discovered. Having been an honor roll student, you'd think Lori could have proofread her mother's badly misspelled "no soliciting" sign before Georgia hung it up on the front door.

Then, to pass some time, I Googled myself and was horrified to find an old photo someone had posted on that Facebook thing that Mattie had told me about. It was a straight-on shot of me leaning back, trying to clear a limbo pole at a party back in the 1980s. My ratty underwear was clearly exposed beneath my skirt, my socks didn't match, and I'd had the most God-awful expression on my face you could ever imagine. The photo was obviously meant to amuse, and it had succeeded, judging by the disparaging comments beneath it and the ridiculous amount of "likes" listed. Someone had even made the comment, "This was the last time I let my alcoholic grandmother go out in public. LOL"

At the time, I was humiliated, but at least

comforted and warmed by the acronym for "lots of love". But later I'd find out from Mattie that "LOL" was also an acronym for "laughing out loud" and the warmth cooled quickly.

As I closed the cover on the iPad, not having the stomach to check out any of the other dozen or so listings under my name, the phone rang. I'd carried the portable receiver out to the back porch and quickly answered it so the noise wouldn't wake my husband.

Wendy was breathless, as if she'd just sprinted up all one hundred and four flights of stairs at the new Freedom Tower in New York. She told me she had actually just run to her office from the basement storeroom where all the autopsy reports from 1991 to the present were stored in file cabinets. I could sense she was anxious to inform me about what she'd discovered.

"Guess what? Tori's autopsy report states she died of cyanide poisoning!" Wendy exclaimed.

"Oh, goodness," I replied. "What are the odds of a coincidence on that scale? Could the same person who killed Trotter with cyanide have killed Tori Piney back in 2005?"

"I suppose so, even though the report indicates there was no sign of foul play."

"Are the cause of death conclusions correct one-hundred-percent of the time?" I asked.

"No, of course not. But I'd say the vast majority are correct. And there's always the possibility it really is just an incredible coincidence."

"It's also possible there's some other connection we're overlooking," I added. "Can you think of any conceivable reason I could use to go back to the Piney home?"

"Not that I can think of offhand. You mean something sneaky and conniving?"

"Um, yes, I guess so."

"Then you need to speak to Mom. Coming up with a sneaky and conniving ploy is definitely in her wheelhouse." Wendy laughed before hanging up the phone.

Not even an hour later, Lexie and I were standing on the Pineys' front porch. She was holding a family heirloom that had been passed down through her family and which would one day belong to Wendy. It was an Anchor Hocking cobalt blue serving bowl her great-grandmother had purchased in 1905, the very year the dishware company was established. Lexie had inherited it when her mother passed away several years ago. She told me her beloved bowl was a very close match to the platter I'd returned to Georgia a couple of days ago. I had to admit it looked very similar to me too.

As we approached the Pineys' front door, Peanut began growling, snarling, and gnashing his teeth inside the house. Lexie turned to walk back to the car as I had the first time I experienced the same frightening situation. "I don't believe I want any part of whatever is behind that door," she said. "The scary woman I shared a cell with would be less terrifying than a protective guard dog that might maul me to death."

I assured her Peanut was not nearly as menacing as he'd have you think. "I hate to use a cliché, but 'his bark is worse than his bite.'"

When the door opened, Georgia's daughter was standing in front of us still wearing P.J.s as if she'd just gotten out of bed. Her baby doll pajamas, with depictions of yellow rubber duckies embroidered onto light blue cotton material, were adorable. I considered asking her where she'd gotten them but decided against it. For one thing, I didn't want to deviate from the task at hand, but also, the detailed and tedious stitching on the P.J.s didn't look cheap. The nightshirt I was currently wearing to bed was plenty comfortable enough anyway. Even with the frayed hem at the bottom of my Dallas Cowboys nightshirt, I figured I could get at least another three or four years out of it.

Lori stared silently at us for several long uncomfortable moments before asking, "Yes?"

"How are you doing, sweetie?" Lexie asked.

"Fine."

"It's nice to see you again, Lori. I just love the duckies," I added.

"Thanks!" She replied, looking down at her pajamas as if having to remind herself what she was wearing.

"Is your momma home?" Lexie asked.

Without responding, Lori turned away from the door and screamed, "Mother! It's for you!"

After telling us her mother would be with us soon, Lori shut the door in our faces. It was at least five minutes before Georgia came to the door. We'd about decided to ring the doorbell again. She appeared surprised to see us and made no comment about the fact Lexie was standing on her doorstep instead of still languishing in a jail cell. She'd probably been glued to the television, waiting for updates about the murder case. She smiled politely, with just a touch of compassion, and said, "Greetings, ladies. What brings you two by this afternoon?"

Lexie held out the bowl and said, "I found this bowl in my pantry and thought it probably belonged to you. It looked very much like the platter that Rapella returned a couple of days ago."

Georgia reached out to grasp the bowl. I was waiting for her to examine it and make some sort of comment about how it was similar but didn't actually match her platter, or that she hadn't even taken the bowl to the party she'd been hired to cater. Instead she said, "Yes, thank you. I must have forgotten I'd taken it over there. Thanks for bringing it by."

I glanced at Lexie, who was standing next to me with her mouth open. After thanking us, Georgia began to close the door to dismiss us. I put my hand out to block the door and said, "Are you certain that's your bowl, Georgia? I told Lexie earlier I was quite sure it wasn't an exact match to your platter. If I remember right, yours had a smooth lip where this one's clearly ridged."

"No, I'm sure this one belongs to me."

Lexie was still standing next to me as if she had no clue what to say or do. She had that same "deer in the headlights" kind of expression on her face that she'd had the night of Trotter's death. I wasn't ready to give up so I said, "This bowl is an Anchor Hocking piece. That's quite an impressive line of dishware, isn't it? Are your bowl and platter Anchor Hocking products too?"

"I'm not positive, but they must be because they look alike for sure."

"Would you mind getting the platter so we can make absolutely sure it's an Anchor Hocking?"

I didn't expect Georgia's reply. She said, "No, I'm quite certain it's mine. No need to go get it just to verify it's an exact match to my bowl here. I really appreciate you two making sure it was returned to me. This blue bowl has a great deal of sentimental value to me. Thanks again."

I was hoping it didn't have a "great deal" of sentimental value to Lexie, because I wasn't sure how we'd demand it back now that she'd adamantly insisted it belonged to her. I looked over at Lexie, who shrugged her shoulders and said, "Uh, well, you're welcome, Georgia."

"Have a nice day, ladies," the caterer remarked.

With that, Georgia began to close the door again and out of desperation, I stuck my right foot between the door and the frame, and said, "Oh dear! I'm in dire need of a restroom all of a sudden. I suffer from spastic colon, and for the last several days I've been so backed up I was beginning to think I was never going to poop again. I'm sure you know how your bowels get all out of whack when you're on vacation. This morning I was plugged up like a cork in a wine bottle. So, you see, I took a couple of stool softeners and now I think they might have worked even better than I'd anticipated."

"Um, well—"

"Hurry, dear, before I make a very unpleasant mess on your porch."

With that vision now in her mind, Georgia swung the door open wide and pointed down a hallway. "It's the second door on the left, Mrs. Ripple."

"Call me Rapella, please," I mumbled as I hurried down the hall. I told Lexie she might as well wait inside while I used the restroom, because it was apt to take me a while. I considered asking for a magazine, but decided that might be over-playing the part. Georgia had little choice but to invite Lexie into her kitchen and offer her a chair at the table.

I'd done all I could do to get us inside the house so we could chat up its owner and see if she had any interesting details to relate. But, with me stuck in the john, it was up to Lexie now to probe for any possible motive Georgia Piney might have had to kill Trotter Hayes, a man she'd told me the last time I visited her "deserved to have his throat slit if anyone did."

I was followed down the hallway by Peanut. I had to push him away with my foot to keep him from joining me in the head. When I stepped into the tiny bathroom, I realized there wouldn't have been room for both of as anyway. After I closed the door, the massive dog whined for a short spell and then plunked down against the other side of the door. Every twenty seconds or so Peanut whimpered to remind me he was still patiently waiting to have his head caressed.

The first order of business was to use the facilities. I wasn't kidding when I told Georgia I needed to use the restroom. I'd been regretting my last three cups of coffee ever since I'd left the inn with Lexie. My short-lived vow to restrict caffeine was only a faint memory now, and I was already anticipating withdrawal symptoms when Rip and I headed north.

I had to waste as much time in the john as I could to give Lexie ample time to grill Georgia. It's not normally in my nature to be nosy, but then I'm not normally trying to prove a friend of mine is not guilty of murder, either. So I opened the medicine cabinet door and sifted through its contents. On the bottom shelf there was a bottle of Xanax prescribed to Georgia by a Dr. Melbourne. It was the same medication Rip had been prescribed by the police force's physician to treat his anxiety when he was involved in a particularly disturbing case involving a serial pedophile. The case took all his time and attention the last year of his career in law enforcement and played a major role in his decision to put in for early retirement.

I was tempted to filch one of the pills. I was feeling a little anxious myself. Compared to the priceless antique bowl Georgia stole from Lexie, one little pill would hardly even register on the theft scale. But even if I'd been seriously considering pinching the pill, my sense of propriety would have never allowed it. I had no desire to lower myself to that level despite the low bar I'd set for myself regarding my involvement in this current situation.

Behind the Xanax bottle I found a prescription bottle of Wellbutrin, which I would later Google and discover was prescribed as a mood enhancer, and also sometimes for help with smoking cessation. I was relatively sure Georgia wasn't a smoker, so I assumed she suffered from depression.

Behind it was another bottle of the exact same medication. First I thought it was the remaining pills of the previous refill. Then, just as I was placing it back on the glass shelf inside the cabinet, I noticed this bottle wasn't prescribed for Georgia, but rather for her daughter. Apparently, Lori suffered from the same troublesome issue as her mother. The penny-pincher in me was hoping they were on some kind of family discount plan.

Two other medicine bottles on the top shelf belonged to Georgia. One was for cholesterol control and the other for lowering blood pressure, neither of which would seem out of the ordinary for a woman Georgia's age. Although not the same brands, Rip regularly took medications for the exact same health issues.

Under the sink, I discovered a large box of Depends. That indicated a bladder-control problem, but I couldn't see how incontinence could play a part in the man's death. I guess everything is within the realm of possibility. But if there was a connection there, I'd be dying to know what it was.

Having securitized everything in the bathroom, I still felt it was too soon to rejoin the ladies in the kitchen. I took a metal file out of my bag and smoothed some ragged edges on both my right thumbnail and the fingernail on my left pinky. Finally, I sprayed the tiny bathroom with a can of Jasmine air freshener I'd found under the sink. It wasn't to cover up a stench resulting from an angry colon, but rather to mask the fact that there *was no* stench.

As I walked down the carpeted hallway, I heard Lexie saying, "I'm so sorry to hear about Peter's brain cancer and am horrified by how you were treated by, um, let's see, my mind's gone blank— where did you say your husband worked?"

I stopped to give Georgia time to respond. I heard her say, "I didn't say, but he worked for a company that manufactures fertilizer. My goodness, your friend must really be having a time with that diarrhea."

"Yes, it sure seems that way," Lexie replied.

I didn't think I could stall any longer so I entered the kitchen and said, "Yes, I most certainly was, Georgia. But I think I'm good to go now. And don't worry, honey, I sprayed your powder room with the freshener before I came out."

"That's a good thing, I imagine," Georgia said as she walked to the door. It was clear she wanted us out of her house before another round of watery bowel movements hit me.

* * *

"I'm glad you were on your toes," Lexie told me on the drive back to the inn. "I was in too much shock to come up with a diversion. I was astonished at how stupidly I'd let Georgia so craftily pilfer my great-grandmother's antique bowl right in front of my face. At least I was able to get a little information out of her. Thank goodness, you were at the top of your game. That spur-of-the-moment inspiration you had made you truly a woman after my own heart."

"I'm sure we can recover that bowl. It's a family heirloom! We can't let her get by with pretending it belonged to her." I was determined to come up with a workable strategy to reclaim it, knowing the valuable bowl meant a lot to my friend.

"Oh, forget about it. I have a number of mementos I've inherited from several generations back. That bowl was just gathering dust in my pantry anyway. I can use the extra space to store more of the staples I can never seem to keep enough of on hand."

"All right, but I'm not giving up that easily," I replied. "So, tell me what you two talked about."

"I knew to look for the photo you'd told me about on the china hutch. I asked Georgia what had happened to Lori's twin sister and, even though she seemed reluctant to discuss it, I badgered her until she did. She told me that Tori had suffered a traumatic incident when she was fourteen and never could get past it. Georgia didn't go into detail about her daughter using cyanide to commit suicide, only that Tori was found unconscious in her bedroom and she was transferred to the hospital where she was pronounced dead. I nonchalantly asked, 'Wheatland Memorial?' and she nodded her head."

"Good information, but I'm guessing it's nearly impossible to dig up a patient's medical records due to the HIPAA Law and patient confidentiality policies," I said. Lexie nodded and continued detailing her conversation with Georgia Piney.

"She told me Tori's death was devastating to both her and Lori, and she feared for several years she'd lose Lori to the same fate. Lori went from being a good student who got high marks, and an athlete and cheerleader who was very popular and active at school, to being a high school dropout. She became a recluse who spent most of her time brooding in the bedroom she'd shared with her twin. Lori had constructed a shrine to her sister on their shared bookcase and began wearing all black clothes and black makeup when she made rare appearances outside her home. It was very alarming and disturbing, Georgia told me. She made the remark, 'It was almost like losing both the girls at the same time.'"

"Goodness, that's very sad. I gotta say, I feel for the woman. Did she mention how Lori was coping now, nine or ten years later?"

"Only to say she was starting to come out of her shell and return to her former personality. Lori still spends entirely too much time brooding in her room though, according to her mother."

I described what I'd discovered in the bathroom about Lori's Xanax prescription and her mother's depression and anxiety issues. We still didn't know how the pieces all fit together or if there was any connection between the Piney family and Trotter's death. For starters, we had no idea if Trotter had played any role in Tori's suicide. And if so, in what way? It was a question we intended to find an answer for.

CHAPTER 17

There were eight of us at the dining room table for supper that evening at the Alexandria Inn. Along with Lexie, Wendy, me, and our partners, Wyatt and his girlfriend had joined us as well. Veronica had come over a couple of hours earlier to whip us up a gourmet dinner. She seemed in better spirits than at our first meeting, and I had to give her credit for being a phenomenal cook.

Our chef's pot roast was so tender, just looking at the savory beef was enough to cause it to fall apart. The new potatoes, pearl onions, and carrots that had stewed along with the beef were just as delicious. And the cole slaw she served as a side dish was to die for. After devouring this meal, I'd definitely be asking her for her recipe. My mouth watered just anticipating the scrumptious dessert that surely awaited us. How such an incredible cook could maintain such a slender build was beyond me. I concluded that she must have way more will power than I even knew existed.

Naturally, the main topic of conversation was the ongoing investigation into Trotter Hayes's mysterious death. Rip and Stone had convinced the lead detective, Russell, to speak with them about the case. Even though Chief Smith had no reservations about pinning Lexie with the crime, Detective Russell was more skeptical. He'd had some interaction with Lexie in the past and couldn't quite believe someone as thoughtful and compassionate as she was would be capable of cold-blooded murder.

During the conversation, the detective told the two men that although it was a taboo topic with the chief, he'd been privy to the fact Trotter Hayes had been called on the carpet more than once for sexual assault on a female. Wendy had not been the only individual to press charges against the randy Casanova in the past. Releasing any specifics about the circumstances behind the charges could lead to the detective's termination with the police department. It was understandable that Detective Russell was reluctant to go into any further detail, but what he did reveal was food for thought.

Could one of those sexual assault charges have stemmed from the traumatic incident Tori Piney had experienced? After all, it'd been apparent the girl's mother had a severe enough grievance against the victim to indicate that he, if anyone, deserved to have his throat slit. According to Lexie, a person as docile as Georgia had always been in past interactions would surely not make such a spiteful statement about a man who had merely broken up with her daughter when she was a teenager. That's an everyday occurrence with high school kids who were reacting to an over-abundance of hormones.

"I wouldn't have let our daughter, Regina, go out with an adult man when she was fourteen," Rip said.

"Nor would I have allowed Wendy to go out with a guy that much older than she was," Lexie added before Rip continued with his line of thinking.

"Trotter was five or six years older than her daughter, or nineteen to her fourteen at the time. If Tori and Trotter had been dating, you'd think Georgia would be as delighted as she could be to see them split up. In fact, I can't imagine her even letting her young daughter go out on a date with a grown man like that in the first place. It was probable that her objection to Hayes had nothing to do with Tori or stemmed from something much more contemptuous."

"What if Georgia was unaware of Trotter's existence before the potential sexual assault? I didn't tell my folks I was messing around with Rip until after I found out there was an unexpected bun in my oven."

Glancing at my husband, I noticed Rip was blushing. He said, "My bad! But even though her pappy threatened me with his twelve-gauge, I'd have married her anyway. Oh, good grief, what in the hell was I thinking?"

After everyone laughed along with Rip, Wendy

spoke for the first time in the discussion. "If Russell's aware of previous sexual assault charges against the victim, there must be a record of those charges. I'm sure there must be more specific details about the charges on a computer file if we could only access it. For instance, if a rape kit was utilized, the results should be included in the report."

"Could Chief Smith have prevented the use of a rape kit if the charges involved his stepson?" Lexie inquired. "In Wendy's case, even though it nearly cost him his job, he was able to sweep the assault charges against Trotter under the rug. And since no actual rape occurred, a rape kit wasn't an issue in that sexual assault."

"I don't think it would have been within Leonard Smith's power to prevent the use of a potentially incriminating tool such as a rape kit if an actual rape had occurred," Wyatt responded. "It's a long-shot, but I might be able to dig up some old criminal report files on the computer at the station. But I'm not well-versed in the applicable program, or computers in general. Where's a skilled hacker when you need one?"

I felt a sudden burst of pride as I said, "I've gotten pretty darn skilled at tracking down information on the Internet. I'm pretty much a first-class Googler now."

Wendy smiled and said, "Yes, you really have advanced a lot more than I could have ever imagined, Rapella. In fact, Mattie and I were just chatting about what a remarkably quick learner you are."

I was beaming like a lighthouse beacon at the two young ladies impressive opinion of me. Wendy went on to expand on her remarks. "However, I'm thinking we should turn this over to Mattie to see if she can get into the police station's criminal records database. She's more highly skilled at this sort of thing than anyone else I know. She can hack with the best of them, and we need your skills elsewhere, Rapella."

I wasn't sure what "hacking" entailed, so I was happy to turn the responsibility over to Mattie Hill. Not to mention, Lexie said they needed my skills elsewhere and I wanted to be where I could do the most good.

Wyatt then remarked that he would be alone at the station again the next day from one o'clock in the afternoon until Detective Travis reported to replace him at one forty-five. If Mattie could meet him there, he'd turn the computer over to her. He knew he was taking a risk as far as his career as a police officer was concerned, but he thought the benefits of any potential damning information Mattie might uncover was worth the gamble. He also knew there wouldn't be much time for Mattie to hack into the files before Detective Travis clocked in, and he'd have to have her out of there before he arrived. I realized he was tentative about letting Mattie have access to the department's computer system, as was evident by his next remark. "I'm probably foolish to even consider this idea to begin with."

After we'd determined our next plan of attack, the conversation switched over to the progress of the repairs on our travel trailer. Boney's Garage had called and told Rip the repairs on the Chartreuse Caboose would be completed, and the unit would be ready to be picked up, by nine the following morning.

Even though we'd be free to be on our way to Chicago, where we were planning to attend a nephew's wedding in a couple of weeks, we had no immediate desire to leave Rockdale. Until Trotter's real killer was arrested, it'd take one of those F-5 tornadoes so prevalent in the Midwest, to remove Rip and me from the Alexandria Inn. And our tabby, Dolly, had the run of the entire antebellum mansion instead of the cramped space in the travel trailer she was accustomed to. There were undoubtedly a lot of things she hadn't had time to sufficiently check out, so I'm sure she was happy to linger at the inn as long as we deemed necessary. The fear of curiosity rendering her dead didn't seem to keep her awake at night, and sleeping eighteen hours a day left little time for Dolly to tackle more arduous endeavors.

We all retreated to the parlor for an after-supper cup of coffee after enjoying the best Crepes Suzette I've ever tasted. And, I swear, that wasn't just the brandy in it talking!

The next day proved to be very illuminating. While Mattie was at the police station hacking into their confidential files, I was employing my new computer skills to research a few intricate details relating to the murder case.

According to Mattie, it didn't take long at all to

access the records she was looking for once she'd hacked her way into the database, which was a compilation of all police reports dating back to 1936, the year the town of Rockdale, Missouri, became the recipient of its own police department.

Peter Piney had filed a police report on September 25, 2004. He reported a sexual assault against his fourteen-year-old daughter, Tori Piney, and alleged the rape was perpetrated by nineteen-year-old Trotter Hayes. Mr. Piney had insisted a rape kit be utilized so the results of the test would be on file. The files indicated the test was performed on the same date at Wheatland Memorial Hospital, but no record of the results could be found in the file.

"And that was the extent of the information available," Mattie told me over the phone. "There was no evidence of charges against the rapist being filed by the Piney family, and Trotter Hayes didn't spend one second in jail for the sexual assault."

"That absolutely sucks, Mattie! How could the scumbag get away with a crime of that nature just by being the police chief's stepson? I can't believe there's no record on file of the results."

"Yeah, me either!"

"Somehow, the chief got them expunged, I'll bet." I was livid at the injustice and was determined to see Chief Leonard Smith be held responsible for the corrupt abuse of his position of authority.

"But guess what?" Mattie asked rhetorically.

"There's a record the chief wasn't able to make disappear into thin air. Working in the women's clinic at Wheatland, I have access to their database too. I found a document on file with the results of that rape kit they performed. It states that Tori Piney tested positive for rape and a subsequent DNA test proved the sperm belonged to that of Trotter P. Hayes. We've got a chokehold on that creep now, *and* his stepfather, Chief Smith!"

"Holy smokes! Good job, Mattie! Your news is music to my ears. Lexie's finally going to be exonerated," I replied enthusiastically.

I was ecstatic when I hung up the phone and rushed to tell Lexie the great news. She wasn't as thrilled as I was for some reason. "Why aren't you jumping for joy like I am, sweetie?"

"Mattie's discovery is absolutely great news and nails Trotter for the rape of Tori Piney. It's a little late to prosecute him for the crime though. And although it might be beneficial to our case, it doesn't prove that Georgia Piney killed him. It's what Judy Jueti would classify as circumstantial evidence, if she even considered it evidence in the murder case at all," Lexie explained.

"But wait!" I replied. "There's more!"

"Like what?"

"I spent the morning on the Internet. For one thing, I learned that the ice that covers Antarctica holds ninety percent of the world's fresh water. And, speaking of water, did you know that by the time you are my age, you'll have drunk an average of nearly twelve thousand gallons of water? In my case, I've probably drunk at least half that in beer and tequila as well."

"That's fascinating, Rapella, but you have wandered far past the subject at hand. I'm guessing that your iPad is no longer going to be used as nothing more than a coaster to prevent water marks on your furniture." She laughed as she teased me.

"Oh, sorry," I said as I smiled and nodded my head at her spot-on remark. "The most important thing I discovered is that one of the main ingredients in fertilizer is cyanide. And Peter Piney worked for years at a fertilizer manufacturing plant so he had access to the chemical. I'm thinking it's likely to be related to how Tori got hold of the cyanide she used to kill herself."

"Hmm, I'm sure you're right!"

"And also, Lexie, the fumes at a fertilizer plant can often cause brain cancer, which is what Georgia's husband died from. I'd think he had to have brought a container of the cyanide home with him for Tori to have had access to the deadly poison. But why? I don't know. I can't imagine any reason he'd want to bring something that toxic into his home to begin with."

"Me either, but I think you might have hit it right on the head," Lexie exclaimed, now as excited as I was. "Do you remember Georgia telling us that Tori couldn't deal with the traumatic incident she suffered, which we now know was being raped by Trotter? I don't know if the girl left a suicide note, but regardless, the

Pineys had obviously felt the sexual assault Trotter perpetrated against their daughter was what caused her to commit suicide a year later. That's why they hired the law firm Candy Crushnut's father works for to file a wrongful death suit against Trotter and his family. What are the chances that Georgia used some of that same cyanide that was left over from Tori's suicide to exact revenge on the man she holds responsible for her daughter's death? She probably felt cheated by the justice system and couldn't bear the thought that Trotter was out attending birthday parties and enjoying life while her daughter is six feet under."

I nodded and added, "Good point! And in the same breath, what are the chances that Lori used some of that leftover cyanide to get retribution for her sister's death? Maybe that's what she needed to ever be able to find any degree of closure. As I mentioned before, identical twins have probably the closest bond amongst all mankind. With the exact same DNA makeup, they're kind of like two halves of a whole. In fact, I read they're classified as 'monozygotic' and are formed from a single fertilized egg. So, in essence, identical twins really are two halves of a whole. The odds of being an identical twin are approximately three in one thousand. And you know how adversely Lori was affected by her sister's death."

"Rapella, you're not getting addicted to Google, are you? Are we going to have to arrange for an intervention?" We both giggled before Lexie turned serious again. "Really, though, I think you're onto something. Georgia may have some inclination or even first-hand knowledge that her surviving daughter had something to do with Trotter's death, and if so, she'd naturally be protecting her. That would explain her behavior when we brought up the subject. It could be either one of the Piney women, or maybe even the two acting as a team, avenging their daughter and sister's death together."

"The only thing that doesn't fit into the puzzle is that you were outside with Georgia when the poison was deposited in the victim's drink. And didn't you say Lori was out arranging the items on the buffet table in the parlor?"

"I actually said I *assumed* she was in the parlor," Lexie replied. I could tell she was reflecting back, trying to visualize the sequence of events leading up to the murder. As she played the scene over in her mind, she said, "But truly, for all I know, Lori could have been in the pantry and rushed out to spike the drink when I went outside to assist her mother. And now that I think about it, the mother/daughter tag team theory is not a totally far-fetched possibility. It was Georgia who asked me to help her carry in the tray of meat, not the other way around. And this was after the woman had hauled in a number of other heavy loads without requesting assistance."

"Yes, and Lori and Georgia could have worked it out in advance on how to coordinate the timing. The only thing that bothers me with this theory is how in the world could they have known Trotter would ask you to make him a drink?"

"Yeah, I'm not clear on that one either. But since all the other pieces of the puzzle fit together so perfectly, I think we have enough evidence to take to the detectives," Lexie said with a grin that showed exactly how relieved she was to have reason to believe the light at the end of the tunnel was drawing near. Now, if the light wasn't glowing from the front of a train that was about to mow us down, we might have just clinched the case and tracked down Trotter's *real* killer.

Standing with Lexie in the police station's parking lot an hour or so later, I said "I hate to use a cliché, but—"

"Rapella, since I've met you I've heard you use every cliché in the book," Lexie said, interrupting me. "Not to mention a few originals I'm sure you concocted yourself. So why stop now?"

"Um, well then, if you put it that way, I—"

"I was kidding, dear. I love your cliché habit. Go on with what you were saying."

"Okay. I was going to say we should have known there'd be a fly in the ointment."

Lexie laughed and replied. "Yes, I agree with you. There's always a fly in the ointment whenever I'm involved in a situation like this."

Lexie and I had planned to relay the information to Detective Russell and then call another pow-wow at the inn. We were anxious to tell Wendy, Stone, Rip, Mattie, Andy, and Veronica our incredible news over supper. We'd even stopped at a local barbecue joint on the way to the station and picked up ribs, beans, and slaw to go. We were both too wound up to take time to scratch up a meal ourselves. Veronica had so graciously prepared a fabulous supper the previous night, and we didn't want to ask her to do so again.

Detective Russell told us he didn't have the leisure of going above his boss, Chief Smith's, head. When he ran our theory past the chief, he was chastised for even listening to two old airheads, one of whom he felt certain had killed his stepson and would concoct any story she could to draw the focus of the investigation away from herself. He stood firm on his decision and couldn't be budged. Chief Smith even told the detective he wasn't going to waste time and manpower chasing down off-the-wall theories and tarnish the reputation of the Piney family without an iron-clad reason. Short of a signed confession by Georgia or Lori Piney, he refused to even consider them as suspects in the murder case. "We don't have the luxury of chasing wild geese all around the county," he had told the lead detective.

"Now that just ticks me off to no end!" I declared.

"Me too!" Lexie agreed. "Especially because the chief's well aware of the rape his stepson perpetrated against Tori Piney ten years ago, and that the Pineys blame Trotter for her suicide. He knows her family's anguish might make for a very strong motive to take revenge on Trotter, as well. But for some reason he'd rather pin the murder on me."

"That really, really ticks me off!" I reiterated. "How dare that moron call us 'airheads', or even worse, 'old'?"

"Well, yeah, that's irritating too," Lexie replied with a chuckle. "But I was actually referring to Chief Smith's attitude. I can't believe he refused to look deeper into what I believe is a very logical and credible supposition. He's so dead-set on charging me with the murder that I don't think any amount of evidence will convince him otherwise. A 'signed confession', that hardhead said. Seriously?"

"We need the Pineys to voluntarily admit on paper that they killed Trotter and then sign their confession to get the chief to even consider them as potential suspects? Seriously?" I guess that really was the word of the month, so I might as well throw it out there every chance I got too. "And here I thought Rip was bullheaded! But the chief's remark about the 'signed confession' made me wonder. Do you reckon there's any way we actually *could* coerce a confession out of one, or both, of the Piney women? Not necessarily signed, but maybe on a tape recording, you think?"

"I don't know, Rapella. But I think we should give it our best shot! Do you have any ideas on how we can get back inside the Piney home? We aren't likely to be welcomed with open arms, nor can we force our way in."

As we walked to Lexie's little car, we contemplated different strategies. An idea hit me just as we took our seats in the Volkswagen. "Think back, Lexie. Do you have any photos that have your Anchor Hocking bowl in them, even just somewhere in the background? I'm determined to get your family heirloom back from that slick swindler. Maybe we can kill two birds with one stone."

I didn't know what caused Lexie to start laughing until she said, "See what I mean about the clichés, Rapella?"

"Oh, yeah, sorry about that! I'll try to work on that. I guess I need to start thinking first before I open my trap."

"Don't you dare! I adore you just the way you are and wouldn't want you to change one little thing about yourself. Your penchant for old clichés just makes you that much more loveable."

"Oh, thank God," I replied. "Cause it'd be nearly impossible for me to turn over a new leaf at my age."

Lexie burst out laughing again. She reached over and slapped me on the knee and said, "That's all right, dear. I understand how hard it is to teach an old dog new tricks."

We were both cracking up when Lexie stopped abruptly and said, "Hey! I just remembered that I have a photo from a long ago Thanksgiving dinner. Grandma's at the end of the table holding that bowl in her hands. I don't recall what was in the bowl—"

"Does it matter what was in the bowl?" I asked. Wendy was right about her mother's habit of getting bogged down in details that had no bearing on the conversation.

"No, I guess not. But it *is* proof it belonged to my family at one time."

"Could you come up with it in fairly short order?" I asked.

"I'm almost certain it's in an old family album I keep in an upstairs closet. I know it'll be easy to locate. And I get where you're going with this. Let's pick up the photo and pay the Pineys another visit. Okay?"

"Sounds like a plan to me!"

While Lexie was going through what had to be six million photos distributed amongst a dozen plastic tubs, I used a small bathroom off the inn's little library. When I reached down to drop a used tissue in the trash can, something behind the can caught my eye. I remembered then that Mattie Hill had utilized the toilet right before she left, so I wasn't surprised to discover it was a cell phone. And since it had an apple engraved on it, I was certain it was the one Mattie had misplaced. I had noticed the apple emblems on her phone and my tablet the evening she tutored me, and I'd asked her what a piece of fruit had to do with all these new-fangled gadgets.

I took the phone into the kitchen to find her work number which Stone had scribbled on a memo pad attached to the freezer door by a magnet. In the process, I accidentally pushed a few of the buttons on the phone's face. At first, I was afraid I'd called the Russian Prime Minister like Rip had previously done, but when I looked at the screen there was a message on it that read, "I dare you to try."

Just at that moment, Lexie walked in holding an older faded photo in her hand. She exclaimed, "Isn't that Mattie's phone?"

"Yes, I'm pretty sure it is," I replied.

When I handed it to her, she looked at the message with a puzzled expression, and said, "This says the text is from Trotter Hayes and was sent to Mattie no more than twenty minutes before he was killed."

"Could she have sent it to him to tell him he'd better leave Wendy alone after Mattie noticed he'd shown up as Joy White's date?" I asked. "Maybe she even told him if he even looked at Wendy, Andy would tear him a new one."

"Probably so." Lexie then pushed a few buttons and came up with another text. "This one's from Mattie to him just a minute or so earlier. It says 'I'm warning you!' So, I'm sure what you just suggested is exactly what happened. As you know, she was not at all happy to see him there, at Wendy's party of all things. She's always been extremely protective of Wendy. Like she said, they've been as close as sisters for many years."

After spreading all the photos out all over the master suite's floor like a five-thousand piece jigsaw puzzle, Lexie finally tracked down the photo she was searching for. Before we left, I called Mattie and told her I'd found her cell phone. I apologized for not thinking to search the bathroom earlier. She assured me it was no big deal and said she'd be right over to pick it up,

even though she'd just purchased a coveted
iPhone 6 to replace it. Mattie was tickled to have
gotten one of the new models that had just been
released by Apple. I told her I'd leave the old
obsolete iPhone 5, that she'd been forced to
tolerate for six long months while the iPhone 6
was being developed, on the kitchen table after
Lexie whispered that Mattie had a key to the front
door and could let herself in.

CHAPTER 18

For the second afternoon in a row, Lexie and I found ourselves standing on the Pineys' front porch. This time our knock went unanswered. We continued to ring the bell and knock off and on for five minutes. Both Georgia and Lori's vehicles were in the driveway so we felt confident at least one of them was home. And Peanut was raising such a fuss, there was no way they couldn't have known someone was at their front door. We knew we were being deliberately ignored.

Finally, Lexie whispered to me. She told me to follow her to the car. We drove about halfway up the block and parked out of view from the plate glass window of the Pineys' home. We walked stealthily through backyards and skirted around the Piney home to a position on the right side of their house.

Lexie pulled out her phone and placed a call to

her daughter. Wendy, whose voice wouldn't be recognizable to Georgia or Lori, put her cell on speakerphone before she called the Pineys on her office phone. With intermittent, and impossible to decipher, responses, we listened to Wendy's side of the conversation.

Wendy asked, "Is this Mrs. Piney?"

"***************"

"Good afternoon, this is your neighbor up the street, Claire Keller."

"***************"

"Oh, well, you see, I just moved in last week. I'm hoping I'll know everyone in the neighborhood soon too."

"***************"

"Thank you. Yes, I'll be happy to stop by for coffee one morning soon to get acquainted with you. Unfortunately, today I'm getting my hair trimmed at the Klip Joint in an hour."

"***************"

"I use Charlene too. And, like you, I wouldn't trust Kerri within ten feet of me with a pair of scissors in her hand. However, the reason I'm calling is to let you know I just drove by your house and saw a package on your porch that UPS probably left there."

"***************"

"I don't have any idea why he didn't ring the bell, ma'am. Are you certain you didn't hear the bell, or perhaps knocking, just a few minutes ago? You know, maybe even a dog barking?"

"***************"

"I agree, wholeheartedly. Solicitors should be

lined up and shot."

"**************"

"I don't have any idea what's in the box, ma'am."

"**************"

"Yes, I understand. Could someone have sent you a gift you're unaware of?"

"**************"

"Nonetheless, Ms. Piney, there's a package on your porch. And whether or not it was meant for you, you probably ought to take it indoors. With my arthritis I can always sense when rain is on the way."

"**************"

"Oh? You too? Well, I'm telling you, if the throbbing in my knees is any indication, this storm's going to be a doozey."

"**************"

"Despite the forecast, ma'am, a fluke shower could pop up. Meteorologists are not always one hundred percent accurate, you know."

"**************"

"I agree. I'm sure I could walk outside on my porch and guess at the forecast just as accurately as most of the weathermen on the tube, too. Oh, dear. The timer on my oven's going off and I don't want to burn the cookies. Anyway, I just wanted to let you know the box was there, just in case whatever's in the package might be damaged if it gets wet."

"**************"

"You're welcome, Ms. Piney. You have a nice day too."

After Georgia rang off we listened to Wendy say, "That should not have been that complicated. But Georgia's heading to the door now, I'm guessing. Better get ready to close in on her."

As we heard the creak of the screen door, we rushed around to the front of the house. Lexie smiled pleasantly and said, "I'm so glad we caught you at home, Georgia."

The look on Georgia's face was priceless. She obviously hadn't seen this ambush coming. This time we didn't feel it was necessary to enter her home. Once Georgia got over her shock of seeing us again, and had greeted us in a fashion that could not have been any less welcoming, Lexie exclaimed, "I know you'll be as pleased as we are that we solved the puzzle about the blue bowl."

"Oh?"

"Yes, ma'am. Here's a photo of my great-grandmother holding the bowl many Thanksgivings ago. I thought maybe you could go get the bowl and we'll compare it to this photo. You know, just to make certain it's the same bowl you forgot at the inn."

"Thanks for bothering, but there's really no need to compare my bowl to the photo. I have absolutely no doubt they wouldn't be a perfect match because my bowl is definitely the one you so graciously returned to me. But I do appreciate you stopping by with your concern."

Lexie must have mentally raised the white flag because her desire to get her bowl back vanished. She looked at me with a resigned expression.

Ever getting Lexie's bowl back seemed a

remote possibility, but I was too stubborn to give up that easily. I'd come up with something eventually. But for now I turned to Georgia and said, "While we're here, dear, we wanted to give you a head's up. We just spoke with the police chief and the lead detective on the Trotter Hayes murder case. They told us they had undeniable proof that your daughter slipped the cyanide in the victim's drink at the party that night, and they plan to apprehend her in an hour or so."

"What in the world are you talking about, lady?" She asked with utter shock on her face. If she'd been holding Lexie's bowl at the time it would have been shattered by then anyway.

"I'm sure you're as astonished as we are, but I'm sure, considering the circumstances, they'll go easy on Lori," Lexie added. I know she was thinking the same thing I was. No mother worth her salt would let her daughter take the fall for her if she herself committed the crime or had any part in the murder whatsoever. So when she didn't take the blame and sincerely appeared stunned by our comments, we felt even more convinced that, unbeknownst to Georgia, her daughter was the sole perpetrator of the crime.

"Pardon me for saying this, but you two ladies are plum crazy!" The irate woman exclaimed loudly in a no-nonsense tone.

"Take it easy, Georgia," I said to calm her down. "We only meant to warn you, not upset you. The investigators dug up the report your husband filed after Tori was assaulted by Trotter Hayes. And further investigation discovered that, although the police chief was able to cover up the crime, he couldn't expunge the rape kit report that concluded Tori was raped, and the rapist was indeed the recent murder victim, Mr. Hayes."

Georgia was staring at me silently. It seemed to me she was considering the possibility her surviving daughter could have committed the crime, given her altered demeanor and odd behavior since the suicide of her twin sister. She finally replied, "I don't need a rape kit report to know Trotter Hayes is the person who assaulted my daughter, ladies. But what does that have to do with Lori? It was her sister he raped, not her."

I ignored her comment because there was no arguing with the facts she'd just pointed out. I continued. "And we know about the cyanide your husband acquired at the fertilizer plant, that not only was the likely cause of his cancer, but also the poison Tori used to kill herself and Lori used to kill Tori's assailant."

I knew Lexie was recording the confrontation with her cell phone. We were hoping we could get Georgia to make some implicative comment that would be as close to a confession as Lexie and I were apt to get from the woman. Hopefully, we could edit out the blatant lies we told Georgia before turning the incriminating tape over to the police. Telling an individual, not even on the authorities' suspect list, that the detectives were planning to apprehend her soon, might not sit well with the investigating team. Regardless, I plunged right in. "We just wanted to give you advance warning that the detectives may already be on their way as we speak. Lexie and I both think it'd be better in the long run for Lori if she went down to the station and turned herself in."

This time Georgia Piney did respond, but not with what we'd hope to hear, which was a confession of guilt. "You two got it all wrong. Yes, Peter did bring home the cyanide for a project he was working on and yes, it did ultimately cause his death. But Lori had absolutely nothing to do with Trotter's death. For one thing, every trace of the cyanide in this house was disposed of after Tori's suicide. More importantly, I know my daughter better than anyone, and can promise you she's not a vicious, revengeful type of person."

Georgia paused for a response from Lexie or me, and when we didn't give one, she continued. "My husband was trying to develop a new and better fertilizer recipe. After the factory he was employed at refused to take responsibility when a co-worker was diagnosed with brain cancer, my husband was determined to create a safer product. Peter worked tirelessly for years trying to develop one, with hopes of getting it approved and patented in his lifetime. He wanted to prevent anyone else from suffering like his friend had in his last year of life. Did you know that it was primarily hydrogen cyanide that was used for mass murder in the extermination camps during the holocaust?"

We didn't, but Lexie and I nodded simultaneously. This woman was sincere. There was no doubt in my mind she was telling us the absolute truth. Mesmerized, we continued to listen.

"Peter was devastated when Tori took some of the cyanide out of his workshop and used it to commit suicide. If you aren't as familiar with cyanide as I am from the years of my husband's devotion to his quest, the chemical compound comes in several forms. The form he was using in his experiments was a white crystal powder."

I actually did know about the various forms of cyanide. I'd read a very informative description of cyanide on something called a "Wikipedia page" and felt I was quite versed on the subject now. And I was sure if it was on the Internet, it had to be true.

I recalled Wendy mentioning that she'd heard from one of her co-workers at the coroner's lab that the sodium cyanide used to kill Trotter was of the crystal variety, which did, in fact, match the form Tori had utilized for her suicide. But she also mentioned it was probably the most commonly utilized form of cyanide, so not a particularly remarkable discovery.

Georgia invited us to sit down on her porch swing before she went on with her story. "Peter disposed of every lick of the remaining poison in his shop, and our daughter's death effectively ended his quest to discover a safer version of the fertilizer. He was a broken man after Tori's death. And ironically, all of his exposure over the years to the fertilizer he was trying to improve caused him to contract the same cancer that had killed his friend. Because of his unauthorized experimenting with the product, Hill Fertilizer Corporation was not held responsible for his death."

I never saw the wrecking ball coming that hit me in the chest at that moment, but it had to have been a large one. The shock waves that went through my body made me shiver from head to toe. I almost fell off the swing.

Breathlessly, I interrupted Georgia to ask, "Where is this Hill Manufacturing Corporation located?"

"The factory's in Mohawk, which is a surprisingly tiny town for such a large factory. It's about twenty minutes east of here."

I glanced at Lexie, who had apparently been hit by the same wrecking ball that nearly took me out. We couldn't apologize to Georgia fast enough. We explained that we'd only used the package ruse to get an opportunity to talk to her. Together, Lexie and I told her the little white lie, embarrassed we'd ever doubted her innocence.

Lexie put an arm around her friend and said, "We never seriously suspected you or Lori of any involvement in Hayes's murder."

"Sure seemed that way," Georgia said with a great deal of resentment in her tone.

I added, "We're sorry, dear. We only hoped we might get some information from you that you'd been reluctant to report to the investigating team for fear of being targeted in the case. And luckily, we succeeded. You made an eye-opening comment that will be a pivotal point in the apprehension of the real killer."

"Please forgive us for upsetting you," Lexie added. "It was unintentional, Georgia. You know I've always thought very highly of you."

When Lexie finished speaking, we stood up to leave. Georgia motioned for us to sit back down on the swing. She was somber as she spoke to us.

"I completely understand, ladies. I've been concerned a great deal about your situation, Lexie. And I want you two to know I'd have helped in any way I could, but I wasn't sure I could handle the emotional turmoil. Lori and I are both seeing a therapist already, and following the added anxiety of Trotter's murder earlier this week, we are both stressed to the limit. It's very disturbing to find yourself feeling delighted about the brutal murder of another human being, even one who you considered despicable. It really makes you wonder what kind of person that makes you in comparison."

We both assured her we understood her dilemma but that she should never compare herself to a loathsome individual like Trotter. After all, she'd never physically harmed anyone and would never even consider doing so.

"No, you're right. I wouldn't. And I appreciate you two putting this all into perspective for me," Georgia replied with tears in her eyes.

We told Georgia we thought we now had the situation under control and the answer to the mystery behind Trotter's murder. We explained that the information she'd shared with us was undoubtedly the break we'd been hoping for and promised her we'd never mention we talked to her when we spoke to the authorities.

She thanked us for keeping her name out of it, because she never wanted the Piney name to be tied to Trotter Hayes's name again in their lifetimes. She said, "I'm not sure what I could possibly have said to help you solve this case, but I'm awfully glad I said it."

Georgia expressed her gratitude to Lexie for the catering jobs she'd passed her way and Lexie replied, "You will always be my go-to caterer, and I'll continue to recommend you to other potential clients too. Without exception, you've always done an exemplary job for us, and we appreciate your high standards."

"Thank you," Georgia said. "I'm sorry you had to make the unnecessary trip over here with the bowl photo."

"No big rip," Lexie remarked. I had to giggle. "No big rip" was one of my husband's favorite sayings, for obvious reasons. Lexie went on to say, "The trip was worth it just to get your insight into the murder case. We hope you and Lori can both find some peace now that Tori's attacker is no longer in the picture."

"I have mixed emotions. I'm glad to know he'll never assault another victim, but sorry he met the ungodly fate he did. I wouldn't wish that on my worst enemy," Georgia said. And then with a sly grin she added, "And I guess my worse enemy would have had to have been Trotter."

We both hugged Georgia and thanked her for the invaluable information she'd related to us. It was apparent in her expression that even though she wasn't aware of what information she'd related, she was relived she'd been able to assist in some way. Oddly, she didn't ask us who we'd determined to be Trotter's killer. Apparently, she didn't care who killed the ruthless bastard, but was just relieved that somebody did.

Walking up her sidewalk to the street, I told Lexie I was sorry my idea to recover her bowl had failed. She replied, "I actually believe she's totally convinced my grandmother's bowl belongs to her. So confident, in fact, she felt no need to verify it. And as I said earlier, it's really not a big deal in the scheme of things."

When we got to the street, we turned right and sprinted to Lexie's car. Mind you, "sprint" is a relative term when you are sixty-eight and the car is seven houses down the street.

As Lexie shifted the car into gear, I asked her if she was thinking the same thing that I was thinking.

In a quivering voice she replied, "I hope not, because I'm thinking my daughter's very best friend, who spent much of her childhood in our home, might possibly have been behind the death of Trotter Hayes."

"Yep! That's exactly what I was thinking too. Or, at the very least, she might have had knowledge of the imminent assault on Trotter Hayes before the party commenced. I'm thinking now the text she sent him was a more chilling warning than we'd first assumed."

"And maybe Trotter's cocky dare is what sent

her over the edge." Lexie was thinking back as she continued to voice the thoughts racing through her mind. "I knew Mattie's father owned a big corporation in Mohawk and probably knew at one time the company manufactured fertilizer. But I'd never heard about cyanide being an ingredient in the product. When the girls were young, Mattie and Wendy would spend the day at the factory on days the nanny was off. Wendy told me on several occasions they'd been told by Mattie's dad to stay away from the areas where the toxic chemicals were stored. But I don't think there was anything actually preventing them from entering the storage centers, other than the threat of a harsh punishment being handed down for disobedience. Her dad was rarely home, but terribly strict on the rare occasions when he was."

"Then Mattie could have acquired the poisonous substance as easily as Peter Piney had," I mused. "But the fact she brought the cyanide to the party with her makes me think she planned the murder and intentionally invited him to the party, hoping to get an opportunity to use it."

"And she'd probably already given him a verbal warning some time prior to the party, maybe even directly after the sexual assault happened," Lexie said. "I just can't imagine a sweetie like Mattie resorting to an act of violence like that, even though, as I said before, she'd do almost anything to protect her best friend."

I agreed and said, "As you know, Wendy asked Mattie to stop by and teach me a few fundamentals about the iPad. Mattie knew I wanted to learn how to research topics on the Internet to further assist with our own little investigation."

"Yes, that was one thing that was bothering me, Rapella. Why would she agree to teach you how to perform a Google search that could later lead to her being caught and charged with murder?"

"I think she agreed to Wendy's request with the idea she could use it as an opportunity to overwhelm me with so much information that I'd ultimately decide it was too much to absorb and give up the notion altogether. I swear she threw every single computer term she could think of into her tutorial. Just before Mattie left that evening, she even joked about trying to teach her grandmother to use a computer, but her elderly student quickly became disenchanted with the idea and decided her time was better spent working in her garden."

"And Mattie knew you'd ask Wendy to teach you when she could find the time if she didn't agree to instruct you, and could have been afraid you'd be more apt to absorb it if Wendy was more patient and only told you what little you needed to learn in order to perform the task you wanted to do," Lexie added, filling in the gaps of my story. When she finished talking, I started up again.

"At the time, I'd even felt a bit like she was trying to discourage me in the same fashion she had her grandmother. But I'd pooh-poohed that idea, figuring it was only because she had other things she needed to get taken care of and didn't have a lot of time to devote to me. I was aware that she had a sick baby in her department she was really concerned about, and I admired her commitment to her job."

"I see," Lexie said with a knowing nod. "She may have decided to aim for the same result with you, but she under-estimated how determined you were. By the way, how did you manage to figure out how to research things on your iPad, considering the boatload of information she fed you in the space of an hour or so?"

"As soon as she began spitting out information like an Uzi spraying bullets, I tuned her out and started thinking about what I wanted to buy Rip's nephew as a wedding gift. Then I said to myself, *Heck! I'll save a little dough and whittle him some kind of trinket, instead.* So then I starting going over wedding-related trinket ideas in my head. When I heard the word 'Google' come out of Mattie's mouth, I tuned her back in and concentrated as hard as I could until she abruptly switched to another task she thought I should learn how to do. She thought I should develop something called a 'spreadsheet' to more easily keep track of our monthly budget. Ha! I wanted to tell her that all I needed to know was that when the well ran dry we needed to stop spending money until it filled up again. But instead I just tuned her out again, and in my mind, to try to memorize the details, I went over and over what she'd explained about how to search topics using a search engine, in my case, Google."

"Good for you, girl!" Lexie exclaimed with sincere praise. "But I'm still puzzled about why Mattie was so involved with our efforts to track down the killer, if she *was* indeed the killer we were trying to track down."

"Have you ever heard the phrase, 'Keep your friends close, and your enemies closer'?"

"Yes, I have. And I get your point," Lexie remarked. "What better way to keep apprised of the developments into the ongoing murder investigation, by both us and the police department, than by inserting herself right into the middle of it? After all, who would suspect someone who seems so set on solving the case?"

"And as far as motive is concerned, as a child growing up without a mother, and an absentee father who left her in the hands of nannies the majority of the time, her friendship with Wendy, and even you, has to be a very special bond to her. She was probably more upset about Trotter's assault on her best friend than even you and Wendy were," I said. "I recall her saying that when someone hurt Wendy, she was hurt just as badly."

"Not to mention," Lexie cut in, "that her mother sacrificed her life to give birth to her. And after she was rendered unable to have children herself, the self-serving abortion of Joy's baby probably put her over the edge. Mattie told us she knew in advance about the 'slaughter', as she put it, of Joy and Trotter's unborn child. Working at the women's clinic, she likely had knowledge of the rape and subsequent suicide of Tori Piney too."

"Wow," was all I could say before Lexie continued.

"And I know Mattie as well as anyone, having served as a substitute mother figure for her all these years. She's a very emotional individual and can be fiercely passionate about a cause, particularly if it involves children. In the past few years, she's seemed to me to be unraveling bit by bit. I've been a little concerned about her and I know Wendy has too. We both worried that her job as a neo-natal nurse was taking an emotional toll on her."

"Of course! It'd take a toll on anyone."

"Except for maybe a psychopath like Trotter Hayes," Lexie said.

"True," I agreed. "You know, I was optimistically hopeful about the Piney theory, but I am dreadfully confident about this new one."

Lexie nodded solemnly and asked, "What do you suggest our next move should be? I'm not thrilled about personally approaching Mattie with our suspicions. After all, it might cause a terrible rift between us, or even an irreparable falling out between Mattie and Wendy. In the event it turns out she had no part in the murder, I wouldn't want to have been the cause of driving a wedge between all three of our inter-relationships. Worse yet would be if an unsubstantiated accusation were to cause my daughter and me to become estranged. That would break my heart, you know."

"It would break mine too," I agreed. "I also have no burning desire to alienate either girl. But given the circumstances, I think it should be Rip and I who approach her. I don't think we should mention anything about this to any of the others until after the fact, especially Wendy. Only Rip should be brought into this situation for now. Don't you agree?"

"Yes, I guess so," she replied, although I knew her heart wasn't in it. I knew she was thinking it might prove very difficult for her to keep something as important as this from her husband, and more difficult still, from her daughter. She suggested a change in dinner plans. "Instead of having the barbecue we purchased for supper, let's save it for lunch tomorrow. I'll come up with a reason to take everyone out to eat and you two can beg off to go pick up your trailer and get some rest, or something else totally believable. Then you can call Mattie and invite her over. Be subtle but make the reason so compelling she'll feel obligated to comply with your request. Maybe you could just casually mention you'd seen the text from Trotter when you picked her phone up off the floor. And then you'll be able to judge how she reacts to your comment. Can you handle that, Rapella?"

"Is the Pope Catholic? Absolutely! Don't worry, Lexie, Rip and I will take care of it. We'll be diplomatic, and, of course, understanding and compassionate. We can just ease into the conversation concerning her exchange of texts with Hayes and maybe she'll give us some clue as to any part she might have played in the murder. We'll be so cunning she won't know what hit her until she's being led away to jail. If she's guilty, that is."

"Oh, my! I don't even want to think about that happening. Don't forget we're operating on a hunch, Rapella. Mattie may be innocent, and we don't want to give her any indication we think she might be guilty of a crime she may not have committed. We certainly don't want to out and out accuse her of murder. You weren't planning to approach your meeting with her tonight that way, were you?" Lexie asked anxiously.

"Do teddy bears poop in the woods?"

"Uh—"

"No, they don't. They're toys, not real animals." I supplied the answer for her. "Don't worry, Lexie. Rip and I can handle this. He's had a lifetime of experience preparing for this kind of confrontation. I'd lay money that Rip could negotiate with a kitten and get it to crawl down a tall tree on its own. He can surely negotiate with Mattie and get her to admit any part she may have played in this matter too. But don't worry, we'll be careful not to cause any irreparable harm if it turns out the girl had nothing to do with Trotter's death. But that's not an eventuality we're apt to have to deal with, I'm afraid."

Lexie didn't appear to be convinced about the diplomacy Rip and I were apt to utilize, but she agreed with the plan. I knew considering the possible outcome of our meeting with Mattie had raised her anxiety level to an all-time high. This time I was praying for everyone's sake that we were dead wrong about the killer.

CHAPTER 19

Rip was no more anxious to confront Mattie Hill than I was. He fought to have Lexie and me contact Detective Russell and turn the information over to him. "I may have a law enforcement background, but I'm nothing but a visiting citizen here in Rockdale, or anywhere else now, for that matter," he argued. "I don't want to overstep my bounds and I can assure you that Wyatt, as a local detective, wouldn't want me to put my nose in where it doesn't belong either. As a former police officer, I know how frustrating it can be when citizens take it upon themselves to exact justice. It's not their place, or yours and mine, to take the law into our own hands. It almost never turns out well, and I can see where this situation could end badly as well. I still think we should bring Detective Johnston into this and let him handle it from here on out."

"I don't want Wyatt to put his neck on the line.

Chief Smith would have his job if he found out Wyatt was going behind his back and taking suggestions from us. The big buffoon considers Lexie and me as no more than 'old airheads'. And if we don't approach Mattie with our suspicions, who will? Besides, do you recall how successful we were in getting the detectives to take our Piney theory seriously?" I asked.

"My point exactly. Do you realize how ridiculous you and Lexie would look right now if you'd been successful in convincing the detectives to raid the Piney residence? The investigating team would never have taken any evidence you two brought them seriously again. For that matter, they'd have sloughed off a written, signed, and notarized confession if you and Lexie had managed to get one from Georgia or Lori. Detective Johnston could decide whether or not to take our suspicions to the investigating team, or not. He might even decide he should take it straight to Chief Smith, providing we hand this matter over to him."

I felt strongly that we'd be wasting our time trying to get any credible tip taken seriously, even if it was Wyatt, a Rockdale detective with sixteen years of service under his belt, who brought it to the chief's attention. It took a lot of begging, complaining, pleading, whining, and worst of all, having to give Rip a lengthy foot massage, before I was able to get my husband to commit to helping Lexie and me put our plan into action. I could convince Rip to tap dance on a table at Applebees if I promised him a foot massage in exchange. And, sorry to say, I wasn't above using that weakness against him.

A couple of hours later, Lexie remarked she'd been too weary to prepare a decent supper and offered to take the two of us, Stone, Wendy, Andy, Wyatt, and Veronica to supper. We begged off with the excuse that I was experiencing a rare migraine and Rip's hip was throbbing so bad he wanted to rest with his feet up all evening. I hadn't had a real migraine in years but Rip's hip was aching nearly 24/7 now, so we didn't have to tell a complete prevarication to get the inn to ourselves for a couple of hours.

I was pacing back and forth across the parlor and Rip was sitting in an ornate, intricately-carved ivory chair, nervously spinning his cane in his hand. As a police officer, Rip had experienced many more nerve-racking confrontations than the one we were preparing for at that moment, but seldom had the outcome meant so much to him on a personal level.

He stopped spinning his cane and looked at me as he asked, "What ruse did you use to convince Mattie to drop everything and rush over here to the inn?"

"I didn't use a ruse," I said. For a second I feared I'd have to pick Rip up off the floor. I can only imagine what he was thinking, and unfortunately, it probably wasn't much off the mark. "I told her the absolute truth."

"Swell." With a sigh, Rip pulled a handkerchief out of his back pocket and wiped perspiration off his bald head. And then he asked me, as he was in a habit of doing, "Do I even want to know?"

"I merely told her we were almost certain we'd determined who killed Trotter Hayes. She asked who we thought killed him, of course. So I told her we were so excited we wanted to tell her all about it in person. Obviously, I didn't let on it'd only be you and me at the inn when she arrived, or that she was the individual we suspected of having committed the murder. She sounded apprehensive as it was when she agreed to head right over."

"And when she gets here and asks who you've discovered the killer is, what are you going to tell her?" Rip asked.

"Oh, yeah, I didn't think about that aspect of it. But maybe I can act confused, like maybe I'd downed too many Miller Lites before I called her and asked her to come over."

"Oh, God." Rip groaned, and then asked, "What the hell was I thinking when I let you talk me into this lunacy? I suppose it's just that I really wanted a foot massage. And I should know by now it's never worth the price I end up having to pay for it."

When I didn't respond, he shrugged his shoulders and said, "I guess it's too late to back out now. So, remember, Rapella, we want to go about this as judiciously as we can. Kind of tiptoe around the subject until we see how she reacts to it. In other words, we don't want to accuse her of anything. We want to try to entice her to offer the information voluntarily."

"I'll be subtly tactful, Rip. I'm nothing if I'm not diplomatic. You know how I am better than anyone."

"Yes, I do. And that's what concerns me."

"Don't be silly. Well, it's six-thirty, so I expect Mattie to be here in about twenty minutes."

As if on cue, the phone rang. I expected it to be Mattie, telling us she was going to be late, or if she had a hunch we'd figured out that she was the perpetrator, she might be begging off altogether. Instead it was Georgia Piney.

"Hi, Rapella, is Lexie there?"

"Not at the moment, dear, but I'd be happy to take a message," I replied.

"No bother. This is Georgia. When I went to put away the blue bowl you two brought by, I took a closer look and realized it wasn't my bowl after all. My bowl was already in the china hutch, and even though they look very similar, mine is not an Anchor Hocking as I'd suspected. Please tell her I'm sorry. I should have taken the time to check it out when you two ladies were here earlier today. I feel badly that I just assumed it was mine."

"Oh, don't worry about it, sweetie. You know Lexie. She'll understand. Would you like us to run by and pick it up tomorrow?" I was relieved to hear Lexie's prized possession was going to be returned to her.

"No, that's all right. You've made enough trips out here on my account. Lori's delivering Lexie's bowl to the inn right now. She should be there in about ten minutes, give or take. I wanted to use it as an excuse to get her out of the house. She's been totally withdrawn this week. Worse than normal even, you know, with the timing of the murder, and all."

Before Georgia hung up, she reminded me to apologize to Lexie for her. I passed on what the phone call was about to Rip and went to sit down in the ivory chair that Rip had just vacated. He was now playing his own rendition of "Chopsticks" on the piano, and after about the seventh time he repeated the tune, it began to grate on my nerves. I considered asking him to give it a rest, but didn't. I was still in his debt for going along with Lexie's and my plan and didn't want to push my luck.

Rip stopped halfway into his eighth playing of the simple tune and said, "If Lori gets here first, take the bowl and send her on her way so she won't be here when Mattie arrives. I don't want her mixed up in this. Lori's under enough emotional strain. And getting Mattie to admit her part in the murder is going to be a delicate enough conversation as it is."

Georgia's comment over the phone about the "timing and all" had intrigued me. Before I'd taken her call, I'd been playing solitaire on the iPad to calm my nerves. When Rip went back to torturing my ears with his piano playing, I Googled Tori Piney's obituary and was astonished to discover that she'd died exactly ten years to the day of the surprise party. Because of the coincidental "timing" as Georgia put it, Tori's death had to be taking a toll on both of the

Pineys' state-of-mind, I realized.

Could that traumatic milestone anniversary have triggered a violent reaction in her identical twin? I asked myself. Could it have been enough to make Lori want to kill the man she held responsible for Tori's death? Could Georgia have no idea what lengths her surviving daughter would go to exact justice for her deceased one?

It was reasonable to believe that at the time of Tori's suicide, her twin had vowed to avenge her sister's death. Because the two sisters shared a room, the odds were good it was Lori who found her dead twin's body there. Could Lori have gotten a hold of some cyanide in the same way her sister had and decided to use it for retribution against Trotter Hayes? And wasn't it possible she'd thought to hide some of it years ago, in the event she ever got a chance to give Trotter Hayes a dose of his own medicine, so to speak?

When the doorbell rang, I was suddenly not sure which of the two girls on their way to the inn was the real killer. And I was now in a quandary about how to find out. Puzzled, I went to the front door, which led through a vestibule and right into the parlor. The opening into the vestibule was situated about fifteen feet from where I sat. I slowly opened the door and was shocked to see Alice Runcan standing on the doorstep with a gaily wrapped present in her hands.

Alice smiled, but her smile quickly changed to one of surprise. "Hey! Ms. Ripple, I didn't know you knew Wendy's family. How are you feeling? I was so disappointed the waitress job at Zen's didn't work out for you."

"Yes, me too, Ms. Runcan. The gout in my big toe is still giving me fits. What can I do for you? I'm afraid we have company coming shortly."

"I was so shook up at the party, I grabbed my birthday gift to Wendy as I walked out the door. It was so nice to be invited, and I didn't want my old friend to think I hadn't thought enough of her to bring her a present." Alice's smile had returned.

"I know Wendy was very happy to see you at the party, too, Alice," I replied politely. And then to hurry her on her way I added, "Thanks for dropping off your gift. I know Wendy will be touched that you made the effort to get it to her. Have a wonderful evening, my dear."

"It had been years since we'd seen each other. It was wonderful to see her, Mattie, Rayleen, Joy, and Tro-ot-ot-ter for the first time in years. In fact, it brought ba-ba-ba-back a lot of mem-mem-mem—"

"Memories?" I asked. Alice's sudden speech impediment caught my attention. It had appeared to me to be triggered by nervous lying the first time I'd spoke with her, and I wondered if this were the case today as well. Now I wasn't so anxious to see her on her way.

"Yes."

"I'll bet seeing another one of the three musketeers show up at the party with Trotter was kind of a shock to your system, wasn't it?"

"Uh-uh-uh, I wa-wa-was —"

"Didn't it take you back to the homecoming

dance all over again?" I asked. "Having both of your best friends stab you in the back like that had to hurt, even if it had been years ago since Trotter humiliated you the way he did."

The unsettled expression on Alice Runcan's face morphed into one of pure hatred. There was an evil glint in her eyes, and I knew I'd touched a nerve. I decided to work on that nerve to see if I could make it jump. With the sudden disappearance of the stuttering, she was furious when she nearly spat at me as she said, "It was Trotter's fault! He lied to them just like he lied to me! He's what caused the three musketeers' friendship to dissolve and all three of us to go our separate ways. I haven't had a really close friend, male or female, since. All I do now is work at the diner, work at all the Baptist Church's events, and work at trying to get —"

Alice stopped talking suddenly. She had the look of a rabid raccoon in a trap, practically foaming at the mouth. I took another stab at that adversely affected nerve by finishing her sentence for her. "By trying to get another man to show interest in you? Like, say, Detective Russell for example? Too bad he was only interested in the photos you took of Lexie standing over your victim, instead of being interested in spending time with you."

The frayed nerve burst like a frozen water pipe. Alice was snarling with fury. I thought back to my conversation with her in the diner. I'd wondered then if she'd been tested for schizophrenia. Now I was almost positive she really did have some kind of mood or personality disorder. Alice Runcan had many different sides to her. She could be the taskmaster boss at her own business, the devout Christian at her church, the kind friend delivering a birthday gift, the shameless hussy throwing herself at a potential suitor, or, as I now suspected, a cold-blooded killer. I didn't think Alice even realized what personality she was exhibiting at any given time.

I took the package out of her hands and set it on a small table in the entryway. Then I grabbed her arm and pulled her into the parlor, as I said, "I'll bet just seeing those two together made you want to kill that son-of-a —"

"You're damn right it did! It was like he was rubbing my nose in it. Taking perverse pleasure in reminding me of that night he snubbed me and made me feel like I would die of embarrassment." As Alice ranted, I signaled to Rip to turn on the voice recorder on his cell phone. I'd watched Lexie do it with her phone before we went to see Georgia, and I'd shown Rip how to do the same thing with his.

Alice was on a roll now, needing no more provoking on my part. She exclaimed, "Yeah, I killed him! I should have done it years ago, but I fought off the temptation. After I heard what happened to Tori Piney, I went to visit her sister. I knew Lori was a potential ally in wanting retribution against Trotter Hayes. She told me her sister had found the key to her father's safe in the desk drawer in his workshop and found a tin container marked 'cyanide' inside it. Lori said her father was devastated when Tori used that cyanide to kill herself, and he always felt responsible for his daughter's death, even though she and her mother blamed only Trotter. Lori was so emotionally distraught the day I visited her that I was able to talk her out of some of the cyanide crystals she'd hidden in an old jacket pocket in her closet. Later, when she'd given it more thought, she asked me to return the poison. Said she wanted to have it destroyed before it could cause any more pain."

"But, you lied to her. Didn't you?" I asked.

"Of course I lied! Do you think I'm stupid, or something? I told her I'd given it more thought too and already destroyed the cyanide."

"I'm curious. Did you know about Joy's abortion?"

"Abortion? No, what are you talking about?"

"Oh, nothing. It's not important. But how did you know Trotter would be at the party?" I asked the clearly disturbed young lady. Alice's face was flushed, the vein in her throat was throbbing in double-time, and even her dilated eyes didn't seem to be blinking at the same time.

"I didn't. For all those years since Tori Piney's death, I've carried the small tin of cyanide around in my purse."

"And gloves, I assume?"

"No, I picked up a pair of the caterer's latex gloves when I went into the kitchen and hid in the pantry, after telling Trotter he could get a mixed drink if he asked Lexie for one. I knew he wouldn't be able to resist."

"And he wanted a Crown and Coke, apparently?"

"Trotter Hayes was a partier and on the verge of being an alcoholic. I doubt he cared what the drink contained as long as it had alcohol in it. Drinking some silly spiked punch was not his style at all though. He stepped right into the trap I'd set for him." Alice was now showing obvious pride in her cunningness in devising such a devious scheme. I found it quite nauseating.

"Lucky for you, huh?" I said, as I glanced over at Rip, who was taking in the conversation silently. I was flattered that he felt I had a good handle on the situation and didn't need his assistance. When I caught Rip's eye, he said, "Don't forget Mattie's due here any second."

The mention of Mattie's name seemed to make her magically appear in the doorway, like a David Copperfield illusion. I'd almost forgotten she was coming over. She'd walked into a situation she hadn't expected and had a puzzled expression on her face.

Mattie Hill really was on our side, and I couldn't have been any happier to discover that *before* I'd launched even a hint of an undeserved accusation at her. The relief that flooded through me at that moment was indescribable. I was so thankful Wendy's best friend wasn't a killer. And I was even more thankful I'd been stopped short of wrongly accusing her of being one. I believe divine intervention occurs at critical times in our lives, and I felt certain this was one of those times.

I was also grateful I hadn't accused Lori Piney of killing Trotter, either. God knew she and her mother had been through enough grief as it was, without having me sling false accusations at her when she was only being kind enough to return Lexie's beloved family heirloom to the inn.

"Go on with your story, Alice. How did the little tin container that had held the poison not get detected by the thorough frisking that the detectives subjected all of us to?" I tried but couldn't resist adding a snide remark. "I'm guessing you enjoyed having that handsome Detective Russell's hands roaming all over your body."

"You really do think I'm an idiot, don't you? If you go in the kitchen right now, you'll find the tin box buried inside the flour canister on the counter. First, with the latex gloves on, I wiped my fingerprints off it with some rubbing alcohol I found in the pantry. I figured the tin, with traces of the poison still in it, would eventually be discovered. But I also figured it would only serve as further evidence it was Lexie Starr who killed Trotter."

"So you deliberately set out to frame Lexie from the beginning?" I asked, incredulously. I was sickened by the fact the nut job was actually boasting about her cleverness in framing an innocent person with her vicious crime. *How could anyone be so mentally deranged that they'd do something so wicked and then wallow in their accomplishment?* I wondered.

"Of course, I did. I had to steer the investigation

toward someone besides myself, didn't I? So, anyway, I had previously researched the fatalness of the cyanide and decided I probably didn't have enough to kill anyone. And that's why I took the cake knife off the table and slashed his throat. Then I quickly tossed the gloves in the trash and hurried back to be in position to take the photo. Michael, er, I mean, Detective Russell, told me the chief of police was convinced that Lexie had disposed of the gloves just before the lights came back on since the trashcan was just a couple of feet from where the worthless prick fell with her standing right next to him."

"How did you know there'd be a knife handy for you to use to finish the job?" I asked.

"I'd seen Lori place it by the cake earlier, before they turned the lights off, and was relieved to find it still there in the dark. I'd only hoped to have the photos to be able to prove I was nowhere near his body at the time. Lexie Starr leaving her blood on the knife and walking up to Trotter when she did were just unexpected strokes of good fortune."

"Well, Alice, those unexpected strokes weren't very fortuitous for my friend, and now your recorded confession is not going to be such a stroke of good fortune for you, either." The callous killer showing such delight in having the blame placed on Lexie instead of herself had rubbed me the wrong way, and now I was going to take even greater delight in turning her over to the police.

Looking as if she'd just been struck in the face

with a cast-iron skillet, Alice's personality disorder took a turn for the worse. She sneered at me when she said, "I ain't going down for this, lady. If you think I'm going to jail for killing that jackass, you're in for a rude awakening. I've got a church bazaar to attend next Monday, and a restaurant to run, for starters. And, I don't believe they serve vegan cuisine at the state pen."

I'd thought Alice had been experiencing a great deal of mental instability, and she proved just how unstable she was when she reached into the bag hanging over her shoulder and pulled out a shiny handgun. I'm sure Rip recognized the model immediately. I knew she wouldn't hesitate to use it on us, but I was also afraid it'd misfire if we tried to get the gun away from her. She aimed the weapon at me first, then Mattie, and finally Rip. Alice continued to wave it back and forth between us.

Alice had a crazed look on her face when she continued speaking. "I lied about not realizing you knew Wendy's family. The night of the party, I saw you chatting with Lexie on several occasions before I killed Trotter. So after you'd asked me those supposedly innocent questions at the diner that day, I had a premonition that made me uneasy. I couldn't get over the feeling that you never really wanted to work at Zen's Diner in the first place, but were just using it as an excuse to question me. I slipped my Glock into my purse before I left to bring Wendy's present over, just in the event something like this confrontation were to take place. And believe me, folks, as you should be aware of by now, I'm not afraid to use this gun."

I froze, but my cool and collected husband calmly advised her to lower her weapon. He said, "Alice, honey, don't be silly. Put the gun down. You don't want to make this situation even worse for yourself by killing three more people. They might go easy on you for the impassioned killing of Trotter, but adding three more point-blank murders to your list of crimes will get you the death penalty almost without question. And don't fool yourself into thinking you're going to get away with this."

"Who's going to know I've even been here? You don't actually think I plan to leave any witnesses, do you?"

"They won't need witnesses, my dear," I said before Rip could reply to the question. "I'm certain the Alexandria Inn's new state-of-the-art security system will have a clear video of your arrival, and will film your departure, as well. There are multiple strategically-placed cameras around the perimeter of the building which are operating 24/7."

I glanced over at Rip just long enough to see him roll his eyes and shake his head in disbelief before I continued. I thought my detailed description of the high-tech system sounded very credible so I continued to elaborate. "When any of the nine cameras detect a body in motion, a facial recognition program automatically activates. If the individual's face is not on the list of approved visitors, the police department is notified and the video files are instantly transmitted to their computer. I can assure you the cops are already in possession of the evidentiary files and are on their way here, young lady."

I knew the inn's "state-of-the-art" security system actually consisted of a cheap worthless chain and a regular locking doorknob that Rip could pick in five seconds with a credit card, but I was hoping my B.S. would fool this loony tune who was cuckoo for Cocoa Puffs to begin with. I doubted anyone in the county had a system like I'd just described. Now if the White House really had been relocated to downtown Rockdale instead of the new Panera Bread, it might have been a different story.

I was quite proud of my ingeniously fabricated remarks, so naturally disappointed when Alice responded with a rude laugh and said, "Yeah, right!"

The crazed nut job was obviously not as dim-witted as I'd given her credit for. She continued to wave the gun back and forth. I'm sure she was considering the ramifications of her actions and mentally going over the pros and cons of shooting us. I didn't think she was a natural born killer, or we'd have already been bleeding out on the floor, almost exactly where her first victim had done the same thing. The thought crossed my mind that the gun might not even be loaded. She could be bluffing, or possibly not even know how to check if there were bullets in the clip or if the safety was off. But there was no safe way to test that theory, so I operated under the assumption that both the gun and Alice were prepared and ready to fire. I figured just the fact she owned a gun was a good sign she was familiar with how to use it.

One thing was obvious that didn't bode well for Rip, Mattie and me. Alice was in dire straits, and her inherent insanity could cause her to do anything, no matter how drastic, in order to save her own skin. I'd antagonized Alice to the point she was threatening to kill the three of us, so I felt it might be an opportune time to let the seasoned law enforcer in the room take over.

Alice held us at bay for another five minutes while Rip attempted to calm her down and reason with her, rubbing his right hip as he spoke. She seemed to become more and more irrational and distraught with each moment that passed. My husband might have been able to talk a kitten down from a tall tree, but he wasn't having much luck talking the bats out of Alice's belfry. And I knew if I held my breath any longer I was going to turn the color of the brick fireplace across the room from the four of us.

Mattie, Rip, and I were standing to one side of the piano, and Alice was standing on the other. Finally Rip told her, "Honey, if you want to kill me, then kill me. But in the meantime I'm going to have to sit down. My hip hurts so badly right now that I won't be able to hold myself up much longer." Without even waiting for Alice's response, Rip walked slowly toward the piano bench, steadying himself with his cane. He must have known instinctively she wouldn't shoot him if he walked toward her in a non-threatening fashion. She kept the Glock pointed directly at him, and he made a point of showing no intention of trying to take her down.

Rip had moved so sluggishly toward the bench that I was as surprised as Alice when he suddenly grasped his end of the bench and thrust it as forcefully as he could in her direction, which was approximately five feet from the other end of the bench. In reaction to his sudden movement, Alice turned away at the last instant, just before the bench hit her squarely in the knees and caused her to topple forward. I could hear the crunch of the wooden bench against the bone of Alice's kneecaps. As she'd tried to retain her balance, the gun had flown out of her hand and hit the face of the piano so hard it had discharged upon impact.

I saw Mattie dive under the piano and heard Rip and Alice gasp in pain almost simultaneously. I knew the bullet had struck my husband, but I didn't know where, or how seriously he'd been hurt. But I had no time to check it out right then. Alice was reaching for the gun again, which was several feet closer to her than it was to Rip or me. Despite his gunshot wound, Rip stretched his left arm out with his cane and whisked the gun out of her reach just as her fingers made contact with the barrel. It flew off the piano keys in my direction, and bounced after it hit the hardwood floor. Out of self-preservation and pure instinct, I dove on the loaded weapon.

It crossed my mind briefly that all those

snickering, spandex-clad, pole-dancing floozies would have been amazed and impressed at the agility I'd just exhibited. With the massive amount of adrenalin coursing through my body, I could have performed the upside-down "grasshopper" flawlessly, or even lifted a burning concrete truck off of Dolly. Considering her ever-increasing weight, perhaps I should say lift Dolly off a burning concrete truck.

I watched Alice struggle to pull herself up to her feet using the piano bench as support. A few seconds later, Alice lunged unsteadily in my direction in a desperate attempt to wrestle the weapon away from me. Using all the force I could muster, I cracked her in an already wounded kneecap with the butt of the gun, all-the-while hoping it didn't accidentally discharge again and blow my nose off in the process. I heard a shattering of glass along with the thud of the gun against Alice's knee. Out of the corner of my eye, I saw Lori Piney standing in the doorway with her hands over her mouth and the blue Anchor Hocking bowl in pieces at her feet. She had walked into the room unaware of the mayhem taking place in the parlor.

As Alice Runcan fell to the floor, I heard her scream, Rip moan, Mattie shout out, Lori gasp, and Wyatt holler, "Freeze! Police!" at the exact same moment. Unbeknownst to all five of us, the detective had rushed in through the parlor door in reaction to the sound of the gunshot he'd heard as he was walking up the front steps into the inn. Wyatt could not have had any idea what he was going to walk into when he entered the house, but after sixteen years on the force, his extensive training had taken over.

I was surprised but greatly relieved to see the detective. Lexie told me later she'd begun to worry at the restaurant about the plan we'd set into motion. When Wendy had excused herself to use the restroom, she'd taken the opportunity to tell the rest of the party briefly what had happened and the real reason Rip and I had not joined them for supper.

Lexie related to us that when Wendy had returned to the table, Wyatt had made a show of putting his phone in his pocket, said, "Sorry folks, but duty calls" and left the restaurant just as the waitress was handing out their drink orders. Wyatt made arrangements for Veronica to ride back to the inn with Lexie and told her he'd stop by to pick her up later.

Wendy hadn't seemed to question Wyatt's excuse to leave the restaurant, which was basically the truth anyway. With a sense of urgency Wyatt had driven to the inn as fast as he safely could. The detective felt he should be there if the confrontation took a bad turn. And the seasoned cop's instincts were correct. The confrontation had taken a very bad turn, indeed.

CHAPTER 20

Lexie explained to me later what had transpired to bring Detective Johnston to the scene at that precise moment. As soon as Wyatt had left the restaurant, Wendy had turned to her mother, and said, "Okay, spill the beans, Mom. I want to know what's going on. I know you well enough to know you're so uptight right now, you won't be able to eat one bite of your food. If there's something going on that's pertinent to the murder case, I think I deserve to know about it."

Lexie had then reached down into her purse and activated the voice recorder on her phone purely on a whim. She played the recording for Rip and me the following morning. We'd listened as Lexie told Wendy about our suspicions that her best friend, Mattie, could have been responsible for Trotter's death. Lexie had felt her daughter really did deserve to know the truth, considering the impact it would have on her. Of course, at the time, Lexie was still under the impression Rip and I were at the inn questioning Mattie about any involvement she might have had in the crime. Lexie knew nothing about what had taken place with Alice Runcan in the interim.

Listening to the recording, we'd heard Wendy say, "Although I don't want to believe it's even possible, it could account for why Mattie's been acting so strangely this week. She told me that she had warned Trotter at the party he'd better leave before I arrived or she'd tell Andy what he did to me, and Andy would make mince-meat of him. Then, when he didn't leave, she sent him a text a few minutes later to remind him of her threat. Naturally, Mattie joked about it, saying she would have never had the guts to do it, knowing I didn't really want Andy to know about the assault. But maybe she'd actually given Trotter a more menacing threat, and couldn't resist his daring her to do it."

We then heard Lexie's voice ask, "Why didn't you tell us about that exchange of texts between Mattie and Trotter?"

To which Wendy replied, "I guess, in retrospect, I should have mentioned it to you all earlier, but I couldn't imagine that my friend, who I thought I knew as well as I knew myself, could ever do something so vicious."

Lexie had then suggested they leave before they placed their meal order, and get back to the inn quickly. She'd told them we still had the barbecue stuff we'd picked up earlier, which we could all eat later as a late supper.

With an apology to the waitress and a ten-dollar tip for her trouble, the remaining five in the party had rushed out to their vehicles and arrived at the inn just a minute or two behind Wyatt. Earlier, they had carpooled to the restaurant in Lexie and Stone's vehicles and Wyatt had met them there in his patrol car. That decision had turned out to be a good one.

With Veronica in the passenger seat, Lexie told me she hadn't even bothered to check her speed as she rushed back to the inn. Her little VW Bug sped through downtown Rockdale, just a yellow streak racing down Main Street, with Stone's truck nearly glued to her bumper.

When I had turned in surprise at Wyatt's voice shouting, "Freeze," it seemed like mere seconds before the rest of the dinner party had flooded into the room. The look on Lexie's face will forever be imprinted in my memory. The scene when they entered the room was that of Rip lying across the piano bench with blood streaming down the right leg of his pants, Mattie on the floor, still hiding under the grand piano, Lori dabbing at a speck of blood on her ankle where a shard of glass from the shattered bowl had cut her, and Alice wailing as she clutched her left knee. To top it off, I was standing in the center of the room like one of Charlie's Angels with the Glock pointed at the helpless restaurant owner on the floor. I'm not sure what had been going through my mind at that moment. But for the record, I was ready to defend my husband, Mattie Hill, Lori Piney, and myself if the sobbing, wounded lady suddenly jumped to her feet and brandished a second revolver she'd had hidden in her no doubt lacy and revealing brassiere.

Wyatt had immediately taken control of the situation. He called the police station for assistance, requesting EMTs and a couple of ambulances. Then he began to apply pressure to the gaping hole in Rip's hip from the close-range shot, to stop the profuse bleeding. He looked over at me and said, "He's going to be all right, Rapella."

Seconds later, Lexie approached me with a questioning expression. I nodded and said, "It's over, Lexie. And Rip's got all the proof we'll need recorded on his phone."

With a smile that spoke of mixed emotions, Lexie said, "I'm glad you've had your wits about you better than I have this week. Let's keep our earlier suspicions about Mattie just between the six of us. I wouldn't want Mattie to find out we ever doubted her honesty and integrity."

"Absolutely!" I agreed. I put my arm around Lexie as the ramifications of the situation had caused Lexie's eyes to pool. Through her tears she thanked me for all Rip and I had done on her behalf.

"I'd do it all again, and I know Rip would too. At least the old bull-headed turd will have to have his hip fixed now, whether he likes it or not."

She smiled at my remark and I heard my husband mumble something that's not fit to repeat. I gave Lexie a tender pat on her back and said, "I hope you aren't terribly upset, but for a short spell you had your great-grandma's bowl back, only to have it shattered to pieces in the ensuing chaos."

"Oh, well. I thought it was gone forever anyway, and had already come to terms with losing it. Not to mention, family heirloom or not, I'd trade it for my freedom and Mattie's innocence any day. So, my friend, considering the ramifications of all that's gone on this week, that old bowl is, as Rip would say, no big rip! But it breaks my heart to think of Alice Runcan's future. She must have been tormented for years by whatever mental illness has taken control of her mind."

"I had a feeling you'd see it that way, my friend. I hate to use a cliché —"

"Of course you do."

"But the poor girl's madder than a wet hen, and maybe that will turn out to be another stroke of good fortune for Alice, regarding her future."

Wyatt tended to the injured with Mattie, a registered nurse, instructing him on how to best assist my husband. In between directions to the detective, she did her best to care for the bloody laceration to Lori's leg. She applied an antibiotic cream and gauze to the wound, items Lexie had brought her from the medicine cabinet in her bathroom. After Lori's inquiry, Mattie assured the young lady that no stitches would be necessary to close the gash which was not as deep or severe as it appeared.

When the room became still as the gravity of the situation sank in, I broke the eerie silence by saying, "Well, Wendy, Rip, and I wanted to attend your birthday party to watch you be surprised by your family and friends. And if everything that happened this past week didn't surprise you, nothing will!"

"Speaking of which," Andy said. "I know this is not the most appropriate time to do this, but it might be the last time we're all in one room at the same time. And it's only a matter of minutes before the room fills up with cops and medical personnel. Wendy, my love, I want to take care of something I'd intended to do at your surprise party and never got the opportunity."

He approached his girlfriend and took her hand. Andy then dropped down on one knee before he spoke again.

"Wendy, you have made me the happiest man in the world. I love you with all my heart, and I'd like nothing better than to spend the rest of my life with you. With your mother's, and my Uncle Stone's blessing, Wendy Marie Starr, will you do me the great honor of becoming my wife, to have and to hold from this day forward?"

Through glistening eyes, Wendy also used words from the traditional wedding vows to reply, "I'd love nothing better than to be married to my best friend, in good times and in bad, in richer or poorer, in sickness and in health, until death do we part. Just promise me, sweetheart, that you won't be in any hurry to have to honor that last one."

The room erupted into laughter, mixed with applause and delighted congratulations. Even

Alice clapped and cheered as she watched Wendy get engaged to the love of her life.

An odd sensation swept through the room at that moment. Two life-altering events had just occurred within minutes of each other and the two emotions the events invoked were polar opposites of each other.

We'd all just learned an emotionally and mentally disturbed young woman was going to be held responsible for a ghastly murder, and also that Wendy would soon marry the man of her dreams, Andy Van Patten. Nearly everyone in the room smiled through their tears. The tears in everyone's eyes were from overwhelming sorrow and overwhelming happiness, and in Rip's case, quite a bit of pain, as well, all mixed into one bittersweet moment.

Lexie and Stone had offered to let us stay at the inn until Rip had completed rehab and was fit to drive again. As much as we appreciated their offer, we'd opted to get a monthly site in a nearby RV Park. The campground was only two blocks from the physical therapy clinic Rip was going to be treated at, and the park owner agreed to let me help out in the office for free rent. And as I said at the beginning of my story, "free" was one of my favorite words.

Compared to the monstrous Alexandria Inn, our abode was tiny and without frills and thrills. There were no mints on our pillows at bedtime, no baskets of fresh fruit on our nightstand, no fancy four-course meals, and no hosts ready to tend to our every need and desire. But to Rip and me it was home. You should know by now how much I hate to use clichés, but home is definitely where the heart is. And to us, our hearts were in the comfortable old Chartreuse Caboose, complete now with a toilet that actually flushed, and no leaks, squeaks, or reeks to be found.

Even Dolly seemed to be content to be back in her favorite napping spot on the back of the couch. She was now spending most of her waking hours staring out the window at the finches and wrens flitting around a feeder the campground owners had hung on a branch of the Mimosa tree located next to our RV site.

I was sitting in a chair next to my husband's hospital bed. After a three-hour operation early that morning, Rip was bullet-free. Better yet, he'd come out of the surgery with a brand-spanking new artificial hip joint, like the one I'd been nagging him to get for months.

Lying on his hard and uncomfortable hospital bed, Rip turned slowly and tenderly in my direction. He looked at me for a few seconds before his face broke out in the most endearing smile I'd ever seen on a man. Then he said, "I've learned a thing or two about you over the years and I know that, because you were itching to know and couldn't stand the suspense, you asked either Lexie or Wendy what was in the wrapped package Alice brought to the inn last night. So, tell me, what was it?"

"Okay, you've got me there," I replied. "Alice

Runcan's birthday gift to Wendy was a very ragged first-edition copy of Arthur Miller's *Death of a Salesman.*"

"Seriously?" Rip asked. I had to laugh at his usage of my new least favorite word.

When I nodded, he said, "How fitting! Now *I'm* itching to ask you something else, knowing without a doubt you will know the answer. What did Trotter Hayes do for a living?"

"According to Wendy, he owned a used car lot in St. Joseph with a rather shady reputation, just like its owner."

Rip chuckled and said, "Considering her gift, I think Ms. Runcan has got that insanity plea option in the bag!"

Even though it was no doubt highly insensitive and inappropriate, Rip started laughing so hard that he was groaning in pain at the same time. Naturally, his amusement cracked me up, and our rowdy laughter enticed one of the night shift nurses to stick her head in the door to make sure her patient was all right.

When we finally got control of ourselves, I asked Rip, "You know the author, George R.R. Martin, whose books the *Game of Thrones* series was adapted from?"

It was a rhetorical question since we both knew Rip couldn't come up with enough authors to use up all ten fingers if he had to. And those few authors included Mark Twain and Dr. Seuss. He'd always said that if God wanted us to read he wouldn't have created the television. I once heard him tell an influential author at a law enforcement seminar that his favorite book was *A Tree Grows in Boston*. I'm pretty sure the writer was not as impressed as Rip had hoped she'd be.

"Well, George R.R. Martin once wrote, 'Shattered legs may heal in time, but some betrayals fester and poison the soul.' I think in this instance, a shattered soul poisoned the betrayer."

"Very clever, sweetheart," Rip said. "Not to mention, I'm impressed you can remember a quote like that but forget where you've left your glasses nine out of ten times."

"Yeah, no kidding! Hey! I almost forgot. I've got good news and even gooder news," I excitedly told my husband.

"*Gooder* news? This from a woman who beat me at Scrabble a few weeks ago with the word 'zyzzyva'?"

"It's a tropical weevil. Everyone knows that."

"Well, I didn't. I thought the word 'weevil' pretty much covered it. And I'm still wondering where you came up with the extra 'z's'."

"Slight of hand, my dear. And just for your information, 'gooder' describes the tail feathers of an albatross."

"No kidding?" Rip asked. "I'd never heard of that."

"Yep! As in 'the large bird's gooder was thinning out as it began to molt,'" I explained, with just a hint of superiority in my voice.

I didn't tell my easily fooled husband he'd fallen for another made-up word with a matching made-up definition. You know, just in case I might want to use the fictional word in a future game of Scrabble. Naturally, if Rip ever tried to use "gooder" as a word in the board game, I'd most certainly challenge it.

"Hey, baby, we got side-tracked. Tell me the good news," Rip requested, as he soothingly caressed my shoulder with his hand.

Our playful bantering may have side-tracked us, but it also seemed to make Rip forget about his pain and discomfort for a few minutes. "Oh, yeah. Sorry. I did go off on a tangent, didn't I? Lexie called while you were in recovery to tell me that first thing this morning, Wendy was offered the promotion to Deputy County Coroner, replacing Max when he retires at the end of the year."

"That's terrific," Rip said. "She deserves it, and I couldn't be more proud of her."

"And the other bit of news is that Alice Runcan was booked on murder charges, as you already knew. However, Lexie told me that Judge Jueti has recommended a mental evaluation be performed on her first. The judge believes Alice really *could* qualify for an insanity plea."

"Outstanding! I was only half kidding about Alice having that option in the bag."

"Oh, and there's one more thing. Chief Leonard Smith has been placed on administrative leave pending an investigation into his alleged misconduct and corruption. At the very least, instead of heading up the Rockdale Police Department, he'll likely be working at Wendy's favorite restaurant in the near future."

"If I owned Wendy's, I wouldn't even hire that louse to ask decent law-abiding folks if they'd like fries with their burgers. But, I gotta say, that's the *goodest* news of all."

After he finished speaking, Rip moaned and gave himself a dose of morphine via his pain pump. I was trying to think of some other silly topic to discuss that might help Rip take his mind off the pain. But before I could come up with anything, he had reached down to take my hand, and asked, "Do you remember me saying I thought our stay here would be a rip roaring good time?"

"Yes, I do, as a matter of fact."

"Well, I was wrong. Dead wrong, in fact! But it's definitely been an experience we won't soon forget."

"You can say that again!"

"But it's definitely been an experience we —"

"Oh, you nut!" I smacked him gently with the pillow I'd been leaning against. I was happy to see that despite the pain Rip was enduring, his sense of humor was still intact. "By the way, I called your brother and told him why we wouldn't be able to make it to Chicago for the wedding next week. He told me to give you his best and tell you he hopes you get back up on your feet quickly."

"Good. Thanks, dear. I was thinking about where we'd head after I get a couple of months of physical therapy under my belt. How do you feel about going home for the holidays? We could stay in that new RV Park overlooking Copano

Bay that was just getting ready to open up for business when we were in Texas for Reggie's fiftieth birthday."

"I think that's a wonderful idea. It'd be nice to see all our friends, and to spend some more time with Reggie. We'd also get an opportunity to get to know her new husband better," I said.

"Yeah, I thought of that too. Other than at their wedding and the few days we were down there in May, we've hardly had a chance to speak with Milo. Regina's over the moon about him, so he must be a pretty terrific guy. I'm just glad she finally found someone she loves after her bitter divorce fifteen years ago."

Rip's expression took on a sorrowful look. He'd been close to our first son-in-law and was really torn up when he and Reggie grew apart and split over irreconcilable differences.

I hated to see Rip's chipper mood darken, so I changed the subject. "I'm looking forward to enjoying some sunshine this winter. So, as far as going home for the holidays, I'm all for it. You'll be able to do more walking if we're in a warmer climate, and that can only be beneficial to having your hip heal well. And, after all, I haven't gotten to cut the rug with my dancing partner for ages."

"I promise you I'll be spinning you around like a top at the Sheets' annual New Year's Eve party," Rip said as he lifted my hand to his lips. "Have I told you lately that I love you, my darling? Being shackled to you for nearly fifty years has been such a pleasure. And once this new hip gets all healed up, I'll be ready for another fifty."

After I assured him I loved him with all my heart too, and that I'd hold him to his promise about dancing with me, he said, "I'm kind of lonely in this hard, uncomfortable bed all by myself. If I can move over without screaming bloody murder, would you join me up here until the nurse chases you out when visiting hours are over?"

"I'd be happy to," I replied. I carefully crawled up onto the bed, making sure I didn't jar Rip's legs. I snuggled up next to him, and asked, "Would you do me a favor? Don't be so darn hard-headed next time you have a problem that can be easily fixed with all this incredible medical technology they're continually improving. It hurts me to see you in such pain."

"Okay, dear, I promise! But only if you do me a favor in return."

"What's that?"

"Remind me in the future not to take a cane to a gunfight!"

Turn the page for an

excerpt from

RIP TIDE

A Ripple Effect Cozy Mystery
Book Two

Jeanne Glidewell

"Fishy, fishy in the brook, come and get on daddy's hook," my husband, Clyde "Rip" Ripple said, as he pretended to cast a heavy duty fishing rod in Tackle Town, a popular sporting goods store in our hometown of Rockport, Texas. I don't think he had any idea how ridiculous he looked when he set the invisible hook on an imaginary fish. When Rip started pretending to reel in a large catch, which was clearly putting up quite a fight, I had to walk away so it wasn't obvious to other shoppers that he was my husband.

After he'd apparently landed the "whopper" successfully, he walked over and placed two identical rod and reel combos in our basket.

"I can't wait to catch a big redfish," he said excitedly.

"Oh, wasn't that what you just caught in the bait bucket aisle? I didn't see you measure it, honey. Are you sure it was of legal size?"

"Oh, good grief! I almost forgot I need to get a couple of those stick-on measuring tapes to apply to our rods. Thanks for reminding me."

"Seriously? I can't wait to see what a $117.29 fish looks like!" I replied.

"What are you talking about?"

"We're buying fishing licenses, expensive rod and reels—"

"I wouldn't want a trophy red to get away because we were using inferior equipment."

"Hand-held nets and neoprene waders—"

"Milo said they like to get out and wade for redfish in the shallows of Aransas and Copano Bays, and we wouldn't want to have to sit in the boat feeding bait to the crabs while Milo and Cooper are catching keeper fish right and left."

"And fishing line, nets, stringers, life jackets, pliers—"

"Duh."

"And why do we need all those six and seven dollar plastic rigs when Milo said we'll be using live bait? Mullet and shrimp, I think he said."

"Well, dear, it's because I had to have something to keep my steel leaders, sinkers, hooks, and all in, and there's no sense having a big tackle box if it's not fully stocked with tackle. It'd be embarrassing. I'd look like a kid fishing with a Mickey Mouse fishing pole. Besides, that way we'll be prepared if the reds aren't biting and the guys decide to 'throw some plastic' for speckled trout, as Milo put it," Rip said in defense of his power-shopping spree.

"Okay, I get it, Donald Trump! My point is that

Milo said we were each allowed to keep three redfish per day. If we both limit out we'll have a total of six fish. Divide six by what this basket-full of stuff's gonna cost us and we'll have about $117.29 invested in each redfish we catch. And that's not including the bait we'll still have to buy!"

"Just be thankful we didn't have to buy the boat, too," Rip said. "You can ask any fisherman and they'll tell you they can buy fish at the grocery store cheaper than they can go out and catch them themselves. But that's of no significance. You don't fish to save money on your grocery bill, you fish for the pure enjoyment of the sport. The same thing goes for hunting, sweetheart."

Rip walked over to a rack of Guy Harvey merchandise; t-shirts, belts, jackets, and ball caps, with depictions of trout, redfish, flounder, tarpon, and other game fish on them. I assumed the fish needed to see which particular fish you were hoping to catch before they decided whether or not to bite down on your bait. Judging by the cap Rip brought back and tossed in the basket, he was hoping to land a hammerhead shark.

"I'm putting my chest waders back if we're going to be out there wading amongst hammerhead sharks," I said.

"Actually, Milo told me we were more in danger of a dolphin grabbing a hold of the fish on our stringer than being attacked by a shark. But he did say a fisherman pulled a five-hundred-pound bull shark out of Aransas Bay a few years ago."

"Thank you, honey. That makes me feel so much better about wading now!" I said. Rip shrugged and turned to head toward a rack of Columbia fishing shirts with cape-like things on the back. "Don't tell me that to have a successful day of fishing we have to look like Harold Ensley, too."

I wondered if Rip was afraid the fish wouldn't take me seriously if I had on my stained Texas Rangers shirt that I was planning to wear. They'd been handing the t-shirts out free at the admissions gate when we attended one of their games nearly twenty years ago. And if something's free, I want it whether I have any use for it, or not. I was much more financially conservative than my husband of nearly fifty years was, as was abundantly clear by the over-flowing basket of merchandise he was now pushing toward the check-out counter. All I'd purchased at the store was a two-dollar tube of lip balm with SPF-30 sun protection in it. I was more concerned about getting blisters on my lip than I was about catching a fish.

Rip and I had sold our home in Rockport about five years ago, when we were only sixty-three, and bought a thirty-foot travel trailer we had nicknamed the "Chartreuse Caboose" after we'd painted it that color with bright sunflowers on both sides to give it a little flair. Now we were full-time RVers, traveling the country and living the good life. Occasionally we'd stay in an RV park for several months and help out the campground owners for free rent, and occasionally a little cash, to boot. Other times we'd drive from place to place just enjoying the scenery and the open road.

But we were spending this entire winter back in our south Texas hometown on the Gulf so we could spend some time with our fifty-year-old daughter, Regina, and get to know her husband a little better. Also, we felt it would give Rip, with his new artificial hip, some much-needed time to recoup and recover in the warmer climate.

We'd found a nice site in a newer RV Park only a matter of blocks from Regina and Milo's home. Reggie, as we call her, and her husband, Milo Moore, were still newlyweds. They worked as a team, buying up properties that needed a little TLC, work which they hired out, and then selling the houses for a profit. They called it "flipping houses". Cooper Claypool was an old friend of Milo's, who'd first gotten him involved in the house-flipping business and had offered to take the three of us out on a fishing trip the following day while Reggie spent the day having her hair done and getting a manicure and pedicure at a local nail salon.

Despite the 'bite' the fishing equipment would take out of our budget, I was looking forward to the fishing excursion. Milo said we'd be launching the boat at the Little Bay boat ramp by Rockport Beach, and crossing the Intercoastal Waterway to fish in the shallow areas along a small piece of land called St. Jo Island, which was about six-and-a-half miles across the ship channel.

I walked toward Rip to join him at the checkout counter. I had resigned myself to the fact that even though our fishing excursion wouldn't come at a cheap price, it would no doubt be a memorable adventure. I was even getting excited at the prospect of landing a trophy fish that I could brag about at the bunko party I was planning to attend the following weekend.

As I approached Rip, his cell phone rang. After a few brief one-word responses to the caller, he ended the call and turned to me. He said, "We need to head straight to Reggie's house when we leave here. She's so riled up that I can't even make out what she's trying to tell me. I'm not sure what, but something has happened to upset her."

RIP TIDE

available in print and ebook

THE RIPPLE EFFECT
COZY MYSTERIES

A Rip Roaring Good Time
Rip Tide

Jeanne Glidewell lives with her husband, Bob, and their chubby cat, Dolly, in Bonner Springs, Kansas. In the winter, the three of them travel to their waterfront condo in south Texas, where Jeanne and Bob enjoy spending time with their Rockport friends, and wade-fishing the bays off the Gulf of Mexico whenever the weather is cooperative. (Dolly would go with them if her servants could find chest-waders that fit her— with four legs instead of only two.)

Besides writing and fishing, Jeanne also enjoys traveling, wildlife photography, and spending time with her four incredible grandchildren, Wyatt, Seth, Marissa, and Dax.

A 2006 pancreas and kidney transplant recipient, Jeanne now volunteers as a mentor for the Gift of Life Program of Kansas City, helping future pancreas and/or kidney recipients prepare mentally and emotionally for their transplants. She's an avid advocate for organ and tissue donation and encourages people to let their families know if they're generous enough to donate their organs once they no longer need them. Marking "organ donor" on a driver's license is not enough to ensure your final wishes are adhered to.

Jeanne is the author of a romance/suspense novel, Soul Survivor, and six books and one holiday novella in her Lexie Starr cozy mystery series. With this cross-over novel she is introducing her new Ripple Effect cozy mystery series.

Jeanne loves hearing from her readers. You can contact Jeanne through her publisher at:
JeanneGlidewell@epublishingworks.com

CPSIA information can be obtained
at www.ICGtesting.com
Printed in the USA
FSOW01n0622120216
16863FS